NEW BEGINNINGS

—— *on* ——

VANCOUVER ISLAND

Lorna Hunting

Published by Goldcrest Books International Ltd
www.goldcrestbooks.com
publish@goldcrestbooks.com

ISBN: 978-1-913719-38-8
eISBN: 978-1-913719-39-5

In memory of Mr and Mrs John Malpass who departed England on 3rd June and arrived in Colville on 27th November 1854

Mr. and Mrs. JOHN MALPASS

PART ONE

CHAPTER ONE

Whitehaven, April 1854

It was Saturday night and Whitehaven was busy entertaining itself. A rogue wind was blowing in from the sea, brisk, cheerless and noisy, seeking warm crevices in which to rest awhile. Despite this, the town was teeming with deckhands just in from Antigua. Men with their caps drawn tight over their ears and their jackets buttoned high were swaying from inn to ale house, seeking excitement.

Stag Liddell and Tom Kennedy, colliers at the Wellington Pit, were settled in a congenial spot in the window seat of the Golden Lion Hotel at the bottom of Roper Street, overlooking the marketplace, taking it all in. The room was smoky from the fire and the clay pipes, its tables seasoned by the ale spills and drips from generations of drinkers, and its stools worn shiny. It was a room that had been privy to secrets and promises, to wagers and arguments, and that evening to Stag, eyes bright and alert, entertaining its patrons with his mouth organ. He'd just finished a fresh arrangement of *The Cumberland Lass*,

7

which had been well received, and was savouring his second ale of the evening. Tom, his workmate and best friend – his "marrer" – could now rely on Stag's full attention.

'I tell you, 'tis true,' he said, wiping away a beery moustache with the back of his hand. 'There's a broadsheet pasted up outside the Savings Bank in Lowther Street, down by the ginnel. There's a likeness of a grand-looking three-masted barque. You should think about coming with us.'

'No. It's not for me.' Stag twirled his mouth organ on the table. 'I'm happy here in Whitehaven.'

'They want colliers like us in Canada, leaving next month. They're divvying up part of the fare up front and setting them on opening the mines. A place called Vancouver Island.'

'It's no good if they only pay part of the fare. No collier's got spare brass to fork out for that sort of journey and besides –'

'Let me finish, will you? The other part's to be worked off during the voyage, so there's nowt to pay to get there. I'm really interested. What say you?'

'I'm sure it all sounds good on paper, but for one thing I couldn't leave Pa. I'm all he's got, except for a few cousins o'er Cockermu'th way, and he doesn't hold with them much.'

'Aye, there's that side, but it's a wonderful opportunity. You're my marrer. I don't want to leave you behind. Won't you at least come with me and read about it?'

The idea of upping and leaving Cumberland held no

attraction for Stag, but seeing Tom's excited face as he waited for an answer, he wavered, and Tom pounced.

'How can I discuss it with you if you don't know the details?'

'All right, you've won me over.' Stag picked up his mouth organ, put it in his pocket, patted it and stood up. 'Look sharp, drink up and we'll go take a gander at your notice. A quick look, mind. I don't want to be hanging around outside. The wind is an angry one. There'll be plenty this night glad they've not put out to sea.'

'That's better. Anyway, you've always said if the opportunity to do better came up, you'd take it. What about that shop you've always wanted to open?'

'Aye, but that hasn't ever included taking off for the other side of the world.'

Outside, Stag and Tom jostled their way through a throng of high-spirited sailors with female followers hanging on their arms. Stag, tall, strongly built with broad shoulders, a mop of fair hair and penetrating blue eyes, was a contrast to Tom, who was shorter and stockier, with dark hair and brown eyes. It was rumoured, despite the Kennedy name, that Tom's family had received their swarthy looks from Spanish sailors seeking refuge in Whitehaven generations ago.

Arriving at the Savings Bank, they found said broadsheet fixed to a tall pillar. Part of it had come unstuck and was flapping about wildly, with the anxiety of a surrender flag. Stag shivered and tried to pull his collar further up his neck.

'It's too cold to stand around here. I'll read this at home later.' He peeled the broadsheet off the wall and folded what came away into four, before stuffing it in his jacket pocket.

After agreeing with Tom to discuss the matter another time, Stag, who had an early stint the next day, made his way up the hillside to his home at New Houses. His pa would be in the Fox and Grapes for at least another hour and he'd have the house to himself.

As it was, however, he'd not been home long, and was putting a lighted taper to the fire, when he heard the click of the latch and his father, Jabe, came in.

'It's raw out there tonight, lad.' Jabe rubbed his hands together and blew on them. 'I thought I'd leave the pub early. When the door opened and a gust of wind came blowing in, I could smell the storm in its tail. Best get off home, I thought, afore it gets set in.'

Stag smiled at his father. 'Shall we sup an ale together, Pa?'

Jabe nodded. 'Aye, reckon that's a good idea.' He opened a small cupboard to the left of the hearth, took two tankards and filled them from a brown earthenware flagon. 'You can tell me what's been about in the town this night.'

Stag pulled the broadsheet from his pocket and held it up. 'I had some bad news this evening. Tom's thinking of leaving and taking up a job in Canada.'

'That's a surprise.'

'Aye, it is. It's come out of the blue.'

'Let me guess. He wants you to go with him?'

'Aye, you're right there. Of course, it's ridiculous. Anyways, I promised I'd read this broadsheet so I'd know what he's talking about.'

Father and son talked over Tom's astonishing decision until Jabe yawned and began damping down the fire. They checked the door lock, set out their bait tins for dinner the next day, then bade each other a good night.

Alone in his bedroom, Stag unfolded the broadsheet and laid it out on a quilt made by his mother in anticipation of her marriage. She'd fashioned it skilfully, stuffing it with cloth clippings and wool she'd gathered from hedgerows. Being now well washed-out it provided little physical warmth, but despite this, over the years Stag had often drawn emotional warmth from its proximity in the early hours, when sleep eluded him.

He stripped off his shirt and shivered from the draught blasting through a broken skylight. The house was in the centre of three long rows of hillside terraces, built seventy years earlier for workmen by James Lowther, Earl of Lonsdale. Despite their age they were still referred to as New Houses. The hill they were built on was so steep, the middle and front terraces of house roofs were level with the cobbled road behind. Passing lads – and, less often, lasses – had taken delight over the years in kicking stones from the road at the skylights, scattering swiftly with loud whoops of joy when a pane shattered. Stag had played the same game as a lad and, as far back as he could remember, his window had been stuffed with brown paper.

The draught slapped his naked back and he pulled on his flannel nightshirt. It was an old one, patched and worn, and were it not for the draught from the broken skylight he would have forsaken it altogether. Sitting up in bed, he pulled the quilt tight up to his neck and began reading. He was amused by Tom's attempts to get him to emigrate, but it saddened him to think his marrer might be leaving. He realised, with some guilt, he'd be pleased if Tom wasn't accepted, or if he decided not to go at the last minute.

At the top of the broadsheet was an engraving of the *Princess Rose* entering a harbour not unlike their own in Whitehaven. In large letters underneath was an appeal by the Hudson's Bay Company for able-bodied men to take their wives and families to the Pacific coast to help set up the mines in Colville, on Vancouver Island. The pay was generous – £78.00 per annum for a daily ten-hour stint. Tom was right: after five years there was the offer of a free passage home.

CHAPTER TWO

The next day Stag was picking up his Davy lamp and handing over his token at the Wellington Pit when the superintendent took him to one side.

'I've to make some gang changes. Brown's had his hand hurt by a falling in, so Devlin, Hibbs and Stevens need a fourth hagger.'

Stag's mood plummeted. If there were three colliers he didn't want to work with, it was those three. Stevens was a big brute of a man not long out of gaol and not a man Stag wanted to fall out with. He wasn't afraid of him; he just didn't want the unpleasantness and aggravation that came with disagreement. Devlin was renowned for using his fists first and asking questions later. Hibbs, dimmer than the other two, had a strange way of looking at people that unnerved Stag. Apart from the fact he just didn't like them, Stag knew he couldn't trust them to work as a team in a crisis. The gang he'd been working alongside for the last year was a close-knit unit and each one of them looked out for the others' backs as a matter of course and duty.

'Why me?' Stag asked.

'Because you're dependable, a good worker, and you might knock some sense into their heads.'

'Is that a compliment?'

'No. Stick with me on this. It's only temporary until Brown's hand heals over. No more than a month at most, I'll wager.'

Stag decided there was no point in protesting. The superintendent was the gaffer and his word was more or less law.

❊ ❊ ❊

All went well for the first two days and they worked and ate together. On the third day, Stevens announced they should not all take their snack break at the same time, because he and the other two had business to discuss. Under normal circumstances Stag would have been disappointed, as he enjoyed the camaraderie of the meal break, but he was now only too pleased not to have to sit with them. It suited him to keep himself to himself. It was only for a month and that time would pass quickly.

On the sixth day Stag realised his bait tin was missing. It had been his grandfather's and as such was irreplaceable. He began retracing his steps, thinking he must have absentmindedly put it down. He wondered if one of the others had picked it up and began making his way to where he knew they'd be having their snack. He could hear the men talking and, out of curiosity, held back in the shadows to listen.

Stevens was holding forth. 'Let me go over it again. I know you're a bit slow, Hibbs. It's going to be easy.

There's a ship in Stromness unloading furs. It's in trouble – hit the dock or something. Anyway, they're making short-term repairs and bringing it down here around the 13th of next month to Brocklebank's, before heading down to Liverpool. It'll have the brass from the sale of the furs on board and that'll be in the Lombard Shipping Office safe while the ship's in dry dock.'

'You can't leave brass on a ship in dry dock,' said Hibbs, tipping his bait tin upside down before banging the base to shake out the breadcrumbs.

'That's right. We could be in and out in no time. Just like this.' Stevens clicked his fingers. 'Money in our pockets, smiles on our faces and lasses on our laps.'

Panic coursed through Stag's body. They were planning a robbery and he didn't want any part of it. He began to retreat, but it was too late. He jumped as he felt a calloused hand land on his bare shoulder. He'd been listening so intently he'd not heard anyone sneak up behind him. He looked round.

Devlin's voice was hostile. 'I didn't take you as someone who'd listen in to private conversations.'

Stevens and Hibbs stopped talking and looked up as Devlin pushed Stag out from the shadows.

'What did he hear?' asked Stevens.

'He knows our plan.' The flat of Devlin's hand was now shoved hard against Stag's naked back.

'I was only looking for my bait tin,' said Stag.

'That's a lie, you were hanging back listening,' said Devlin. 'I watched you.'

'Sit down,' said Stevens.

15

Devlin pushed Stag forward, causing him to stumble. Stag sat down amongst the coal detritus on the pit floor. In the dim light, Stevens and Hibbs were staring at him intently. Stevens, eyes cold as glass marbles, stared out from a face black with coal soot, while Hibbs' cheeks were all puffed out with cold tatie pie.

As if he could read Stag's mind, Stevens, leering at him, put his head on one side and said, 'You're wondering what to do now aren't you?'

'I was just looking for my bait tin, that's all.'

'Never mind your bloody bait tin.' Stevens scratched his chin. 'You've got several roads. You can pretend you didn't hear, but we know you did. You can say you won't say anything, but how do we know you'll not be tempted to shop us?

'He's an accessory now, isn't he, Stevens?' said Hibbs.

'Button up, I was coming to that.' The words came out in a hiss.

'Aye, he's an accessory,' said Devlin.

Stevens nodded. He took a knife and a stick from his pocket and, all the while looking at Stag, began whittling one end into a sharp point. Miners often whittled sticks, but with Stevens the action took on a certain unpleasantness. 'There's another road.' He hawked and spat. 'You can join us. We need another man to keep look out.'

'What?' said Devlin. He spoke as if Stag wasn't there. 'What are you thinking of? He's not right for a job like this. He's not one of us. I bet he's never broken the law in all his years.'

'I know what I'm saying. He's part of it now. We can't

let this job slip away because of him.' Stevens turned to Stag, who was fighting a panic reflex to get up and run. 'What say you? Are you with us or agin us?'

Being the focus of the three men's attention, all eagerly awaiting his response, was making Stag even more nervous. Even though he knew he was clutching at straws, he said, 'Devlin's right. I wouldn't be any use. You don't want me in on this.'

'Oh, but we do,' said Stevens

Stag tried another tack. 'I'm not going to commit myself until I know what the full plan is. That's fair enough, isn't it?' He was hoping he could dissuade them, but to do that would make him a party to knowledge he didn't want to possess. Still, it was the only path left open to him. He had to convince them the whole idea was doomed and he couldn't do that without the details.

Stevens scratched behind his ear with the sharp end of the stick and considered the matter for a few minutes. 'All right, but remember, it doesn't take much to upset me.' He turned to Hibbs and Devlin. 'Are we to tell him, lads?' Devlin nodded straightaway. Hibbs paused before nodding, but his face indicated he was unhappy about it.

Stevens laid out the bare bones of the robbery. Had Stag not felt so anxious and out of sorts he would have been tempted to laugh at their naivety.

'Are you really suggesting the four of us should break into the Lombard Steamship Company offices and empty the safe?' He looked at each man in turn.

Stevens cracked his knuckles. 'You know I'm walking out with Bella who works there?'

Stag nodded, thinking, as he had done several times before, he wouldn't be happy coming across an angry inebriated Stevens in a dark alley. Or a stone-cold sober one for that matter.

'Bella knows everything that happens there.'

Stag knew Bella. She was big too, and brazen. The perfect companion for Stevens and together they made a fearsome couple. 'What does Bella think? Is it her idea?'

'No, she's not got wind of it. Too much of a blabbermouth. She's my canary, sings away and tells me everything without me having to ask. No, it's all my idea and a grand one too, isn't it?' Stevens smirked.

'Why now?' asked Stag, ignoring the question. 'What's brought this on all of a sudden?'

'Don't give us that,' said Devlin. 'You heard, I know you did. The ship carrying the brass is going into dry dock here in Whitehaven.'

'You think that makes it an easy target? Surely they'll put the money straight into the bank.'

'No, they're not going to, and this is the beauty of it. Bella says Lombard's got a good safe and the manager, Donal, thinks the fewer people know, the better. If they put it in the bank more people know, and it makes it public. She told me he said "Nothing much happens in Whitehaven".'

Devlin threw his head back and laughed. 'He doesn't look at the papers, then.'

'Bella'll know when the money's in the safe,' said Stevens.

'How will you get in the safe?' Stag asked, exasperated that they couldn't see the obvious problems.

'We'll persuade Donal to open it.'

'You want your brains washing. What if he won't?'

'Then a quick tap on the bonce with my shillelagh and he'll hand over the key.'

Stag didn't doubt for one minute Stevens would carry out such an action. The man was a monster with no sense of humanity.

'Donal will be able to describe you. You'll never get away with it. I don't want to hear any more. You're all going to end up on a convict ship. It's madness.'

Stevens ignored him. 'I'm thinking we need four strong men we can trust. Two to keep watch and two to break in.'

'That's us, then,' said Devlin. 'I'm warming to the idea of Stag being with us more as every minute passes.'

Stag looked at Hibbs, who was still looking uncomfortable. For the one who seemed to have the least brains he appeared to be seeing the most reason.

'Right enough, us four then. You'll be going along with us then, Stag?'

'No, I'm telling you I'm not for it. I'm not ending up in Carlisle gaol.'

'Can't we manage with three?' asked Hibbs.

Stag wanted to shout at them. Why couldn't the other two see the project was doomed?

'Aye, but it'll not be as easy.'

'Stag, you've no choice now. We can teach you the ropes, don't worry. I'm sure you'll take to it like a duck to water.' Stevens' smirk had evolved into a full-blown sneer. It was as if he had something to prove and Stag refusing to go along was now a thorn in his side. Stag wondered if he was using him to establish his authority within the group, which would make it much more difficult to talk his way out of it. The man, as well as being a brute, seemed to have some elements of madness in his being.

'No, I don't want anything to do with it. First, I'm not a thief and second, what if something goes wrong and someone gets hurt? That puts a whole new tail on the fish. My advice to you is to forget the whole thing. It's doomed. I've heard nowt and seen nowt.'

'But the trouble is you *have* heard, haven't you?' Stevens was holding a smile that didn't reach his eyes. 'I'm a decent man. I'll give you a day to think it over. I'm sure you'll come round.'

Stag's chin lifted slightly. He'd not missed the menace in Stevens' comment, but he wasn't going to be swayed. True, he could do with some spare brass, as could any collier, but not illegal gains. He worked for his rewards in life. He looked round at the three of them. He wouldn't trust them to organise a pony ride round the harbour, never mind plan a robbery. There weren't enough brains for it between the ears of all three of them put together. No, it was plain daft, there was no other word for it, but why couldn't they see it? *Greed*, he thought. Just for one fleeting moment he felt pity for the three of them. Born into houses lacking in morality, coached in thievery, what chance had they ever had?

The next day Stag was walking home after his shift when Stevens caught up with him.

'I'm not interested,' said Stag, straightaway hastening his pace.

Stevens kicked out at a stone. 'You're not with us, but how "not with us" are you?'

'Thinking you're wrong and not wanting to join you doesn't mean I'm going to shop you.'

'With a fourth man it'll be so much easier.'

Stag stopped walking, stood in front of Stevens and put his fists on his hips. He assessed the situation. He was taller than Stevens, but lighter of body. If it came to fisticuffs Stevens would down him with one blow.

'You've been thieving all your life. Your pa was a thief and his pa before him. It's your family's way of life. Your choices. I was brought up differently.'

Stevens took a step closer and straightened up. 'Are you saying you're better than me?'

'I'm saying I'm not like you. Call it all off.'

'When that brass is there for the picking?'

'Any fool can see it's not going to work.'

'Think I'm a fool now, do you?' Stevens clenched his fists but didn't raise them.

'Aye, on this occasion I do.'

Stevens grabbed hold of Stag's arm and began to speak, all the time gradually tightening his grip.

'So far you've said you're better than me and my family, that the three of us working in the gang alongside you are stupid and that I'm a fool.' He pushed Stag away so that he stumbled. 'You're not pleasing me, Liddell, you're making me cross. I'm thinking that if it should all go wrong, I can take you with me. The others'll back me up. I'll say you were in it from the start. You're in it, no matter what.'

21

Stag's mouth went dry and he felt a bit sick. Stevens might be able to smell his fear, but he was damned if he was going to show it.

'Think about it, my fellow marrer.' Stevens held Stag's eyes, challenging him to look away. 'Or if I were you, I'd start watching my back.' He drew his index finger over his neck in a slashing movement, turned and walked away.

Even though the immediate menace was over, Stag's legs began to tremble, and in an attempt to calm himself he paused halfway down the cliff and looked out over the town. How could everything look just the same when his own life was being turned upside down? The slate roofs, the ships in the harbour being serviced, the sailors and townsfolk going about their business were all there as they always were. The seagulls mewing overhead, occasionally landing, their fat bodies unstable on their spindly legs. To his left he could see the candlestick chimney and the castellated buildings of the Wellington Pit, all just the same. The smell of the sea, always present, was neither sharper nor sweeter. What he couldn't see was anything different, yet everything was different for him, just because he knew things he hadn't sought to know.

When Stevens had returned to the pit after serving his last sentence Stag had had misgivings and kept his distance. He knew now he should have queried the superintendent's order. He'd been soft, too quick to please. He could have talked his way out of it if he'd tried. He pondered taking Hibbs to one side, to dissuade him, since he was the weakest link in the whole scheme. But better to try and put as much distance between himself and the three of them as he could. He'd make arrangements to change his work gang the next day. He'd come up with a valid reason, even if he had to say he was sick.

✻ ✻ ✻

Two days later, Stag and Tom were walking together on their way up to the pit.

'I heard you got out of working with the Stevens trio.'

'When I went to ask to be changed, Hockenhull said he was surprised I'd lasted as long as I did. I almost think he was waiting for me to ask to be moved.'

'You're a good worker, he knows that. He won't want to put your nose out of joint for long. He's sent in one of the new ones from Cockermu'th, poor bugger.'

Stag yawned.

'Tired?'

'It's nothing. I didn't sleep well, that's all.' He changed the subject. 'Are you really serious about emigrating?'

'Aye, but we can't say 'til all's known,' said Tom.

'Even with Lavinia expecting a bairn in a few months?'

'Aye. This could be a chance to break the Kennedy family pattern of always talking about a better future, but never trying to do anything about it. To strike out, get out, make a name for myself. Having this bairn is making me feel differently 'bout things.'

'What does Lavinia think?'

'She's all for it. Working at the bank manager's house on Church Street before we wed showed her the way other people live. Anyway, her pa is behind it all. It was him mentioned it in the first place.'

'Owen and Queenie are thinking of leaving too?'

'Aye, I know Lavinia won't leave unless her ma does. And it means the family won't have to be split up. In all truth, you should think about leaving too. What is there for you here except always being a collier, when you could be free, with brass to spare in five years?'

'There's saying you want to make changes and there's doing it. Anyway, I told you there's Pa to think of being on his own.'

'Aye, there's a saying "Once a collier always a collier", but it ain't true. Maybe years ago, but not now. Suit yourself, but you could be back in five years making his life more comfortable with all your earnings, and setting up that shop you've talked about. You've no wife or bairns to sap your wages.'

'No, that's right enough. I'd still like to open the shop.'

He wanted to tell Tom he didn't want him to go. That they'd grown up together, that he would really miss him, but the time wasn't right. Those sentiments would have to wait for another day.

'Even if you're not interested, you ought to come to the meeting the day after the morrow. There's folk can't make it and as secretary of the Pitmen's Club you should be there on their behalf. There's more to being secretary than walking at the front of a funeral wearing a white headband and holding an unfurled banner.' Tom made the motions of holding up a banner and twirling it around.

'You just want me to come with you.'

'I'll not deny it'd be a bonus. Apart from us being marrers we've our pact. That binds us.'

'Aye, I haven't forgotten the pact. It may be a long way back, but it's always there.'

'I didn't for one minute think you'd forgotten. It's not something either of us could easily forget. It's part of what bonds us. I'll see you at the Globe on the morrow for the meeting then?'

'Aye, you will.'

Later, preparing for his stint, Stag was waiting in line at the mine when he saw Stevens and Devlin in front of him. Seeing them and worrying they might look round made him uncomfortable. To distract himself he went over his conversation with Tom, but it was no good – his thoughts kept straying to the predicament he now found himself in.

CHAPTER THREE

The coffee room at the Globe Hotel on King Street was a good ten-minute walk from New Houses. Stag allowed himself just under half an hour to secure a good position. Even so, when he arrived the room was already crowded, with standing room only. Colliers of all ages and skills had already taken up the prime positions. He wondered how many had been lured by the promise of the free ale and then decided that, apart from those who had signed the Pledge, that would be most of them. There was a gap in the crowd on the side wall to Stag's right and he pushed his way through and eased himself into it. He leant back and looked around. Plenty of familiar faces, which didn't surprise him. Devlin, Stevens and Hibbs were at the front. Stevens' eyes narrowed when he saw Stag and he was sure, had the room not been so crowded, the three of them would have made their way over to him. Just seeing them made him feel under threat again.

Tom was standing with his father-in law at the opposite side of the room. Stag caught his eye. He wanted to tell him about the position he found himself in. The three men were out to get him, of that Stag had no doubt, but he couldn't tell Tom for fear he would want to do something, and then Stag would be exposed as a grass.

He studied the Hudson's Bay Company representative who, in a businessman's frockcoat with neatly fitting striped trousers, was by far the best-dressed man in the room. Beside him were two other men less formally dressed. He stepped onto a makeshift platform and waited for his audience to notice him. He was a tall, distinguished-looking man with greying, bushy sideburns that merged with a full beard over plump cheeks.

When all faces were turned towards him, he spoke. 'My name is Robert Liversedge and I represent the Hudson's Bay Company. The Company is anxious to engage the right sort of emigrants and we are hopeful we can find them here.'

He had the kind of clipped voice Stag associated with the businessmen of the town. An efficient 'I can get things done' type of voice. To his surprise, Stag found he was intrigued by all Mr Liversedge had to say about the new mine in Colville, on Vancouver Island.

'The *Princess Rose* will pass round the Horn to arrive on Vancouver Island in November. She will depart Liverpool on Saturday May 16th, with transport from here via the Steam Navigation Company on the Friday. We're looking for dependable men and their families. Why their families, you may ask? In our Company we know it's the men who must work and the women who keep the hearth. We want a happy community built on sound social foundations.'

He paused to stroke his lower chin whiskers, turning them into a 'V' shape, before pulling down the front of his waistcoat. 'We need men who are true in body and spirit to their families and who will serve the Company honestly.' He pulled out his pocket watch and checked the time. 'I should make it clear we do not accept vagabonds or feckless men, any who are of ill health in body or mind, or any who have spent time in gaol.'

As the last words were spoken, several men turned to look at Stevens, Devlin and Hibbs. They stood their ground. Stag assumed they did so in anticipation of more free beer, or perhaps – and this was an awful thought – perhaps they were going to lay in wait for him at the end. Just as Whitehaven seemed to be a different place, so he himself had changed. He couldn't go anywhere now without wondering if he was going to run into them or if they were going to come for him. He didn't want to spend his days continually looking over his shoulder.

From his position with his back against the side wall, Stag could see the faces of the men listening. He knew them all and tried to put himself in the position of Mr Liversedge, who didn't know their backgrounds, and had to make decisions visually on accepting or rejecting each man. He imagined the Company representative disregarding one man because he looked shifty and another because he was wilting under the stuffy atmosphere of the room.

His voice interrupted Stag's thoughts. 'I've not been on the journey myself, but I always inspect the passenger ships before they leave and I know discomfort below decks is unavoidable. You colliers are usually able to adapt well, but it's curious how different a confined space on a ship is to that down a mine, and some find it hard. This is not a journey to be undertaken lightly, but the rewards on arrival are, in my opinion, well worth the travail.'

A voice, sounding slightly tipsy, shouted out from the back of the room. 'Yer would say that, wouldn't yer?'

Mr Liversedge glanced at the men who'd arrived with him. There was a break while he waited for them to make their way to the back of the room and eject the owner of the voice before he continued, 'I estimate three-quarters of you are here for the free ale. Of the rest, most of you will be interested, but unable to persuade your wives to leave kith and kin. Of the remainder I may be fortunate and sign up six or eight men with families, and a few single men. We are offering opportunity; the rest will be up to you.'

He held up a smaller version of the broadsheet and handed a pile of papers to the two men to distribute. 'All the fine details are on this paper. Kindly take one. A doctor and teacher will travel with you. The Company will provide guaranteed work and a bonus of half-a-crown for every ton of coal over 45 tons. You'll be provided with one acre of land close to your dwelling for one pound per year. Don't hold back if your experience is limited. We need men of varying skill levels.'

At 10 o'clock Mr Liversedge drew the meeting to a close. 'I hope you will pass tonight's information on to those unable to attend. I shall be holding interviews tomorrow morning in room 14 at the Lonsdale Hotel from 10 o'clock onwards and I will be available all day, so no need to change your stint. Leave your name with my associate here.' He pointed to one of the men who had ejected the heckler.

Stag waited in the public bar until the coffee room had cleared. This was partly to avoid a meeting with Devlin, Stevens or Hibbs, but the main purpose was to waylay Mr Liversedge as he left. He'd made a decision and, hearing Mr Liversedge's voice, he left the bar and stepped out into the corridor. He removed his cap.

'Excuse me, sir,' he said, his hands twisting his cap. 'I'd like an appointment.' He told himself he wasn't committing to anything. He could change his mind – he was keeping a door open, nothing more. It was just that since he'd discussed things with Tom, everything had changed. He didn't want to leave Whitehaven, but his life had suddenly taken a most disagreeable turn. He noticed that asking for the appointment out loud brought him some relief. He now had options. The words gave him a way out, a possible escape from the hell he was experiencing. He even hoped his imaginings in the room had been accurate and that Mr Liversedge, seeing him leaning against the wall, had marked him out as a suitable applicant. He was just putting a toe in the water, he told himself, not leaping in.

Mr Liversedge examined the strongly built fair-haired lad standing in front of him. 'I said to give your name to one of my men. Why haven't you done that?'

'It's a bit tricky for me, sir, because I don't want people to know I'm leaving.' Stag was unsure how to explain he was thinking of emigrating without it appearing as if he was a criminal fleeing justice, when the truth was, he was fleeing to avoid being called a criminal.

'Got some girl in trouble?' Mr Liversedge was scrutinising him in a knowing way.

Stag was startled. The man was blunt for a gentleman. He thought quickly. If necessary, he needed to be away from Whitehaven at least five days before the ship sailed on the 16th in order to be far away if the robbery took place. No, he couldn't give the real reason.

'Can I take it by your silence this is the case?' The representative pointedly took out his watch.

'No, sir, nothing like that.' *What if he won't take me?* thought Stag. *Then what?* 'I just don't want everybody knowing my business.' It was a lame reply and surely Mr Liversedge could sense he wasn't telling the truth. However, he showed no sign of thinking Stag had just lied to him.

'Name?'

'Liddell. Stag Liddell, sir.'

The representative pulled a small black notebook from his pocket and wrote it down. 'Be at my room at 6 o'clock tomorrow evening in the Lonsdale Hotel. I'll see you before I leave and I'll know better then what availability of space there is. Does that time fit with your stint?'

Stag nodded. 'Aye, sir, I can make that time. Room 14.'

'It's no certainty I'll accept you.'

'No, sir, but I thank you already for the consideration.'

'I've a word of advice for you.'

'Aye?' Stag was unsure, suddenly anxious about what was coming.

'If you really want to leave in secret, tell no one of your plan. Do you understand? Trust no one.'

'No, sir, I won't. Understood. Not a soul, except my pa, and I must tell him.'

'Good. Let's save time right now. Have you ever been in trouble with the constable? Because if that's your reason for leaving secretly, I'll find out.'

'No, sir.'

'I'll check, you know.'

Stag looked him straight in the eye. 'No, sir, I'm not in trouble with the police.' He was thinking – *but I'm probably going to be in trouble if I stay.*

As he walked home, Stag's thoughts were all over the place. He relived the conversation he'd had with Tom the day before and reflected, not for the first time, that others he liked or admired were planning to emigrate. Lavinia's pa, Owen Jefferson, was a first-rate foreman respected by all. He'd be an asset in any new mine. Queenie, his wife, was a jolly, level-headed woman any person would be glad to turn to in a crisis. It was a big step he was pondering, going away for five years, although maybe with friends to support him it'd be easier. Stag kept his misgivings over Lavinia's suitability to himself. Tom, as her husband, was in a much better position to assess her ability to adapt to a new country.

That night he fell asleep almost immediately, only to wake when the room was still dark, with his brain fully alert after dreaming he was falling off a cliff. It was his recurrent bad dream and always an indication something was troubling him. He never reached the bottom of the cliff, but death seemed certain until the last minute, and he always woke in a cold sweat. After that it would be a long night if he couldn't get back to sleep quickly.

That early morning, following much tossing and turning that served only to tangle his bedding, Stag gave up lying there listening to the seagulls. He lit his lamp and had another look at the broadsheet.

When all was said and done, there was only one decision to make, but it was an enormous one. Should he stay or should he go? He wondered if it was more truthful to describe his dilemma as should he stay or should he run? He was in a hole, and there was no denying it was a deep hole.

By first light he could see both a carrot and a stick. An excellent salary in a job he was good at, with the option of coming back to open his shop, at the cost of leaving his father for five years. What if Pa died before he returned? That was too awful to dwell on. Or, staying put with the risk of being caught up in the aftermath of a robbery that anyone could see was going to be a total disaster, with maybe even a stint in gaol, followed by a lifetime as a collier.

Stag heard his pa rise and rake through the coals. He began to dress, knowing he'd things to see to that day: to keep his appointment with Mr Liversedge and to discuss the situation with his pa. He'd hesitated all his life; he wasn't going to anymore, he wasn't being allowed to. He'd begin by talking with his pa.

CHAPTER FOUR

With the town's church bells summoning the faithful, Stag sought out a pail and made for the communal pump to fetch water. There was already a short queue. Nobody spoke. It was an unwritten rule that at the pump on the Sabbath, before church, it was sufficient greeting to nod at one's neighbours. After returning and setting the pail down by the hearth, Stag fingered the folded broadsheet in his pocket, waiting while his pa prepared breakfast and then settled to eat it in his favourite seat by the hearth. On Sundays, for reasons he had never shared, Jabe chose to dress in the manner of an agricultural worker rather than a collier. This consisted of best breeches and a linen shirt with smocked top and braces. For church, usually in the evening, he would add a worn tweed jacket that had belonged to his father and grandfather before him, along with his best cap.

'You're fidgety, lad,' he said. 'Wriggling like an eel. Owt to say? I heard you light your lamp in the night.'

There was no easy way; Stag was just going to have to blurt it out. 'I've got myself in a spot of bother.'

Jabe helped himself to a thick wedge of bread and spread it with a layer of dripping. 'What bother?'

'I'm not sure I can tell you.'

'What do you mean?' Jabe leaned forward in his chair, giving Stag his complete attention. 'Summat you can't tell your pa? In trouble with the constable?'

In the last twenty-four hours Stag had been asked that question twice, never having been asked it in his whole life before. 'No. Well, not yet, but I could be.' He outlined the situation to his father, stressing that he told him only upon pain of death and that he didn't want his father to do anything about it for fear of retribution upon them both, especially on Jabe.

His father was silent for a few minutes. 'I know the men. Stevens and Devlin are nasty pieces of work, Hibbs is gormless and easily led. It's been said Stevens has been known to swap his hewer token for a tub with another's coals if it looks heavier. 'Appen maybe they're just clarten about and you're mithering o'er nowt?'

'No, Stevens is after me. I think he's got something to prove over the other two.'

'You've told them you're having no part of it?'

'Aye. Over and over. In fact I'm thinking of emigrating to get away.' There. It was out. He'd said it.

Jabe didn't say anything for a few minutes. His face grew sad and he put a hand on the back of his head and rubbed his hair. 'You're thinking of going with Tom, then?'

'It's a thought. I don't know. I don't know what to do. Can you advise me, Pa?'

'I can see you're in a tight spot, but North America? It's such a long way, another land, another country.'

'I'm thinking perhaps I can make something good out of this whole thing. In five years, with a bit more brass and some business training, I can really set myself up and come back and everything will be easier for us. I could go into business. You know I've always thought about opening a shop, but never had the means.'

'You're your mother's lad, all reet. She always wanted to open a shop like her pa, and she'd have inherited his if he hadn't lost it through drink. She'd such plans for us all about going into business. God bless her. Taken from us before her time.' His father's eyes grew misty. 'She'd be sad to see you looking so drawn and ill at ease as you are now.'

Stag handed over the folded broadsheet. 'You can read about it here.'

Jabe glanced at the sheet then handed it back. 'Read it to me, lad, whilst I'm eating.'

With an eye out for his father's reaction, Stag relayed the relevant parts. Jabe refrained from comment until he'd finished, then cut more bread from the loaf by his side.

'Is it right to grasp this opportunity?' asked Stag.

His father supped his tea and gave a big sigh. 'Let me think on it, lad, but if you really must, then take that road. It goes without saying I'll miss you dreadfully.' He turned his face away and Stag knew, without having to see, that his father's eyes were moist.

'I know I'm running away, but this could be my only chance to make something of my life. Staying here, I'll always be down the pit.'

Jabe pulled out a handkerchief and blew his nose. 'True,

that's not what your ma had in mind for you when she worked so hard on your learning. Thinking of her again reminds me, you look like her more and more these days. It surprises me a son can resemble his ma so closely. It's the same blue eyes, I think, and she was always smiling, or looking as if she was about to laugh. You can be like that sometimes. That's apart from when she was ailing. You've a strong body, whereas she was always fragile in health.'

'I've a lot to thank her for, I know that. Teaching me to read, showing me picture books of the world, taking me for walks and talking about the trees and animals along the way.'

'All in the past now, but she sowed summat good in you. The Good Lord knows, I don't want you to leave, and if I thought it were going to be for ever it'd be an arrow through my heart, but I'm a fair man and I reckon were I in the same boat, I'd maybe want to steer the same course. I don't want to push you away, but there's some soundness in going away and five years is not long if it's going to be for the better.'

'It all seems so unfair, being pushed like this. I've been living a quiet life and now everything's all over the place.'

'Aye, but if you can work something good out of it then it might come right in the end. Let's talk after you've had your appointment. We can go and pay respects to your ma and talk about it then. How's that?'

'What if I have to make a decision there and then?'

'You'll know what to say. If the head and the heart agree, then it'll be the right decision, whatever you decide.'

✻ ✻ ✻

Upon his arrival at the Lonsdale Hotel, Stag's nervousness was compounded by the hotel's liveried doorman looking him up and down before directing him to the service stairs. Although glad of the chance to keep his appointment from public view, he resented the fact that, just because he was a collier, he was a second-class citizen in the town. Without the colliers' sweat there'd be no grand hotel, no visiting dignitaries, just a small town with a deep harbour. It was coal that made Whitehaven rich and stoked Irish fires, and his sweat was responsible for some of that. It was something he was proud of, and he wondered if he would have the same pride in setting out the mines in another country, should he choose that path.

At 6.05 pm Stag was ushered into Mr Liversedge's presence and directed to a wooden chair with a rush seat that had seen better days. His immediate thought was how out of place it was in the ornately decorated room, with its gilt mirrors and expensive drapes. The hotel management, no doubt fearing the effects of honest workingmen's dust upon their fine upholstery, must have placed it there as a hygiene measure.

Mr Liversedge, somewhat imperiously, took up his pen and motioned to Stag to sit down. 'I've made a few enquiries. The police sergeant speaks highly of you and says you appear to be a responsible citizen. I have told him all enquiries are confidential. He assures me he will say nothing that will cause you any problems or alert any third party.'

Stag knew it was more than the sergeant's job was worth to upset the Hudson's Bay Company representative.

'How long have you been a collier?'

'Ten years, sir. I started at fourteen, filling my pa's carts. Then I was a hurrier pulling other's carts and now I'm a hagger, cutting coal at the face.'

'How much are you earning?'

"Two pounds a week, sir, but I've to pay my own filler and hurrier now. Would I need to do that in Colville?'

'No.' Mr Liversedge wrote everything down in a green ledger in a swirly copperplate hand. 'Stand and walk around.'

Stag relaxed a little. He knew he stood well, with a straight build.

'Thank you. Any sickness or shortage of breath?'

Stag shook his head but, as he didn't look up from his writing, Mr Liversedge missed his response. He looked up. 'Well?'

'No, sir, none.'

'Spittle?'

'Begging your pardon, sir, do you want me to spit?'

Mr Liversedge sighed. 'No. Is your spittle clear and healthy? Is it black?'

'Oh, you mean "Black Spit"? No, sir, nothing like that.'

'Do you drink?'

What collier doesn't? Stag thought. 'No more than any other collier, sir, although I haven't signed the Pledge.'

'We are not looking for Pledgers, or water bellies. No need to fear if you like a drink now and then. It's thirsty work down in those pits, I am sure.'

'I like some ale most nights. I'm not what's called a drinking man in these parts.' It was difficult to know how to answer some of the questions. He wasn't a saint and he wasn't going to pretend to be one, but he needed to be accepted.

'Any relations still living? I think you mentioned your father yesterday.'

'That's Pa. Jabe Liddell. He's a foreman at the pit.' Stag instinctively nodded his head in the direction of the pit entrance. It was so much a part of his life, he always knew where he was in relation to it. 'Ma's been gone twelve years since.'

Mr Liversedge gave no verbal condolence, but he did glance up with a kindly expression at the young man in front of him whose voice had softened as he spoke of his mother. 'Accident or disease?'

'Disease, sir…The cough.'

Liversedge nodded. 'Common in industrial areas these days, and the cause of much suffering for those inflicted with it and sadness for those left to mourn. I come across it a lot.'

'It's a slow death, sir.'

'Do you need time to consider? Perhaps to consult with your father?'

This was the moment. Stag shook his head. 'No, I don't need to speak with Pa.' His brain was racing. It wasn't just Stevens' physical threat – it was that he could be branded a criminal, and he was an honest man. He could end up in Carlisle gaol, or worse. The safest course of action would be to leave Whitehaven, and not just for a month or so. That way he could never be linked with the robbery if it took place. His head told him to run and his heart told him there was every chance it would come good in the end. He'd always made the best of a bad job and he could be back in five years, financially secure.

He took a deep breath before saying, 'I wish to sign here and now if you'll have me.' He acknowledged the significance of the moment to himself. His life was now going to take a different path, a very different one, although Mr Liversedge, not being privy to Stag's thoughts, probably regarded the moment as just the signing up of another collier.

'I am at liberty to inform you that if you pass the on-board medical, we will engage you. Our doctor examines everyone on board before setting sail.'

'That is good, sir. There's one thing. I understand the Company is paying for the journey from Whitehaven to Liverpool. Would it be possible for me to travel earlier?'

'That would depend on the reason.'

'I've cousins there I've not seen for a long time. I'd like to spend time with them since I may never come back.' It was a necessary lie. He just couldn't run the risk of being in Whitehaven when the robbery took place.

'I can provide you with the cost of transport and one night's accommodation, which is what the others will receive. The ship sails on the 16th. What date are you thinking of?'

'Monday the 11th?' That would put him either side of the robbery, which he thought was going to be that week. It would be even better if the Irish Sea was rough and the ship arrived later.

'You are truly decided? Once you have signed, it is a legal commitment. You understand that, don't you?'

'Pa's kin came in from farming the fells when the rents went up. I'll not be the first Liddell to pick up roots and start again.'

'I'll sign you up now. Can you read well?'

'Aye, compared to many others here. Ma taught me. She said it was important, so I've read from an early age, but I'm no good with legal writing.'

'In that case I will read your contract aloud.' Liversedge withdrew an Indenture Contract of Service from the leather case on the desk, and showed it to Stag. The margins were decorated with scrolling leaves and the script was elegant copperplate engraving. Stag admired the fine lettering; it was impressive, and he felt proud he would soon be part of such a company.

Mr Liversedge began reading: 'Stag Liddell doth hereby bind himself to the said Governor and Company of Adventurers of England trading into Hudson's Bay to serve them as a working collier, miner, sinker, or labourer in the ship or vessel, but not bound to go aloft, from the date of embarkation after mentioned until his arrival in Vancouver Island, North America, and thereafter, during and until the full and complete term of five years from thence next ensuing...' As he continued, Stag tried to give the appearance of listening, but he wasn't really interested. He'd thrown his cap into the ring – there was no going back. When the reading came to an end, Mr Liversedge, with a finger that could be described as delicate, pointed to the place where Stag was to sign. There was no hesitation. Stag wrote in a clear bold hand. The representative blotted the ink and added his signature beneath Stag's, on behalf of the Hudson's Bay Company.

He wrote on a piece of paper, folded it and passed it over. 'Take this. It's the address of a good lodging-house. Mrs Hudley, the keeper, will look after you, and I will settle with her directly. Shall I inform her to expect you, or will you be staying with your cousins?'

'I'm not sure. One night at the lodging-house will be very useful. Thank you.'

Liversedge closed his marbled ledger with a flourish and began gathering his papers, indicating the meeting was at an end.

'Aye, thank you, sir, and for all your help.' Stag turned to go, but had only gone halfway across the room when Liversedge called out, 'What's that in your pocket?'

Stag pulled out his mouth organ.

'Can you play?'

'Aye, sir, I can indeed. I can make even a rough ploughman dance a fine jig with my tunes.'

'Be sure to take it with you. There's not much to do if the ship's becalmed and you'll be in great demand as the journey progresses.'

Stag returned the mouth organ to his pocket and patted it as he always did, out of habit. He left with his fate sealed and a sense of deliverance in his heart. Emerging from the hotel, he collided with the police sergeant.

'Steady, lad, you'll not get anywhere if you're always in such a rush.' The sergeant gave no indication he knew where Stag had been or where he was planning on going.

My secret's safe, thought Stag.

* * *

The next morning, Stag told his pa he'd signed up with the Company. Jabe nodded. 'I thought you would. We'll talk more this evening.'

'Is it so painful for you?' Guilt's fingers were tapping a fast rhythm on Stag's shoulder.

'No, it's not that. It's that I want to be near your ma when we talk about it. She's our family. We should respect that, and it's a peaceful place, just right for the things we have to talk over. Come with me after stint and we'll talk then.'

Stag sensed his father wanted to be alone with his thoughts, so he held back, letting him get well in front before he too set off for the pit.

Having a few minutes to spare, he called in at Mrs Giles' shop for some taffy toffee. It tasted good and kept his mouth moist underground. He was just coming out, turning towards the path to the mine, when he saw a figure walking up the cobbled way. It was Stevens, the sides of his coat flapping about as he strode along. Stag's heart sank. There was going to be a confrontation – he didn't have much choice. He wasn't going to give the bully the satisfaction of seeing him run away. It seemed an eternity before Stevens caught up with him, yet it was only a minute or two.

'Morning, Stag.'

Stag could smell last night's ale on the man's breath. He instinctively wrinkled his nose and took a step back.

Stevens put his head back and laughed. 'You don't seem pleased to see me.'

'Do we have business, you and I?' asked Stag.

'Indeed we do. We've a job to get done. I doubt it's slipped your mind.'

'For the last time, I'm telling you I want nothing to do with it. Get someone of your own kind and persuasion to help you. For a start, they'll be better at it than me.'

Stevens leant forward so his face was close. His stale breath hit Stag's face with the force of air escaping from a pair of fireside bellows. 'I don't want anyone else. I want you, because it's the only way I can rely on you keeping your mouth shut. I'm worried you're going to suddenly feel you have to do the right thing and blab. You should be pleased. It's not every man I want watching my back and it's not as if you won't come out of it with a pretty penny to your name.'

There was nothing to say. The man standing leering in front of him in the grubby oversized jacket, with half-closed eyes and foul breath, was not one either to see sense or back down. And Stag doubted that, even if he was in a mind to agree, he'd be lucky to see any payment from the crime.

'I'll be in touch when we've had word from Bella that the brass has come into Lombard's.'

'When will that be?'

As if he took the question as an indication of submission, Stevens grinned. 'In the week of the 11th, most likely the 13th. Like I say, I'll be in touch.'

That evening, Stag and Jabe took the low road to St Bees, leading inland from the town and the sea to the cemetery.

They went straight to the graveside, close by the ornate wrought-iron entrance gates. It was a cheerless spot and Stag remembered the day they'd placed his mother in the ground. Hers had been one of the first graves in what was then the new cemetery, and the spot had seemed exposed and gloomy. It was no less dispiriting now. Stag had always thought it an inappropriate resting place for such a life-loving wife and mother, but it was the plot the town clerk had allocated her: Mary Alice Liddell, 1808 – 1842, Plot 8. At least it was an even number; she'd always preferred those. She'd buy four apples, never three, always an even number. 'Nothing odd about me,' she'd say and laugh. She was now immortally recorded on the cemetery's plot chart, lodged in the inner sanctum of the Town Hall's cellars. Jabe had occasionally nagged his son for not returning to help tend the grave, but Stag always replied that when someone was gone, that was it, and there was no good dwelling on the loss as it only extended grief. It was a lie. He often thought of his ma.

The two men removed their flat caps and looked down at the carefully tended grave to which Jabe remained a regular visitor.

'So, you've signed up, lad?'

'Aye. I think I can make something good from this mess.'

'What about Stevens and the other two?'

'He collared me this morning outside Mrs Giles' shop. He's going to come looking for me the week of the 13th, when they know for sure the money's in.'

'He thinks you're going along with it?'

'I didn't say I would, just asked when he thought it would be.'

'You'll be gone that day. I'll cover for you, send him off in the wrong direction. I'll say you've gone to Cockermu'th for a day or two.'

'What if they take it out on you? Come round and threaten you?'

'If they threaten me, I'll tell them I'm going to shop them. You'll be long gone and they can't pin anything on me, like they can on you, lad, having worked alongside them. Better I keep mum and well out of it, but if it comes to it, I've got friends I can call on to knock a few heads together. People who owe me a few favours.'

Stag was amazed. He couldn't imagine his pa arranging anything that might involve violence. He'd never been one for fisticuffs.

'You look shocked. You're my son. You may be a man, but I'm still going to protect you in whatever way is necessary.'

'I'm still afraid for you.' Stag looked at his father's old jacket and old boots. As soon as he had some spare brass, he would buy him new ones.

'Let's put your fear to one side. I can look after myself. You've no need to worry, and besides, we're here with your ma now, and she wouldn't like all this kind of talk. I'm glad you've chosen to visit afore leaving for good. I'd always thought you didn't care o'er much.'

'It's because I care I don't come and see her in this place. I hate to see her here in such a solemn setting, but now I wish I'd visited more.' Stag wondered if he would ever see it again. Looking round at the tombstones with their carved citations, angels and crosses, all new memorials that had appeared since his last visit several years ago, he took heart. 'She's not so alone anymore,' he said.

'I'll take my place with her here in due course. You needn't worry 'bout where to put me, lad. I've done a lot of thinking in this spot recently, and I want you to know I may not be going with you on this journey, but I'm with you in spirit.'

'And I with you.' Stag put out his hand and touched his father's arm. He wanted to hold on to the memory of them gathered in this place for the last time as a family, even though it was a place associated with death and grief. 'I've a lot to thank you for, Pa.'

'Remember this, lad – no matter how we try, things never come out the way we expect. I'm truly wretched in my heart to see you go, but you're making a new life. If you're wanting peace of mind, ask yourself what your ma would have said, and if you think she'd have been agreeable, then you leave with my blessing too. For what it's worth, I've a mind she'd not have stood in your way.'

CHAPTER FIVE

Having told Tom the previous evening he'd signed up, and entreated him to tell no one, least of all his wife Lavinia, on Monday, May 11th, Stag slipped away, making for the coast road to catch the coach to Ravensglass station. From there he took the train to Barrow before transferring to the Liverpool post-boat. As they approached Liverpool from the river, the city appeared to exist within a cocoon of murkiness. One minute Stag and his fellow passengers on deck were bathed in mid-May sunshine, then, as if the boat had passed through an invisible frontier, they found themselves in a different world, where everything was grey, including the river. Thick black smoke hung over the city and the foul air caught the back of Stag's throat, setting him off coughing. Unfamiliar and unpleasant odours assaulted his nasal passages, and the soft tissues of his mouth acquired a metallic taste. The city was not at all how he'd imagined it, even though he'd seen prints in books. He'd expected an exciting place: all he saw was drabness and grime. He'd never seen so many buildings, so many ships or so many people.

Stag's unease grew when the boat docked and he was carried forward by the disembarking crowd. The quay was buzzing, and although no one paid him any attention, he felt conspicuous in his town clothes, with his battered carpet bag. A gentleman's portmanteau it was not, but it served its purpose. The crowds were busy seeing to their affairs and he was relieved they had no interest in the Whitehaven lad in their midst. The city folk were dressed in fancy fashions and Stag was particularly intrigued by the lace-up boots worn by some of the men. He was also struck by the women passing by, with their toes squeezed into narrow-ended slippers. He was reminded of a missionary lecture where they'd said the Chinese bandaged women's feet to keep them small. He didn't believe it; they'd never be able to walk. He took off his flat cap and stuffed it deep into his back pocket, beside his mouth organ.

'Carry yer bag, mister?' A shabbily dressed young man with a small wooden handcart was blocking his way.

'No, I can manage.' Stag studied the curious creature. He appeared malnourished, but it could just have been that his jacket was at least two sizes too big that made him appear so.

The young man nodded towards Stag's bag. 'Yer things, mister. Walk and I'll carry 'em for yer on me cart.' He gestured to the handcart which, on close inspection, was held together by frayed ropes that had been tied using numerous ingenious-looking knots. The man was obviously resourceful in maintaining the tools of his trade.

'Please, mister, I've 'ad no luck all day.' He put his head on one side, as a child might when pleading for a toffee.

Stag felt sorry for the poor wretch. He could carry his own bag, but since he didn't even know in which direction the boarding-house lay, the porter could be useful. 'Maybe, then, if you're not too costly?'

'Cheaper yer'll not find in all Liverpool, mister. Where to?'

Stag searched for the piece of paper with the lodging-house's address and thrust it at the man. The porter peered at it for several moments, until it struck Stag he couldn't read.

'Dale Street, number 74,' he said.

They settled terms and Stag placed his bag on the cart. It was heavy, although not unreasonably so, and he felt a moment's indecision, before deciding to leave it where it was.

The man picked up the back of the cart. 'Right, mister, I knows the place. Let's be goin'. I'll lead. Mind yer keep up, I'm a fast carrier.'

They set off at a pace, and had Stag not been so fit he'd have had to ask the man to slow down. After five minutes' hard walking, they were joined by another man of smarter appearance.

'I wonder, my good man, may I enquire about your footwear?' The man was looking at Stag's clogs.

'What about them?'

'Are those Lancastrian clogs?'

'No, they're Cumbrian.'

'That's interesting. Is there a difference?'

'Aye, the soles are different.'

'Ah, I see. I wonder if I may take a look. I'm a shoe manufacturer and have a genuine interest. I'd very much like to see the size of the sole nails.'

It was too late. The shoe manufacturer's intervention had brought Stag to a standstill, while the curious man with the handcart had quickened his pace. Stag was just beginning to realise what was happening when the handcart turned right and disappeared down a side alley a short distance ahead. The shoe manufacturer came in close to him, laughed, gave him a wink, did an about turn, and ran off.

Stag darted forward to follow the handcart, turning right into what he thought was the same alley, although he was unsure. He found himself confronted by a mass of courts, from which led further forbidding alleyways. A group of women, all wearing stained and well-worn aprons, eyed him suspiciously as they waited in an untidy line to draw water from a street pump. There was a stench of decaying vegetation and rotten fish. Even though his main purpose was finding the man with the handcart, he registered how grim it was.

Stag shouted out to the women, 'Where'd he go? A man with a cart's run off with my bag.'

A small barefooted child chasing a rolling ball tried to squeeze between him and the court wall. Stag managed to grab hold of the boy's arm. The boy yelled, kicked out at Stag's ankle, found his mark and spat on Stag's hand. Stag cursed, wiped the spittle off with his sleeve and went as if to cuff the boy, as he would have done in Whitehaven, until he saw the women had turned their attention to him. As one, they began coming towards him to protect their communal child and see him off. He let go of the struggling urchin and retreated the way he'd come, without looking back. In the main thoroughfare there was no sign of either of the two men or his bag, as he'd known there wouldn't be.

Stag threw his hands up in the air. How could he be so gormless as to fall for such an old trick? He immediately began ticking off what he'd lost: all his clothes, a spare cap, some books, some letters – and then he remembered, and a great sadness swept over him. It was the final straw. His body reacted immediately; his stomach turned over and there was a rushing water sound in his ears. He felt tears of anger forming, but made no effort to hold them back or brush them away. He'd lost the one possession he valued more than anything else: his mother's quilt.

It was as if the fates had decided he needed to experience the loss to mark the passing of the old and the commencement of the new.

✳ ✳ ✳

Mr Liversedge was true to his word and when Stag finally arrived at Dale Street, Mrs Hudley was expecting him. She was a cheerful middle-aged woman with an unfortunate squint, and she greeted him as she might a long-lost friend.

'Come in, you'll be exhausted from your travelling. Did you have a good journey? What do you think of the city?' Mrs Hudley continued with a stream of trivial observations and comments. Words slithered out of her with the same ease as from a country auctioneer as she escorted him to his room.

'I've put you up here at the top, in the garret, seeing as how you're an emigrant. Mr Liversedge never takes any that aren't fit and well, so the steep stairs won't cause you any bother. If you give me tuppence, I'll send Our Mary out for some ale before you die of thirst. I know you Cumbrian men enjoy refreshment, especially colliers.'

Stag put his hand into his jacket pocket, pulled out his wallet and froze. It was a wallet he'd never seen before and he knew instinctively that it would be empty. He remembered how the 'shoe manufacturer' had leaned in close before rushing off. Stag had patted his jacket pocket to make sure he still had his wallet. He hadn't looked, he'd just patted. They'd been clever enough to switch his wallet with another one and get everything except for some small change in his breeches pocket and the five shillings emergency money his pa had given him that was hidden inside his shirt. He had five shillings and seven pence, that was all, and lodgings to sort out and pay for.

If she noticed Stag suddenly turn pale, Mrs Hudley didn't mention it. She was standing smiling at him, holding out her hand for the tuppence. In shock, he took two pennies from his pocket and handed them to her. He needed a drink more than ever now.

Mrs Hudley disappeared down the stairs and Stag could hear her chattering away to someone he presumed was Our Mary. Even though he was agitated by his loss, he looked round the room. It was grand compared to the home he'd left in Whitehaven and not at all how he'd imagined a lodging-house in Liverpool would be. It was clean, and the furniture and brass-work around the small fireplace shone in what sunlight was able to find its way through the heavily netted windows. He leant back into a high-backed chair, stretched his arms out in front of him and listened to the city's sounds outside his window: carriages bumping over uneven cobbles, horses neighing, people calling to each other, children laughing.

A quarter of an hour later Mrs Hudley returned. 'I've sent Our Mary to the Cross Keys for your ale. She'll be back in no time at all.' She looked around the room as it dawned on her. 'No bag? Is it coming along later?'

Stag related how he'd been parted from his bag. When he'd finished, she smiled and, patting his hand in a maiden aunt fashion, said, 'Never you mind. I'd say it's an omen. A good one too. A true start to a new life in a fresh country.' He didn't tell her about the wallet, as he judged she wouldn't want a practically penniless emigrant under her roof.

A short while later a slim, blonde-haired young girl of uncertain age arrived, carrying a large jug of ale in one hand and a pewter pot in the other. She had ringlets on each side of her face, in front of her ears, and a white muslin cap perched on the back of her head. She smiled shyly at Stag then leant forward to whisper in his ear, 'Mrs 'Udley's been tellin' me. They didn't take everythin', did they?'

Stag thought she must have read his face for she went on to say, 'Oh no. I'm sorry. I'll not tell Mrs 'Udley.'

'I could understand taking a wallet, but I can't think why they even bothered with my bag. It's not as if I look like I've got owt, and if I had, I'd never put a bag with money on a handcart.'

'It was to distract. They wanted yer money,' said Our Mary. 'I was thinkin' you'd probably lost all your brass.' She wiped her hands on her apron front. 'What about your ticket and your contract? Have they gone with your bag? You'll need them to get through the port gates.'

'I've my ticket and my contract. All's well there, but I feel foolish being conned like a country bumpkin, even if I am one.' He didn't mention the quilt. Our Mary probably wouldn't understand.

'No use fretting over it now. Maybe the Bay Company can give you a sub?'

'I hadn't thought of that.' Stag warmed to the servant girl, who seemed as upset as he was about the loss of his funds.

* * *

The next morning, Tuesday the 12th, after Our Mary had cleared the breakfast things away, Stag got up from the table and Mrs Hudley looked him up and down. 'You'll be needing to get yourself some clothes for your trip.'

'I'd thank you for any advice you can give me.' Stag was enjoying being mothered by her, although she used a very strong scent, which he suspected was what was making his eyes water.

'You're not thinking of all new clothes, are you? That'll be expensive. If you're not, then St John's Market is the place for you. There's a good choice and you can haggle with them. Seeing as how you've a whole wardrobe to buy, you can probably get quite a few bob knocked off.' Unaware of the state of Stag's precarious finances she produced a piece of paper and began drawing a map. 'From here you cut through to Whitechapel and you'll see St George's Hall just on your left.' She drew a long building. 'You can't miss it. It's got rows of pillars outside, and it's brand new. There's going to be a big do in September when it opens for concerts and they're getting a big organ next year. It's just the gaol now. Do you like music?'

Stag put his hand in his pocket and brought out his mouth organ.

Mrs Hudley's face lit up.' Can you play well?'

He put the mouth organ to his lips and played the opening bars of *Greensleeves*.

'Oh, that was lovely. Play some more and I'll fetch Our Mary. She loves music.' She disappeared and returned with the servant girl, who was wiping her hands on a towel. 'You can play now.'

After playing *Greensleeves* and being begged for more, Stag launched into *D'yer Ken John Peel*.

'That's wonderful, Mr Liddell.' Mrs Hudley clapped her hands like a schoolgirl, delight etched all over her face.

'You can call me Stag.'

'Oh no, I call all my gentlemen by their proper names. You'll stay another night will you? Or maybe longer?'

'I'd like to.' He reasoned he could afford one more night, although that meant he was relying on the Hudson's Bay Company to advance some pay. He put the thought that they might refuse out of his mind.

'So you'll be in for supper?'

'Aye.'

'On Tuesday evenings I like to play the piano for a few of my lady friends. We usually do hymns. Perhaps you'd join us?'

Stag hesitated a moment. 'I don't know as I'm good enough for that. It's most likely an occasion.'

'Nonsense, that was beautiful.' Mrs Hudley sent Our Mary back to the scullery. 'What if you just come for a short while at the start and entertain us, and I'll say a thank you with a jug of ale that you can take to your room when you've finished? It'll make such a pleasant diversion for our little assembly.'

'If you're sure.' Stag put his mouth organ back in his pocket, gave it the usual pat and glanced down at Mrs Hudley's map.

'Oh yes, where was I?'

'St George's Hall.'

She put her finger on the long building. 'Here it is. Then you veer off onto the right and St John's Market is there.' She drew a large star. 'If you get lost anywhere in Liverpool you can always ask for St George's Hall. Everyone knows it.'

Later, Stag was making ready to leave for the Hudson's Bay Company offices when there was a tap on his door. He opened it to see Our Mary standing in the hallway.

'I just thought as I'd tell yer, since yer won't know, yer could make a bit o' brass playin' yer mouth organ. Then maybe yer needn't tap up that Bay Company.'

Stag stepped out. 'Aye?'

'Wednesday afternoons there's a matinee at the Adelphi Supper Rooms. It's like a theatre wi' dancin' and music. People sing and play for money. They do it then 'cos it's a double day.'

'What's that?'

'They get the people comin' out o' the matinee and then the people goin' in for the evenin' show, so double the takin's. That's why it's double day. Yer playin's just right for that. Well, maybe yer'd be better playin' a few faster tunes, since that's what makes folk 'appy and so they give more. Yer'll be goin' near there today. Why don't yer go and 'ave a gander? Likely there'll be a few people playin', but as I say, tomorrow's a better day. Wednesdays and Saturdays are best. Anyways, wherever you end up, tonight's tea's special: pig's cheek broth and apple pie, so make sure yer back in plenty o' time.'

Stag thanked her and wrote the name of the theatre on a piece of paper, promising he'd be back in time for the broth and the pie. He'd have liked to have given her a small coin for her trouble, but he couldn't afford it.

✻ ✻ ✻

As he'd been told, St George's Hall couldn't be missed, and, with the sun shining directly on its tall columns, parts of it shone out amongst its soot-pitted older neighbours. He wondered how long it would take for it too to turn grey. St John's Market was no less impressive. It had a grand entrance with three turrets: one over the central entrance and one at each end. He was beginning to see that despite the greyness and the atmosphere, the city's buildings were impressive, and he was getting used to the bustle. When Mrs Hudley mentioned going to the market, he'd never envisaged such a grand place. For him, a market was stalls in the street, carts, horses and lots of clamour.

The clamour was in full flow, and there was much more of it. Its source was not just the stall-holders bustling about greeting each other, whistling, and shouting out, but also the squeaking and rattling of their barrows as they pushed them along. The empty ones, with chains and ropes rolling free, were louder than the laden. The major difference with the market back home was the stalls: they were like miniature shops, each permanently sited with its own gaily painted fascia board extolling the name of the merchant and the goods available. At last, he'd found somewhere bright and colourful in the city.

First, he had to find the Adelphi and assess the moneymaking possibilities. After leaving the market behind, he knew when he was near the Adelphi because he could hear music playing. Another grand building, he thought, when it came fully into view. Playing that afternoon were a tin whistler, a fiddler and an acrobat who could have been drunk, because he kept falling over. Stag assessed the site with a practical eye. It was busy enough as it was, so if Wednesday was a double day, as Our Mary had said, he was sure he could make money. He looked around to see where he could stand. Not having worked as a street musician before didn't mean he didn't know pitch was all important. He could sort that out. What worried him most was how, if he made any brass, was he going to keep hold of it? It would be easy for someone to pretend to put money in a hat while taking it out, or even to pick the hat up and run off with it. He'd give thought to that.

Suitably buoyed and trusting in his ability to entertain, Stag decided to return to the market. After wandering around for half an hour he found an area of stalls specialising in second-hand clothes, so he picked the one run by the man he thought looked the easiest to haggle with. After the transaction was completed there was a lot to carry, so he asked if he could collect his items later in the day. The stall-holder registered surprise, as if he'd never been asked such a thing before. He checked the area around him, pulled a bag from a small box, stuffed the clothes inside and plonked it on the floor next to his chair.

'Long as yer back by five. It's a ha'penny for the bag,' was the reply.

Stag's face fell.

'That's a sour face yer've got on yer all of a sudden. If yer's that poor I'll throw in the bag.' The stall-holder was suddenly looking sorry for the lad, as if he knew what it was like to be short of a bob or two. Stag wondered if he looked like a working man on his uppers, as he certainly felt like one.

'I'm going to play my mouth organ outside the Adelphi tomorrow,' he said, then wondered why he'd felt it necessary to tell a stranger his business.

''Old on to yer brass. There's a lot more dippers up there than in 'ere. Not just in the evenin'. All day. Yer don't look as if yer from 'ere, and anyone can tell that, as soon as yer open yer gob, so be careful. Watch out for anyone tryin' to get close to yer.'

'Pickpockets?' *I know all about those*, thought Stag.

'Aye, we calls 'em "dippers" cos they dip in yer pockets. I wouldn't usually say owt, but seein' as yer've done good business wi' me this day I'm makin' an exception.'

'Thank you, I'll be careful.' Stag had hoped he was looking confident, despite there not having been a moment when he didn't worry about having something stolen again.

✳ ✳ ✳

That evening, Mrs Hudley's parlour assembly was enjoyed by all. Stag held the floor as a soloist for just short of twenty minutes before asking if they knew the new hymn *Abide with Me*. Since they did, and since they usually sang hymns, he suggested it would be appropriate if he finished with it. They sang the final hymn with Mrs Hudley accompanying on the piano and himself on the mouth organ. At the end, Mrs Hudley was so appreciative she sent Our Mary to buy two pots of ale for Stag, which the girl duly delivered to his room.

'Did yer go see the Adelphi?' asked Our Mary.

'Aye, I did, and it was busy. I think I could make brass if I set my mind to it.'

'Are yer goin' to do it?'

'I've got to. I've played in inns and ale houses for years, but never on the street for brass. Only thing is after losing my bag I feel I'm a target for thieving in a place like that. If I put my cap on the ground, what's to say someone won't skim it and it'll all be gone?'

''ow 'bout if I went with yer as an 'at lady? Wednesday afternoons I'm off. As long as I'm back in time to cook tea

I can come. Give me a share o' the takin's, buy me an 'ot tatie and I'll do it for the fun.'

'You mean you'll collect the brass?' Stag smiled as she negotiated her service. He was seeing a new side to Our Mary.

'That's right. I pass round the 'at while yer play. I've done it afore for a lad.'

Before he'd arrived, Stag had worried how he was going to spend five days in Liverpool on his own visiting imaginary cousins. Never had he imagined for a single second he'd be considering a business proposition. *Why not?* he thought.

'All right. How'll we split the takings?'

'That's up to yer. We can see what we make and yer can give me what yer think's fair.'

'We might make nothing.'

'With me 'olding the 'at we will. Anyways, if we don't then yer only two pennies out of pocket for an 'ot tatie.'

* * *

True to her word, Our Mary met him at the appointed hour the next day, outside St George's Hall.

'Good job yer not late. It's busy,' she said.

If he hadn't seen it, Stag would never have believed it. Our Mary, free from Mrs Hudley's, was a completely different vision. Gone were the uniform, ringlets and white cap, and in their place were a bun at the nape of her neck, a red and black tartan dress, a grey jacket and a small black velvet bonnet with a spray of roses attached to one side.

'Looks like maybe we've left it a bit late,' said Stag, looking round. 'There's a lot more here than I thought there'd be. That fiddler and tin whistler were here yesterday. Looks like they've got prime positions.'

'The dancing' monkey's new,' said Our Mary.

'That juggler knows how to work a crowd. He's got a full circle round him.'

'Over there, quick.' She indicated a space underneath an advertising board listing the week's top billings: 'Abel and His Wonderful Dogs' and 'The Minstrel Singers and Songs of the Deep South'. 'Best get started and 'ave the 'ot tatie when we're done,' she said.

Not one person passed that Our Mary did not waylay with a winning smile and cheeky grin, to great effect. She told everyone Stag had just arrived from Cumberland and had his pocket picked and needed the brass. She only stopped when the hat became too full and she had to empty it in Stag's bag.

After two hours Stag was beginning to tire. 'Shall we have the taties?'

'Not yet. Look.' She pointed to a group of young men dressed up to the nines, holding silver- or gold-topped canes and sporting tall top hats, such as that worn by Mr Liversedge. Each of them was carrying a small posy of flowers. ''Ere come the "Gentlemen".'

'Who?'

'The men who take out the theatre girls. The dancers, singers, actresses. That's who the flowers are for.' Our Mary was looking at him as if he was a halfwit.

'They watch the show then wait outside to take the girls to wine and dine?' he asked.

64

'Wine, dine and more.' She laughed and raised an eyebrow. 'How do I look?'

'Pretty as a picture,' said Stag, watching in awe as she pulled off her velvet cap and loosened her hair so it fell down onto her shoulders.

She approached a group of "Gentlemen", smiling and swaying her hips at them in such a way as to make them look in her direction, without it being too vulgar. 'Afternoon, gents. Come to see the ladies, 'ave yer? Well, while yer 'ere, appreciate the dulcet tones of my friend 'ere.' She turned to Stag. 'Play a merry tune for the gentlemen, Stag.'

He led off with *John Peel* and, to his surprise, Our Mary began dancing and swirling her skirts. She was a girl of many talents.

One of the men stepped forward and placed a shilling in the velvet hat.

'You've pretty ankles there, miss,' he said, smiling at her. 'Shame I'm already spoken for this afternoon.'

'Maybe another day,' said Our Mary, quickly turning to another group of men, with a winning smile and cheeky expression.

After the "Gentlemen" had passed by, she handed the hat over to Stag, and he was surprised by the weight of it. With the men having disappeared into the theatre, the street musicians and artistes began packing up.

Stag put his mouth organ in his pocket and tapped it.

'Do you always do that?'

'Do what?'

'Tap yer pocket after yer've put yer mouth organ away. I saw yer do it yesterday.'

'Aye, I do it for good luck.'

'Does it work?'

'I don't think so. I've done it for so long it feels odd if I don't. That's all.'

Stag bought their taties from a strange lady dressed in black, with a fat pug dog wearing a sailor's hat by her side, and they ate them in the street, walking back to Mrs Hudley's.

'Yer'll 'ave to eat another tea,' said Our Mary, 'and it'll be a big 'un. Mrs 'Udley's taken a great shine to yer.'

Just before they got back to the house there was a small park, where they sat down on a bench. Stag counted the money and handed her half.

'I can't. It's more'n a week's wage.'

'Take it. You've earned it and I can make more.'

'Ta. I'll buy a new bonnet. And yer?'

'Nothing yet, but I'm sure I can get some more over the next two days. Then I'll get a new bag to put my things in and a new mouth organ so I've a spare one, in case I drop one overboard on the journey.'

'Yer not as wet be'ind the ears now, are yer? Yer'll not let anyone run off with yer takin's.'

'I'll put one foot on the cap and keep a close eye.'

On their return, Stag went straight upstairs to his room. Within five minutes Mrs Hudley was at the door.

'We need to settle up. Are you leaving tomorrow? There's this night to pay for.' She didn't actually put out a cupped hand – rather, her face was set in such a way that it implied it was pay up time.

'I was planning on moving on, but...' He looked around the room; it would make a good base.

Mrs Hudley's face lit up at the prospect of his extending his stay. 'I can offer you a good rate if you change your mind. With meals, if you pay in advance. Good meals too. You could do with a bit of fattening up. I'll get you more ale – you'll be wanting some.'

She made her way to the desk by the window, where she wrote a short note containing her charges and handed it to Stag. It was a bit more than he'd thought it was going to be, but then he remembered it included meals, and that he was going to be on a ship for the next six months. He deserved a bit of comfort. He handed over the money he had just earned as payment for the next night and told her she could have the rest the following evening. For a moment the landlady looked as if she was going to protest, but then her expression changed. She counted the money carefully before putting it in her pocket, then pressed a bell for Our Mary. When, after two minutes, the girl failed to appear, Mrs Hudley shouted through the open door, 'Our Mary, come here this instant!'

Our Mary appeared, looking flustered. She was in her maid's uniform and her hair was back in ringlets. 'I'm cookin' the fish and veg for 'is tea.' She pointed at Stag. 'I'm already runnin' late.'

Mrs Hudley ignored Our Mary's disgruntled mutterings and handed her the note. 'Fetch Mr Liddell some more ale. I'll watch over the supper.'

Stag smiled. He rather liked being called Mr Liddell.

❊ ❊ ❊

Thursday and Friday passed quickly and although Stag didn't have Our Mary to drum up custom, he did well enough. In the mornings there was much to see and the weather was kind with the sun making an appearance Friday morning. Yet, despite there being much to distract him, the closer it came to Saturday the more his thoughts kept returning to Whitehaven and the proposed robbery. Surely they'd seen sense and called it off? Wouldn't they?

CHAPTER SIX

The first thing Kate McAvoy registered when she and her family stepped out of the brougham onto Liverpool Dock was the ship. The *Princess Rose* was smaller than she'd imagined, but looked seaworthy enough. She looked around to find there was no one she recognised, but she knew the occupation of her fellow-travellers straightaway. Their stance, their hands and the remains of coal dust deep in the creases on their faces and necks marked them as colliers. Some were standing, mouths open, staring up at the rigging as if they'd never seen a ship close up before. Kate thought that was probably the case. Most were chatting while a few were silent, appearing almost fearful.

Kate's father and mother stepped out to stand beside her. Pa was looking distinguished, with his handlebar moustache, white shirt and intricately decorated waistcoat. Her ma was wearing a fashionable light brown plaid dress for the embarkation, the sleeves exceptionally wide at the wrist and edged in black velvet with white lace cuffs. Her

69

hair was parted in the middle under a small lace cap and drawn back into a braided bun.

Kate, too, had dressed fashionably, in a similar gown to her mother's, but with narrower cuffs. Around her shoulders was a dark blue cotton shawl, delicately embroidered with a design of scrolling blue and pink blooms amongst flowing foliage.

Her two younger brothers began charging around as soon as they left the brougham, getting in everyone's way. It was too much to expect them to wait as patiently as their elders. Kate smiled good-naturedly as they darted in and out of the passenger groups. Then, when they veered too close to the edge of the quay, she felt the need to intervene.

'Steady down, Seamus and Bartley.' Her voice was authoritative, without being dictatorial. The boys paused and looked at her. 'You see that man with the top hat and fancy waistcoat walking down the gangway?' She pointed. 'I'll say he's coming over here to talk to you two, you're running around so much. You're probably making him dizzy just looking at you.'

The boys looked at the man with interest. The young woman hoped they thought he was a bit scary and then maybe they would settle down a bit. The important-looking gentleman stepped down from the gangway and did indeed make his way over.

'A good morning to the McAvoy family.' He bent down so the two boys could see him more clearly. They stood stock still. 'Good afternoon, boys, my name is Mr Liversedge. It is a great day for you and the family.

The start of an adventure, travelling over the oceans to pastures new.' He waved his arm in the direction of the ships in the dock. 'All sorts of new sights and sounds. A phantasmagorical adventure for young children and you will enjoy yourselves, I am certain.' The boys were struck dumb. Mr Liversedge turned to Kate's father and they shook hands. 'How are you this morning, Patrick? Does the McAvoy family have its sea legs prepared?'

'Indeed, we are ready, and we are all well,' replied Patrick. 'Allow me, sir, to introduce my wife, Mrs Hannah McAvoy.'

'Very pleased to meet you, ma'am.' Mr Liversedge raised his hat and extended his hand. 'Your husband and I have enjoyed our meetings planning this journey. The Company is delighted he has agreed to take up the teaching position.' Then he turned his attention to Kate.

'This must be your daughter?' He smiled at her and extended his hand. 'You are also a teacher, I understand?'

Kate smiled back. 'Yes, I have been teaching at my father's school now for two years.'

'I'm sure he was very happy to have you by his side. Do you plan to help him on board and in Colville?'

'Most certainly if the opportunity arises.'

'It will keep her in practice,' said Patrick, pride for his daughter showing on his face.

Mr Liversedge was nothing like Kate thought he would be. She'd imagined an overweight, overbearing individual, probably smelling of cigar smoke, yet he appeared charming and was finely dressed. However, she reminded herself, it remained his fault they were leaving Liverpool.

It was he who had enticed her father away from the school where he was a well-respected headmaster, filling his head with dreams of a new life. It was his fault they had had to sell everything and were now heading to a land she had hardly heard of and a place she had no wish to go. She wondered if her unhappiness showed.

After Mr Liversedge had taken his leave and was walking back up the ship's gangway, Kate felt in her pocket for some barley sugars. She pulled out a twisted paper cone and saw her handkerchief had become lodged in one of the paper folds. As she unwrapped the packet to take out two barley sugars, the handkerchief freed itself and dropped to the ground. She passed the sweets to the boys then bent down to gather it up. As she straightened up, a rogue gust of wind blew in off the river, catching the wide brim of her hat and tipping it back, loosening the ties. Kate, off balance, put a hand up to steady the slipping bonnet, which was tottering precariously. Unfortunately, before she could take a firm hold, to her acute embarrassment it blew off, rolling a little way on its brim like a runaway cartwheel before coming to rest at the feet of a tall, fair-haired young man. He'd just arrived at the quay and was being greeted by a young couple. The young man picked up the hat and looked around. Kate, cringing inside, rushed forward and stood looking up at him. Lips clenched, she felt the rush of a sudden flush and knew her face was now bright red. Their eyes met. Kate ran a hand with open fingers through her hair and put out the other hand for her bonnet.

'This must be yours,' he said, dusting off the hat and

handing it to her. Kate thanked him and put the hat back on.

'I'm Stag,' he added with a half-smile. 'Stag Liddell.'

Kate nodded, while failing to volunteer her own name.

All the while, another young woman had been watching. Although she'd placed a gloved hand in front of her mouth in a half-hearted attempt to cover a smile, she was unsuccessful in smothering a laugh.

Kate transferred her gaze from Stag to the young woman. Despite the colour that flamed with even greater fury on her cheeks, and which was now also invading her neck, she held the girl's gaze with unblinking eyes. Out of the corner of her eye she registered a shocked expression on Stag's face, which she attributed to his response at the girl's rudeness. *This is not a good start*, she thought. *Not a good start at all.* She turned her back and moved away, but not far enough not to be able to hear the girl's words spoken to an older woman who was standing by her side.

'Well, she was all hoity-toity, Ma, wasn't she?'

'It's a beautiful shawl she's wearing,' said her mother.

'Yes, but mine is pure printed cotton. The best Mary Williamson's Establishment of 71 King St, Whitehaven, can provide.'

'I'm not comparing, Lavinia, or saying yours is dowdy. Just saying how lovely hers is.'

CHAPTER SEVEN

With the upset over the interruption of the hat dealt with, Tom turned to Stag. 'We really are so pleased to see you.' He slapped him playfully on the back.

Stag grinned. 'Did you think I wouldn't be here?'

'No, I knew you would be.'

'Is that a new bag?' Lavinia put out a hand to touch it, as if she wanted to check it was real.

'Aye, I made some brass playing my mouth organ and bought myself a present.' This gave him the opening he needed to launch into the tale of his stolen bag.

A member of the crew, standing on the quay, short of stature, round of body with vivid green eyes and unruly blonde hair, blew a high-pitched whistle. Stag stopped relating his experiences and paid attention along with the others.

'Gather round, gather round all. My name is Billy Botcher. Second Mate on the *Princess Rose*. It's my job t' welcome you today. They've chosen me because I've got such a loud voice. I've been with the Company since I was fifteen. I'm an Orcadian by birth and proud of it.'

'What's that?' whispered Tom.

'He was born in Orkney,' replied Stag. 'I've heard sailors from there called that before.'

Billy held up a hand, palm facing outwards. 'I see some late arrivals. We'll wait a minute for them.'

While they were waiting, Stag appraised the ship. It was one he was going to spend six months living and working on. He'd grown up seeing ships of all sizes every day of his life and knew people who not only sailed in them, but built them. Over the years he'd learned how to check rigging was in good order and hulls were sound, so he was relieved all seemed in fine fettle. He hadn't thought it wouldn't be, but he was trusting his life to this ship. He wasn't so relaxed about the crew members he'd seen so far since most of them, with their wild beards and multiple tattoos, looked hard and rough, and he was going to be working alongside them. Then he thought it was probably fortunate they were like that, since it was their strength, skill and expertise that would determine everyone's safety and they needed to be robust men. Stag looked at Tom, who, from his serious expression, he guessed was probably having similar thoughts to his own. What the Brierley Hill colliers were thinking, he had no idea. It was likely many of them had never seen a ship up so close, or perhaps even seen the sea. Judging by their faces, the majority were nervous and likely having second thoughts. Several were looking at the ship with dread. He could understand that. Colliers, so firmly at one with the earth and its depths, could be expected to be nervous about taking to the ocean.

Billy blew his whistle again and repeated his earlier introduction for the benefit of the latecomers. 'We're still liftin' and shiftin', but since we've a while t'wait, 'ow 'bout I give you a little learnin' on this beautiful lady 'ere?' He swung his arm out in an ostentatious arc to point to the ship behind him. 'We 'ave 'ere a lovely lady of the sea. Our own Princess, the *Princess Rose*, beloved by all 'er crew.' All heads turned again to the ship which towered above them. 'Right now, you're all spectators, but come the morrow you'll be carried in the bosom of our dear *Rose*.' Several of the single men sniggered and Billy acknowledged them with a grin and a tap on the side of his nose.

Stag saw a frown pass across some of the women's faces at Billy's crude joke. He could see the young woman who had lost her hat, and when Billy asked those who had never been to sea in a ship like the *Princess Rose* to raise their hands, she did so. *I must find out her name*, he said to himself. *I can't keep thinking of her as the girl who lost her hat.* When Billy asked who had never seen the sea, all but one of the group he judged to be from Brierley Hill raised their hands.

Billy carried on. 'As you'll see, our lovely lady's got three masts and the sails right now are furled.'

Stag thought he spoke of 'this lovely lady' as if referring to the Virgin Mary.

'See the ratllins – oops, beggin' your pardon, *rat lines* for those of you that's takin' notes.'

Stag laughed along with many others. When the laughter died down, Billy's demeanour became more serious.

'You see them black ropes 'tween the sails that makes a ladder? We climb up 'em in all weathers. Let me tell you, if you fall from there, you're probably goin' t'be dead as a rock after you 'it the deck.' There was a murmur through the group and some furrowed brows. 'Don't you worry, though. Only crew climbs up there. It's so dangerous, if we catch you 'urryin' aloft we'll tie you to 'em, and t'get down'll cost you a bottle o' rum. That should keep you curious ones on deck.'

Stag wasn't learning anything new, and his attention began to wander. There was a man on deck watching the crewmen as they went about their business. From his waistcoat and breeches, and the fact that his dress was of a higher quality than the other crewmen he'd seen so far, Stag guessed it was the ship's first mate. The crewman was ignoring Billy Botcher going through his quayside performance, and was bellowing orders that were incomprehensible to Stag watching from ashore. Crates and casks were being loaded by seamen and dockers, who lifted their burdens with little effort. Fresh beef, vegetables and soft bread were loaded, along with two pigs that trotted up the gangway. Sacks of flour and rice were tossed around like feather cushions. Stag marvelled at how skilled the men were and that not once was anything dropped or harmed in any way. He supposed it was something they did every day. Then it occurred to him they would probably have been similarly impressed by the amount of coal a Wellington pit collier could amass in a day.

One big crate in particular needed two men to carry it. There was a notice pasted on the side saying 'HANDLE WITH CARE. Dr MacDonald's library. DELIVER TO CABIN'.

Queenie nudged Stag and pointed out an overweight man on board who was holding lots of papers. 'Who's that?' she asked.

Owen joined the conversation. 'Must be the cook with that fat belly, and with him inspecting everything so carefully.'

Queenie laughed. 'Trust you, Mr Jefferson. Always thinking of your insides. Isn't that right?'

After Billy had finished educating everyone about the ship, Stag finished his tale about losing his bag and his money. He was about to regale everyone with his other Liverpudlian adventures when Tom butted in.

'There's been a bit of excitement since you've been gone.'

'Oh?' Stag put his hand in his jacket pocket and wrapped it around his mouth organ. *I must not show any involvement*, he said to himself. *I must keep calm.*

'Aye,' said Lavinia. 'You'll never guess.'

I probably can, he thought, hoping the anxiety creeping over him was not showing itself outwardly.

Tom turned to Lavinia. 'You tell him.'

'No, you.'

'No, it's your story Lavinia.'

'All right. You'll never believe it.' She paused for what seemed an eternity. 'Mrs Woodley's run off with her lodger.'

'No!' said Stag. Was that it? Just a bit of gossip? What a relief.

'Aye. Hear tell they've set up house in Cockermu'th.'

'Mrs Woodley the church organist? The widow?'

'Aye, the very one. Turns out she's having a bairn too.'

''Appen she's been doing more'n fix his supper,' said Queenie.

Stag's laugh was louder than it should have been, but he couldn't help it. His relief was instantaneous. *Thank you, Mrs Woodley*, he thought. *Thank you very much.* He let go of his mouth organ and took his hand out of his pocket, and was wondering which of his Liverpudlian experiences to relate next when Owen spoke up.

'There's more.'

Owen was chomping at the bit to tell him and Stag felt himself freeze. If he could have stopped time at that point to calm himself and settle his nerves, he would have done.

'There's been an attempted robbery. A big one.'

Stag had practised this moment all week, but now it was upon him his mind went blank. *Questions, that's what I must do. Ask questions as if I don't know anything about it. Ask what, though?* With some effort he managed to say, 'Where?'

'Lombard's Steamship Offices. Three men broke in wearing masks.'

'When was this?'

'Last Wednesday. You missed all the excitement. The constable has been round questioning everyone. Tom told us you've been visiting your cousins in Liverpool.'

'Do they know who did it?' *Let them say 'no'*, his brain was screaming. *Just let them say 'no'.*

'No, but I reckon they will. Someone must know something.'

Hearing they didn't know who'd committed the robbery was enough to make Stag lightheaded. The idiots, they'd gone ahead and tried it. He was surprised they'd not been caught. It was going to be all right; everything was going to work out.

'Shame about Donal Little,' said Queenie.

Stag felt his stomach lurch. 'What happened?'

'He was locking up when they arrived. One of them demanded the key to the safe so he gave it to them, and when they opened the safe it was empty, apart from some petty cash. That would have been an end to it if they'd run off, but one of them was so put out he set about Donal with a shillelagh. The police think it was a weighted one, because it knocked him unconscious with the first blow.'

That'll be Stevens, thought Stag. He could picture him bringing a shillelagh down on someone's head without giving it a second thought. 'Is he going to be all right?' He couldn't think straight. There was a sound in his head like a rushing waterfall.

'He came round enough to say what had happened, then a couple of hours later had a terrible headache and passed out. He was still like that when we left. Must've been a dreadful shock.'

'The police are saying it's attempted murder,' said Lavinia.

'Can't Donal tell the police who they were?' Stag tensed as he waited for the answer.

'I already told you, they were wearing masks,' said

Owen. 'Maybe when he's recovered from the shock, he might be able to tell them more.'

Lavinia adjusted her shawl. 'That's if he *does* recover. There was talk he might not.'

'Did they think there was money in the safe?' Stag was hoping he was asking all the right questions. It was becoming quite a strain trying not to indicate he had any prior knowledge.

'Yes, there was a whole load of it from fur sales in Stromness, but Mr Liversedge'd already seen to it. He'd come up Sunday evening on the *Whitehaven Queen* to finish some business and interview two families who'd changed their minds and decided to join at the last minute. They're over there.' Owen pointed to a group standing by the gangway. 'Anyways, apparently this fur money was taken off and put in Lombard's safe because the ship, on its way from Stromness to Liverpool, had to stop at Whitehaven and go into dry dock –'

'And you can't leave brass on a ship in dry dock,' said Tom.

'As I was about to say,' said Owen, glowering at Tom, 'the money was needed in Liverpool to pay off some crew, so Liversedge was given instructions to load the money on the *Whitehaven Queen* Wednesday afternoon and accompany it back. I reckon it was probably clearing the harbour wall just as they were staring into an empty safe.'

'If it wasn't for Donal, it'd be a grand jest,' said Queenie.

The one thing everyone wanted to carry on talking about was the attempted robbery, which was the one thing Stag most wanted not to. They weren't giving him time to gather his thoughts and it would be a disaster if he made a slip-up. He looked almost longingly at the ship's gangway. Though it seemed he'd avoided implication in the robbery, how relieved he was going to be walking onto that ship to a new life.

The time came for them to board ship. The man who had been overseeing the loading came down the gangway and introduced himself as Mr Ward. Stag had been correct: he was the first mate. It suddenly came to Stag that the man was going to be his boss during the voyage, and he looked at him with renewed interest. In a way he was pleased, because he'd been impressed by the way Ward had handled things earlier. He was strong, like the other crewmen, and being older was more weathered. His was a face that had seen many storms and sweated under many suns.

A few moments later the first mate was joined by a man who, judging by his deportment and dress, could be none other than Captain Fleming, the man Billy had told them was master of the ship. He made an imposing figure, worthy of his command – the absolute ruler of his kingdom, the *Princess Rose*. He was dark, in a broody way, with deep-set eyes and a square chin. He showed no sign of wanting to speak with any of his passengers, nor that he wished them to speak with him. He said something to Mr Ward, who nodded, stepped forward and looked around.

'Passengers Mr and Mrs McAvoy and Miss Kate. Will you please make yourselves known to me?' he called in a clear voice that carried well, at the same time moving his head from side to side, seeking them out. Stag watched as the well-dressed couple and the boys began walking forward, followed by the young woman who had lost her hat, whose name, he had just learned, was Miss Kate. He had also learned something else – that she was not married. He, along with everyone else, watched as the family moved to the front of the queue for the gangway. Unlike many women of her age, who took small steps and looked as if they could fall over given only the slightest push, Kate walked confidently, with her head held high. Gone was the young woman who had been so embarrassed earlier. As she approached the gangway Stag saw her pause before stepping on it and thought for a moment she was going to turn back. However, she carried on. It had been just the slightest pause, but he'd noticed it and he wondered if she was unhappy about leaving. What was she leaving behind? Or perhaps 'who' was she leaving behind?

Earlier Stag had wanted nothing more than to be on the gangway, but as the time approached, he moved to the back of the queue. Seeing Kate pause had made him think twice too. He was now in no hurry to board.

After around fifteen minutes, Mr Liversedge arrived and went up to Captain Fleming.

'I have the necessary papers.' He put them down on a nearby table that was being used for the loading list paperwork. 'You've seen the list. There's Dr MacDonald, Patrick McAvoy the teacher, with his wife Hannah, their two boys and daughter Kate, and the rest are the colliers you've seen on the quay. Ordinary God-fearing people from Whitehaven and Brierley Hill, hoping for a better life, or running away from this one.'

'There's no ordinary mining folk. Those that live like beasts crawling around underground spend too long in the darkness. It gives them strange ideas.'

The two men were talking as if Stag wasn't there. It should have been obvious to them that he and several others could hear what they were saying. Then it dawned upon him. He was only an emigrant collier, soon to be a temporary crewman. He was so low in the ranks on board that, to them, he was more or less invisible. He wondered what strange ideas he was supposed to have.

'I dare say you'll help them see God's light,' said Mr Liversedge.

'The Lord knows, I've tried with all men, but while we're passing the Horn, I always find Divine Service attendance improves greatly. Frightens the life out of them. Nothing like some of God's vengeance by way of wind and wave to stir souls up a bit. Likewise, there's always an upsurge in attendance at Divine Service after every storm.' The captain looked upwards to the heavens. 'There's nothing as cleansing as a wrestle with the power of the Almighty.'

Stag wondered if the captain was expecting to see angels with trumpets flying overhead. He wasn't afraid of a storm, but some of the women might be. He'd learned something else too. That Kate was the schoolteacher's daughter and, from his accent, he deduced the captain was a Scot.

The captain signed the papers and the two men shook hands.

'Congratulations, Captain Fleming. You are now responsible for twenty-seven families, the crew, and the Norwegian boys we engaged in London.'

'They're in safe hands, sir. This will be my fourth trip to Vancouver Island and I've lost count of the number of times I've rounded the Horn en route to San Francisco. They'll be safe with me, as will the Company's cargo on the return journey.'

After taking his leave, Mr Liversedge made his departure from beside the *Princess Rose*, passing the remaining emigrants waiting to embark, nodding briefly to those who looked his way. Stag mused over whether he would ever set eyes on Mr Liversedge again, then moved on to ask himself whether he would ever set foot on English soil again.

CHAPTER EIGHT

Dr MacDonald, a solidly built man with a long body and short legs who still boasted a full head of dark curly hair, visited the McAvoys in their cabin. He asked them if they felt feverish, looked at their eyes, placed a hand on their foreheads and signed them off in his record book as healthy.

'Do you think you will have to turn anyone away in your examinations?' asked Kate.

'I will be most surprised if I have to. I expect there'll be a fair share of healed pit injuries, eye infections, rotten teeth and sprains, that sort of thing. All to be expected.'

Kate had noticed that some of the older colliers on the quay, despite looking healthy with broad chests and strong arms, stooped a little as they walked. She had seen one with a bad scar running across his cheek, from just below his eye almost to the edge of his mouth, and had done her best not to stare. She thought Stag would pass with no problem. He kept entering her thoughts unexpectedly.

'If I were you, I'd get out on deck while you still can. You've six months to unpack,' said Dr MacDonald.

Kate and the boys took the doctor's advice, leaving her parents to keep an appointment with the captain. The crew were moving around at quite a pace, checking ropes and carrying boxes. After watching them at work for a while, she thought it best if they tucked themselves away, and assessed the best place to be close by the other emigrants towards the stern, where the boys would be entertained. She was shocked to see Dr MacDonald carrying out the medical examinations in full view of everyone. She had assumed they would be somewhere private. Was it seemly of her to see them? But no one else seemed to mind and there wasn't really anywhere else to go. She was not slow to admit to herself she was curious about her fellow travellers. She would try to listen in without seeming to.

The doctor scarcely looked up as he asked his questions and he was quite brusque with some of the male emigrants. It was not until he came to a petite girl who was heavy with child that he expressed any concern. She was the sort of person who didn't seem to take up much space, neither in a physical sense nor in her bearing. Kate estimated she was well under five feet in height. A man much taller than her was by her side, looking anxious and unsettled.

'Your name?'

The man answered for her. 'She's Evie Gray and I'm Sam Gray. We're from Whitehaven.'

Dr Robertson wrote the names down in his book then looked at Evie for a while before speaking.

'When is your confinement?' When she didn't answer

Dr MacDonald repeated the question in a gentler tone. 'Don't be afraid. When is your time?'

'A month, I expects.' Evie spoke in a soft voice, keeping her head down.

Only a month, thought Kate. What courage she must have to think of undertaking the journey. Probably she'd had no choice.

Dr MacDonald leaned towards her, lifted her head and gently pulled down her lower eyelids, before placing a hand flat against her forehead. 'No fever, but you're very pale and you could do to eat more.'

'Aye, doctor, sir, my wife don't get out much, being a hard-working lass and always helping her ma. She always looks like this.'

'The last thing I need is a complicated confinement on board,' said Dr MacDonald, opening his medicine bag. 'Her looks could be due to fatigue. If you have any pains, send for me immediately. I've seen emigrants wait too long before they seek help. I don't mean to frighten you, just to make sure you heed my words. I've a job to do and it pays to be cautious over these things.' Handing Evie a small box, he said, 'Take two of these every morning and get out on deck. You could do with some sunshine.'

Sam took the box and read the label. 'Dr Rigby's Pills.'

Kate saw him turn it over as if looking for something, then he put his hand in his inside jacket pocket and brought out some change. 'How much?' he asked. As he looked up, he caught Kate's eye, and she looked away in embarrassment. It must have been obvious she'd been listening.

'There's no charge in this instance. The Company provides certain medical supplies.' The doctor closed his bag. 'Take your wife below and sit her down in a quiet corner.' With those words, his attention moved to the next person in the queue, a young Norwegian boy, and Kate went to find Seamus and Bartley. She'd been so engrossed in Evie's examination, she'd taken her eye off them.

They were standing in front of some other children, chattering away. She gathered them up and, on the way back to their cabin, Bartley, two years younger than Seamus, said, 'Those children sound funny.'

'It's a Cumberland accent,' said Seamus, always happy to help with the education of his little brother.

'Will they talk like that where we're going?' asked Bartley.

'I don't know how they'll talk,' said Kate. It wasn't something she had given any thought to. In fact, she hadn't given much thought at all to their destination, since thinking about it would make it more real.

✻ ✻ ✻

Below deck, in steerage, there was an overall gloominess and a dankness that invaded everyone's nostrils and would, no doubt, soon invade beings and belongings.

Tom voiced his opinion to Stag. 'I know we're used to cramped conditions in the mine, but at least we could come up for air every night. We're stuck down here for the next six or so months. I don't know how the lasses are going to cope.'

'Not so bad for those of us working part-passage. We'll get some air but...' Stag's voice trailed off as he looked around at the women and children, who would be more or less cooped up until November. It was already crowded and there were more people to come down. His spirits sank. The only light came from oil lamps hanging from chains looped into hooks in the roof which, he had no doubt, would pitch with the ship. With no penetrating daylight or portholes that he could see, the lights would have to burn constantly, and they would smell. High up, some wooden grilles allowed a little fresh air to penetrate, but any air sneaking in there, or when the hatch was opened, would be swallowed up in what would soon be a fetid atmosphere. Stag also thought rain would come in through the holes in the grilles and he made a mental note to remember not to sit under them in bad weather.

'It'll be a miracle if we don't all turn on each other like rats in a sack,' said Tom. He turned around and saw Sam and Evie and called them over. 'Let's put the "soon to be ma's" together.'

After greeting Evie with a hug, Lavinia screwed up her face. 'It's proper foisty. This smell reminds me of a dishrag I once found dried out hard as a rock in the bottom of a bucket. It's disgusting.' She put her hand over her nose and mouth.

A crew member with short tufty hair and bulging eyes, who was supervising their luggage, laughed at them. He identified himself as Jim. 'You'll soon get used to it.' he said. 'You won't even notice it in a week. A month ago we came back from Hudson's Bay with a cargo of timber and beaver pelts. We were three weeks in Stromness offloading the pelts, then down to London with the timber. Now we're back in Liverpool, the good timber smell's gone, but the pelts – well, they're like corpses, so the smell tends to linger.'

Stag watched the colour drain from Evie's face and suggested Sam sit her down on a nearby case. He looked around at the open space, furnished only with some roughly hewn bunks and trestle tables piled up to one side. There were no proper beds or even hammocks.

'Are we to sleep in those boxes?' asked Lavinia.

'That's what most do, or string up hammocks,' said Jim. 'You'll see there's spaces marked out on the floor. My advice is find yourselves a space quick like. Get your bags in it and then, if you want some privacy for yourselves, rig up some sheets or something.' He pointed first to some hooks in the ceiling, and then to his right. 'I wouldn't go over there if I was you. It looks inviting being near the ladder hatch for air, but that's where we stack the big privy pot in the morning. You don't want to be over there. Especially when the babies arrive.'

Sam thanked him and he, Evie, Tom, the pregnant Lavinia and the Jeffersons staked their claims well away from the privy pot holding area.

'You,' said Jim, looking at Stag. 'You a single fella?'

Stag nodded. Jim pointed to an area about twenty feet away. 'Singles over there.'

✻ ✻ ✻

Kate's parents were still with the captain. She gave the boys a book each to look at and considered their cabin. How were they all going to fit in? Where would their things go?

There were four bunks – she assumed the adults would have a bunk each and the boys would share. If either of the boys were ill, the well one would have to come in with one of the adults. She made a mental note to make sure her parents had some privacy, then wondered if that was ever going to be possible.

She thought back to when she'd first learned the news that the family were emigrating. It had been such a shock and she'd immediately felt shivery and short of breath. She remembered trying to breathe deeply, to expand her chest, to bring in more air, but her ribs had been constricted by her laced bodice. She'd experienced similar feelings when her grandmamma had passed away: a sense of something lost never to be regained.

That evening she'd lost a city, a future. She'd planned to teach so that the next generation could have the advantages she enjoyed from enlightened parents. Then she would probably marry, although that was not a given, but she would like to have children. This was all still open to her, but the backdrop had always been Liverpool, the city she loved. The bustle of its maritime business and the friendliness of its people fascinated her, and she'd been grateful to her parents for leaving Dublin when she was a child. She looked around the cabin and felt tears prick her eyes.

Her parents returned and she could smell whisky on her father's breath.

'Captain Fleming shared a wee dram with me. He's a very devout man. I'm sure we'll all get on very well. He was born in Dundee, but hasn't been back there for years.'

'He ran away to sea when he was a boy,' said Hannah.

Kate wanted to tell her parents she was not the least bit interested in the captain's past life. Her mind was firmly set on how they were going to manage in such a cramped space.

Her father sat down on a bunk. 'It's a bit cramped, but at least we've got a porthole. I've a feeling, compared to steerage, this is luxury.'

'You'll find out soon enough when you begin the schooling,' said Hannah.

'Nevertheless whichever deck people are on, this is the beginning of an exciting adventure for everyone.'

It was the beginning of something, but quite what, Kate wasn't sure. So far it had all been a waking nightmare. Her mind went back to the embarrassing incident on the quay, having to chase her hat and retrieve it from a stranger. The young man, Stag, had been friendly, but the girl had been rude. Kate stopped herself. She wasn't going to waste time thinking about her.

Her mother was busying herself folding clothes and trying to stow them. 'It's certainly a change; last week you were a renowned headmaster living in a respectable part of town. This week you're on a ship bound for North America, furniture and belongings sold, with goodness knows what to come.'

'Yes, but it's all so enlivening.' Patrick couldn't keep still, and neither could the boys. They were sitting on the opposite bunk, swinging their legs backwards and forwards in time with each other.

'I don't think I've felt so alive since we celebrated your

brother's fortieth birthday,' Patrick went on. 'That was a night of revelry and indulgence.'

'I remember,' said Hannah, smiling. 'That tin whistler came across from Dublin Town and how he could play.'

'That's because he was a true Dubliner, raised in The Liberties.'

'We danced until we were nearly exhausted.'

'True, and all the lasses had such rosy cheeks, such as we rarely saw in Liverpool. That was the year we welcomed Bartley into the family.' Patrick gave his wife a sideways glance. Hannah blushed and he laughed. 'Now you're the one with the rosy cheeks.'

'Father!' said Kate.

'The captain suggested you might hold some classes for the women. To keep them occupied, was how he put it. What do you think? There's no additional salary, but it will help you all pass the time. Shall I put it to them?'

'And you will get to know some of them,' added her mother.

The idea appealed to Kate. 'There's no harm in offering them a class and I would enjoy that.'

'Excellent, that's splendid.'

Watching and listening to her parents, Kate was glad they were happy.

Her mother's voice broke into her thoughts. 'You look sad. We know this is hard for you, but can we appeal to your sense of adventure?'

'I don't think she wants to leave Liverpool,' said Seamus. 'She looks as if she's going to cry.'

Patrick put his arm around Kate. 'I remember my grandmamma saying to me one day: "A woman must go where her man goes and if he decides to take a path into the wilderness, then his wife and children must follow." This is a new beginning for us. It's a new beginning for every one of the passengers on this ship.'

Kate looked around the cramped cabin they would share for the next six months. Were they really undertaking a journey to the Promised Land? Or would they find themselves marooned in the wilderness?

CHAPTER NINE

On May 16th at 6.10 pm, the men positioned in the rigging raised their caps and gave three hearty cheers to signal to one and all that the *Princess Rose* was ready. When the ship was released from her moorings, the whole crew took up chanting *Blow the Man Down* while the ship was towed out of the river Mersey into the Irish Sea. The captain had, reluctantly, given permission for those who wished to stand on deck for a last glimpse of England. As the ship cleared the dock there was a sudden lurch. Stag was pitched forward against the ship's rail and his cap fell over the side into the water.

'Damn!' he said to Tom, who was standing by his side. They looked down at the cap as it bobbed up and down and whirled around in the water churning between the ship's side and the dock.

'Can't you keep a hold on any of your clothing?' Tom grinned at his own joke and Stag threw his head back and let out a laugh rich with the essence of newfound freedom.

'That cap's a final symbol of all my cares and worries. I'm glad to leave it behind. Don't fret, I've got a new one.' He put an arm around Tom's shoulders. Tom reciprocated with an arm around Stag, placing the other around Lavinia's swollen waist.

✤ ✤ ✤

Further along the rail, Kate felt a lump forming in her throat. Although she swallowed hard to try and control herself, tears began to fall. She pulled her handkerchief from her pocket and wiped them away. They were a nuisance, hampering her efforts to scrutinise the faces of the people waving to them from the quay. Her mother called out to her, but she didn't hear what she was saying due to the cheering and the sound made by the churning water. The crush at the handrail was too great for Hannah to reach her daughter, so she smiled at her encouragingly. Kate was just able to make out the smile through her tears. Even though her eyes were smarting and her nose was running, she kept looking at the city she loved as the ship moved down the river and the figures on the quay became smaller and smaller. 'Goodbye, Liverpool,' she said under her breath. 'I must start afresh.'

✤ ✤ ✤

Just before they hit the open sea, Mr Ward ordered everyone below. Tom asked him for permission to speak privately to Stag before going down. 'It's important,' he said.

Mr Ward looked at Stag, who shrugged his shoulders, being none the wiser himself.

'All right, be quick about it. We'll be getting strong movement soon and you're not used to it yet. It's for your own safety, mind.'

'What is it?' asked Stag, when Ward was out of earshot.

'What was the name of your grandfather's farm?'

'Why do you want to know that?'

'I'll tell you in a minute.'

'Barn Hill Farm. Yon side of Frizington.'

'What was his first name?'

'Oliver. Oliver Liddell.'

'Was there something special about your bait tin?'

'It was like any other, but had a brass plate with O.L. and Barn Hill Farm stamped on it. It was my grandfather's. I lost it a few weeks back. I was quite upset and I spent time looking for it. Why?'

'Damn. I thought so. I'm afraid to say this, but you need to know.'

'What?' Stag was beginning to get slightly irritated. Out on the river it was growing colder. Why couldn't Tom ask him all this below?

Tom shuffled his feet and looked down. 'It's been found with just a small dint in it.'

'I can tell there's more, where is it?' said Stag.

'It was found next to the safe at Lombard's after the robbery on Wednesday.'

'What?' Stag went cold inside. His hands gripped the ship's rail so tightly his knuckles went white. 'I was in Liverpool.'

'Aye, I know. It's all very strange. The constable's got it and he's been asking questions. I knew it was yours straightaway.'

'And you didn't say?

'No, I didn't let on. I know you weren't involved. He came round on Thursday and anyway we were all leaving the next day.'

'Are they looking for me?' Stag's thoughts were racing. He felt dizzy.

'They don't know it's yours. I haven't told anyone. Not even Lavinia. You're my marrer and we have the pact, our secret. You know I'll never let you down.'

'No, of course not. I know that, but they're bound to find out.'

'By which time you'll be long gone.'

'It doesn't look good me disappearing for the week of the robbery then emigrating.'

'I can't think why it would be there, can you?'

'Aye,' said Stag 'I can. I've been set up. Hibbs, Devlin and Stevens wanted me to join them in the robbery. I refused and Stevens threatened to implicate me.'

'Why didn't you tell me?'

'I wanted to protect you and your family. It was better you knew nothing about it. And I thought you'd think I was a coward, not standing up to them, or that you'd want to fight it out with them and put your own emigration plans at risk. I know it makes me look weak, running away. I thought I could just get away from it all and leave the whole mess behind.'

Tom put a hand out to steady himself as the ship began to pick up speed and roll. 'That's why you left for Liverpool early. I thought it was a bit odd. You never mentioned cousins before.'

'Yes, so I wouldn't be there if they carried it out. I knew it was doomed. Now people'll think I was involved and only pretending to be in Liverpool. Anyways, I didn't think I needed to tell you.'

'Don't fret yourself. Nothing's going to happen here on the ship. We'll mull it over.'

'I wonder how they got the tin. Maybe I didn't lose it, after all. Maybe one of them stole it.' He tried to remember if there was a time when he'd left it unattended. 'Anyway, there's one good thing.'

'What's that?'

'I told Pa about Stevens and the other two, so he'll know I'm innocent.'

'Do you think he'll shop them?'

'No. I warned him not to. If he does, they'll go after him. But he says he has friends who can sort them out if necessary, and from the way he said it I believe him.'

Tom put his other hand on the rail. 'We'll talk again. Best get below, it's getting choppy. Don't worry.'

'But there *is* something to worry about. Donal getting hit on the head. It had to be Stevens. He said if there was any trouble about getting the safe key, he'd hit them over the head with his shillelagh. Owen said the police are calling it attempted murder.'

'Like I say, there's nothing going to happen on this ship. I just thought you ought to know.'

'Do the others know?'

'No. Come on, let's get below afore the wind really picks up and we're lifted up and blown back on shore.'

In steerage, Stag kept going over and over in his mind what Tom had told him. His bait tin had been found at the scene of a robbery in which a man had been set upon and might die, and it looked as if he'd been involved and run off to avoid arrest. He comforted himself that if the police did follow him up in Liverpool, Mrs Hudley and Our Mary would vouch for him not even being in Whitehaven. But no one knew where he'd stayed except for Mr Liversedge, and no one'd think to seek him out and ask him.

* * *

The next morning the ship sailed into bright light after a fair dawn, but the crew were the only ones able to appreciate it. Everyone in steerage was 'shooting the cat'. It was debatable whether this was due to the rolling of the ship in open water or the surroundings in which they found themselves. The hatch leading to steerage was lifted. Stag propped himself up on one elbow and saw Captain Fleming descending the ladder. Halfway down he stopped and cleared his throat before addressing the ailing passengers as if delivering a sermon.

'I know this is a difficult time for you all. It's always like this with passengers when we get fully underway. I'd like to see if I can help you along a wee bit.'

At the bottom of the ladder, he peered into the gloom then moved closer to one of the hanging lamps, which swung to and fro, so that the light falling on the book he was holding passed back and forth over the pages. He began reading to the groaning emigrants.

'They that go down to the sea in ships and occupy their business in great waters; these men see the works of the Lord and his wonder in the deep...'

Stag looked across at Tom. His friend met his gaze and raised his eyes up to the heavens as the captain droned on.

'They reel to and fro, and stagger like a drunken man, and are at their wits' end...'

'Aye, I know how they feel,' said Stag. He buried his face deep into his pillow to drown out the recitation and the groans of the sick.

'I didn't think it would be this bad,' said Lavinia.

After what seemed an age, Captain Fleming closed his book with a thud. He surveyed the room with a gratified smile before withdrawing, with a lighter step than when he'd descended.

'Why did he do that?' asked Evie.

'He probably thinks it makes us feel better,' said Sam. 'Cleanses our hearts and minds.'

'I'm not so sure on that,' said Owen. 'I think it makes *him* feel better.'

'Never mind cleansing our hearts and minds,' said Tom, 'It's our stomachs need cleansing, and preaching to us won't do that.'

❖ ❖ ❖

On his first visit back up on deck, Stag saw the McAvoy boys playing with some of the other children. He looked around for Kate, but they were on their own. A crewman was supervising them, while splicing ropes at the same time. As Stag drew nearer he recognised Billy Botcher, the man who had delivered the welcome patter on the quay. He was overseeing games of leapfrog and tag and it was obvious he had a way with children. Stag guessed he must have some of his own, or nephews and nieces, he seemed so relaxed with them. They, in turn, appeared to be really taken with him.

Billy saw Stag looking. 'This is just a temporary measure until lessons begin and that won't be until the schoolmaster finds his sea legs.'

'He's poorly, is he?' asked Stag.

'The whole family is suffering in a bad way, apart from the boys. That's why they're out here with me. Hooker'll be along in a moment. He'll be setting you on scrubbing some of the canvas gear.'

'Hooker?'

'You'll see,' said Billy. 'Here he comes along with one of the other colliers.'

A tall man as thin as a bean pole was advancing, with Tom by his side. Stag had noticed the man when they were loading up on the quay. He'd been using a large iron hook to pick up sacks and carry them up the gangway. What Stag hadn't realised until he was well in view was that the hook was attached to him, where his right hand should have been.

Stag pointed to it. 'That's different,' he said. 'How'd you end up like that?'

'A flying chain from the rigging came down and lopped off my arm. Years ago.' He made a quick chopping motion with his good hand just above his hook, making Stag shudder. 'It was a poor day. I lost a hand and the ship lost a logline; it got carried away over the side.' Then, as a proud afterthought, he added, 'I made an entry in the ship's log that day.'

'Was it the logline or your hand got carried away?' asked Tom.

'Both.'

'A logline? What's that?' asked one of the Brierley Hill colliers, coming up to join them.

'It's a bit of wood with rope attached that's got knots in it,' said Stag. 'They throw it over the side.' It was interesting how ignorant the Brierley Hill men were of the ways of the sea.

'What for?'

'To see how fast we're going,' said Hooker.

'How does that work?'

'We count the number of knots going over. Anyways, that day when the chain came down and lopped off my hand, I dropped the reel and the whole thing bounced up and scampered over the side. Our first mate was not happy, I can tell you.'

'What about your hand?' asked Tom.

'He picked it up and chucked it over the side.'

Tom grimaced. 'God's truth?'

'Aye, but the Company paid for me to have this hook fitted, so it's all mended now. I'm used to it and it's given me a good name. From the Mile End Road to Honolulu in the Sandwich Islands, everyone knows who Hooker is. Now back to work.'

'Can Stag play us a tune?' asked Tom. 'To lighten the mood?'

'Since I'm in a fine humour and the weather's fair, if the rest of you start work, I can turn a blind eye for ten minutes.'

Stag took his mouth organ from his pocket. He would be careful on board: he valued his hands.

* * *

In all her years of teaching, from being a student to being certificated, it was the strangest class Kate had ever stood in front of. Mr Ward had agreed women's classes could be held outside three times a week for an hour in good weather. Any other classes were to be held below in steerage. Twelve of the women had asked her father if they could attend.

Kate suddenly felt unsure of herself. With children, she was in charge and they did as she bid without question. Looking at the women sitting on benches she realised she had nothing at all in common with them and she didn't know where to begin. She didn't even know if they could all read, and if they could, then to what level. They were gossiping among themselves, paying her no notice. How was she to begin? Normally she would have clapped her hands, the children would have said, 'Good morning, Miss McAvoy,' and she would have begun taking the register. Today, her class was gossiping, knitting, mending clothing, and one was smoking a clay pipe. Kate recognised one of the knitters as Evie Gray, who was working on a shawl, and she saw she had not yet had her baby. She didn't look well at all and Kate wondered briefly if she was still taking the tablets Dr Macdonald had given her.

Kate realised what she had planned for the lesson was of no use at all. She was going to have to adapt, and do it quickly.

She coughed as loudly as she could. 'Good morning, ladies.'

A few heads shot up, and one of the women said, '*Ladies*. We've never been called that before.'

The others laughed, but Kate had caught their attention and they were now all looking at her expectantly.

'As this is our first lesson, I think it would be a good idea if we each gave our names and said a little bit about ourselves.'

The woman spoke again. 'We've been living together for two weeks now. We know all there is to know about each other, and things we don't want to know.' There was laughter again and Kate guessed she had uncovered the class clown. She was undernourished rather than thin, with high cheekbones, lively eyes and auburn hair. Kate judged her to be a few years older than herself.

'Yes, how silly of me, of course you do,' she said. She was sinking fast, she knew it, and they knew it too. 'However, I don't know you, so what if we just go round and you give me your names and I'll write them down.'

This worked quite well, and as each gave her name, Kate tried to think of something she could remember that was distinctive about them to add to her list later. It took a few minutes to get all the names, which allowed the knitters and menders to pick up their needles, return to their handiwork and lower their heads.

'What I think would be a good idea is for you to tell me what it is you want to learn,' Kate said. 'How can I help you?' No one spoke. As she waited for a response, she saw Evie's face. She was panicking, and it dawned on

Kate that whilst she herself was happy to speak in public, the women were not used to speaking out, apart from the clown, who she now knew referred to herself as the fiddler's wife.

'I have an idea.' She looked around the group. 'I'll put you in groups of three and each one of you think of a reason why you want to be here and choose one of you to tell the rest of us.' This seemed to be agreeable, and surely one of the three would be able to speak up. The women put their heads together. When it looked as if they were ready, Kate asked the fiddler's wife what her group were looking for.

'We want to be out in the open air, to be able to help the children with reading and to be able to tell them stories.'

It soon became clear the main reason for being there was to get above deck, and Kate could understand that. Other reasons were: help with adding up, getting away from steerage and escaping from the menfolk, who were always playing cards, or 'making a racket', as one of the women said. Kate knew for sure now most of them were not there to learn – they wanted physical and mental space for themselves in the fresh air. There was one reply in particular that she thought could be useful. The spokeswoman for Evie's group said one of them wanted to know about faraway places, and Kate guessed it might be Evie herself who had suggested that. Seamus had a book with prints of capital cities, and she could probably do something with that.

Kate could see she was going to have to be inventive. She would ask her father for guidance, but not straightaway.

It seemed the majority in her classes would need to be set on to entertain each other in some way so she could give the remaining few individual help. And from the way they looked at her it was apparent some of them resented her. She wasn't yet sure why, but she suspected it was because her speech, manner of dress and education formed a barrier. She would have to try to reach them all in some way, although it wasn't going to be easy.

Kate struggled on for a week. On one occasion she'd looked up to see Stag standing to one side, watching her. He was with a group of collier crewmen swabbing the decks. He began to smile, then seemed to change his mind. She looked away, pretending not to have seen him, and when she looked back, he had his back to her. Evie was smiling and Kate realised she'd been watching her. She felt herself blush.

That evening, when the boys were sleeping, she consulted her father. 'The women are happy to listen to you, but I think some of them resent me. They gossip when I'm trying to talk and they keep their heads down. I heard some of them today say it's not right for a woman to know so much.'

Her father looked concerned. 'Really?'

'I wanted to tell them it was fiddlesticks, and that education should be for all. You taught me that. If they'd voiced their grievances to my face, I could have said something, but overhearing it meant I couldn't defend myself. I know there are more women who would come to be taught, but not by me. They want you.'

'They want a man because they see education as a man's world and you will seem second best,' said Hannah.'

Patrick nodded. 'There's truth in that, I'm sure. However, Kate is right, Hannah my dear, because the women asked if they could attend.'

'They come because they've nothing better to do,' said Hannah, hands on hips. 'An educated woman shows them up.'

'I can't be teaching all the children and the women as well,' Patrick said. 'If Kate is free and able to help, I see no reason why she shouldn't do so. She's passed her letters and is a recognised teacher. It's good practice for her too.'

'This is all too foolish,' said Kate sighing. 'Isn't it more appropriate for a woman to instruct them?'

'You may think so,' said Hannah, 'but, like I say, to my mind they see you as adding score to how little they know. Your pa's the teacher, he's supposed to know more than they do, but you're just a girl to them. You know nothing of their world.'

Patrick nodded, 'Your mother's right. It's something I should have anticipated.'

'You're not thinking of cancelling the lessons, are you? This is a real opportunity for some of them. We can't take that away from them and if I can just connect with all those that want to learn I can really help them. I'm sure more will want to come forward if they see the others improving with their reading.' Kate reflected how the other women passed their time gossiping about their hometowns and the mines. 'Even if I want to converse with them, I can't. I've no idea what they're talking about. Pitheads and "marrers" and so on.'

'They're not looking for friends,' said her mother. 'They see you as different. Not one of them. For a start you're up here in this cabin, not down there in steerage, and this singles you out straightaway. You'll have a much easier passage than they will and they'll likely be resenting it. If not now, certainly later, when we hit the colder weather and the sea gets rougher. You don't even smell like they do; they've got the steerage smell on them and their clothes, and you haven't. Patrick, what are you thinking of doing about this?'

'I don't know. I'll think about it.' He stood up to leave.

Kate put out a hand to delay him. 'There may be a solution. Why don't you take the women and I'll take the children?'

Patrick rubbed the side of his nose with his forefinger. 'It could work, but I'm contracted as the schoolteacher by the Company. I can't break my contract.'

'You don't have to. I don't suppose it states how old your pupils have to be?'

'No,' said Patrick. 'But I have a better idea. Let us share the teaching. It will give us the opportunity to identify those women who really want to learn, and if you continue then I think they will lower their defences as they get to know you. If that is successful, you can take a small group of your own.'

✳ ✳ ✳

A week later, with the weather poor and the sea rough, classes were being held in steerage. Evie had missed class three days running. Kate went looking for her after she'd finished teaching the children. Usually, she left as soon as she reasonably felt she could, but she was concerned about Evie, who was turning out to be one of the women who wanted to learn.

When Kate found her, she was sitting on a bench in the shadows, leaning against the hull. The deterioration in her appearance in just three days was shocking. They'd all lost weight during their bouts of seasickness, but Evie, being thin to start with, had wasted away more than most. The skin of her cheeks was drawn so tight it was pulling the corners of her mouth sideways. Her eyes were beady, like a hungry bird's.

Kate sat down next to her on the bench. 'I hope I'm not disturbing you, but I thought I'd see how you're getting on, since I haven't seen you for a few days.'

'Yes, I'm sorry, I've been very tired,' she said, in her quiet voice. 'I think my bairn will be here soon. I should have sent you a message to say I'm going to be busy and that I won't be able to come to the classes anymore.'

'That's a very special reason for not being able to come,' said Kate. 'You must be looking forward to it. It's your first baby, isn't it?'

Evie nodded. She seemed reluctant for Kate to leave, yet appeared to have no more to say. Kate was about to stand up when a woman she had seen several times, but did not know, came bustling up to sit down on the other side of Evie.

'Miss McAvoy. I'm Queenie. We don't know each other yet, do we?'

Kate was a bit taken aback. She didn't want to appear unfriendly, so she smiled. 'No, we do not.'

'I've just been peeling potatoes and I saw you talking

with Evie, and I thought I'd come over and introduce myself, didn't I? How is your mother? And your father?'

'They are both well, thank you for enquiring.'

'I'm Lavinia's mother. She's expecting a bairn too. Do you remember her from the quayside? When your hat blew off?'

Kate did remember and was about to answer, but it seemed Queenie didn't wait for replies to her many questions.

The older woman turned to Evie. 'How are you, lass? Feeling well? Why so glum? I saw you place your hand on your stomach a few times in the last half hour. Is the bairn playing football with your insides?'

'I'm just tired.' Evie gave a half-hearted smile.

'Are you sure that's all?' asked Queenie, concern in her voice. This time she waited for a response.

'Really, I'm well enough, with the noise and the smell and the ship pitching.' Evie paused before adding, 'Most of the time.'

Kate suddenly felt all was not well.

Queenie, too, seemed unsatisfied by Evie's answer. 'I've borne a bairn. I'll wager something's not right with you. You're too fidgety. Are you having pains?'

Evie's eyes filled with tears and she turned her face away from Queenie's penetrating gaze.

'If you want to tell me what's wrong, I may be able to help.'

Evie wiped her nose on her sleeve. 'I can't feel the baby moving no more.'

Queenie's outward expression did not change. She

put her arms around Evie, who began sobbing into her shoulder. Queenie ran her arms protectively up and down her back, as if rubbing away a small child's hurt following a sudden tumble. She locked worried eyes with Kate over Evie's shoulder. No one else paid much notice; it was not uncommon in steerage for women to burst into tears. Queenie pulled an embroidered handkerchief from her pocket and handed it to Evie.

'Now then, moppet, dry your tears with this.'

Evie shivered despite the stuffy warmth of steerage, blew her nose, sniffed and appeared to try to pull herself together.

In a tiny voice that Queenie and Kate could only just hear, she said, 'I'm sorry for carrying on so like this, but I haven't really felt the bairn for a while. At first, I was too seasick to notice and then I realised I was sleeping without waking up through the night from the bairn's moving.' She placed both hands on her swollen body and raised her head. She looked first at Queenie, then at Kate. 'Do you think there's something wrong?'

'Let me send the lady schoolteacher here to fetch the doctor,' said Queenie, biting down on her bottom lip. 'He's the one to ask about this. I'll wager it's nothing. More likely you've a lazy boy who'll run you ragged once he's here.'

'The doctor said we could call him if we needed to.'

'That's all good then,' said Queenie.

Although Kate had initially found Queenie's intervention tiresome, she could see she was a caring woman with Evie's best interests at heart.

Queenie guided Evie back to her berth and Kate departed to seek out Dr MacDonald.

✵ ✵ ✵

The doctor was in his cabin. It was the first time Kate had visited it and she was surprised to see piles of books stacked around the room. It looked as if he was in the process of cataloguing them, since a large ledger was open next to one of the piles and he had obviously just put a pen down beside it. The ink on the nib was still wet.

'Dr MacDonald, I've just left steerage and Evie Gray, the girl expecting the baby, is not very well.'

'She's started labour, has she?' The doctor reached down and picked his medical bag up from the floor.

'No, it's not that. She says her baby's not moving anymore and hasn't been for some time.' Kate could see he was trying to place Evie. He probably hadn't seen her since her medical examination.

'The small girl?'

'Yes.'

'I can see her now in the sick room.'

Kate paused. She thought the doctor should visit Evie, but how to say it without seeming assertive and telling him what to do? After all, she had little idea of childbirth and labour and he must have plenty. 'She doesn't look well at all and in my opinion, which of course is not medical, I don't think she can climb the steps out of steerage. She can scarcely walk, she's so weak.'

Dr MacDonald nodded. 'In that case, I will visit her myself.'

Kate hesitated. Should she let him go on his own or should she accompany him? She didn't want to abandon Evie, yet she didn't know her very well at all.

Dr MacDonald solved her dilemma by asking her to accompany him to act as a chaperone.

Back in steerage they found Queenie sitting beside Evie, who was now lying in her berth. Queenie made to step away, but Evie called out, 'Please stay. I want you to stay.' She looked from Dr MacDonald to Queenie and back again. Then she saw Kate. 'And you too, Miss McAvoy. Please.'

Dr MacDonald put his bag down. 'I remember you. Have you been taking the tablets I prescribed?' Evie nodded. She seemed to have folded up into herself, taking up even less space than usual.

The doctor was professional, and, as seemed to be his way, almost stern, but the examination was efficient and considerate. Evie answered the doctor's questions as best she could and looked relieved when he stepped back and said, 'I think we should send for your husband before I deliver my prognosis.' He looked at Kate. 'Will you seek him out?'

* * *

Kate found Sam almost immediately and she was thankful for that blessing. She outlined the situation, aware she was a stranger to him and it was a very personal time for him.

'Is the baby coming?' Concern showed all over his face.

'No, not yet.' Should she tell him what Evie had said about the baby not moving? Would that prepare him for if the baby had died? Maybe he already knew – although she guessed probably not.

'I pray the bairn's all right,' he said. 'All she's ever wanted is a loving husband – which she has in me – and children. She told me she didn't mind where she raised her family, and she was happy to come on this journey. If we lose this bairn, I'll blame myself.'

'Don't think like that,' said Kate. It was inadequate, she knew that, but she could think of nothing else to say.

'She's so kind and loving in nature. Always there in the background. She'll make a wonderful mother.'

'I'm sure she will.' And Kate meant it.

When they arrived in steerage, Kate could tell by the look on Dr MacDonald's face that the baby had died. This was confirmed after a few moments, when a wolf-like howl came from behind the curtain that had been erected in Kate's absence to provide Evie with some privacy. Steerage fell silent as they all listened to her sobs. Kate felt tears prick her eyes and, knowing there was nothing she could do and that Sam was there to comfort his wife, she went up on deck, where she could sob quietly in private.

CHAPTER TEN

The following day, Owen gathered everyone together for a meeting. He climbed on one of the benches and blew two sharp blasts on his whistle. All those present, which was almost everyone in steerage not on working duty, including Stag, began looking expectantly in his direction. Sewing needles were put down, books placed on laps, card games and conversations paused. Owen cleared his throat, put his whistle in his pocket and fiddled with his necktie.

'June 16th, one calendar month at sea.' This was greeted with sighs and groans. 'I know, I know, it seems like six months.' He raised his hands palms outwards for silence. 'With this anniversary, and our fiddler's daughter's seventh birthday the day after tomorrow, we should celebrate.'

Stag sought out a striking blonde-haired child, missing a front tooth, peeping from behind her mother's skirts.

'The news is Queenie, and me, are thinking a dance will be in order.'

There was an instant buzz. Stag, too, was all for it.

'What say you?' asked Owen of the gathered passengers.

A voice called out, 'Can't have a dance with diddly squat to drink.' Heads nodded.

'Reet enough,' said another.

Lavinia spoke up. 'There's not enough room.'

Owen clapped his hands. 'I've thoughts on that. We'll have a concert to begin with – Frank on his fiddle and Stag on his mouth organ.' Owen looked across at him and Stag stood up and gave an exaggerated mock bow.

Owen continued, 'We can ask that crewman Jim for a shanty. The ones they're always singing when they pull the ropes. He's the one that leads them.'

'Aye, but what about drink?' It was the same voice that had raised the issue before.

'I'll ask the first mate to tap the captain for a rum issue. I understand he can do that for passengers in times of need.'

'Need?' shouted out one of the Brierley Hill colliers. 'I'll say we're needy. No ale for a month. It's as if we've signed the Pledge.'

'Are we in agreement a little joviality will do us all good, then? Let's have what we call back home a "Merry Neet", like we do at Christmas, even though it isn't. All in favour say "aye"!'

There was a loud positive response, accompanied by cheering and waving of hands.

'Any naysayers? All those against – say "nay"!'

A trickle of voices responded. Stag noticed that, although he didn't say anything, Sam was looking worried.

No wonder, he thought, with Evie close to delivering her stillborn bairn. The noise would be an ordeal for her, never mind the heat their dancing would generate. It would not be a "Merry Neet" for her.

'That's a solid victory in favour. Well, I've a surprise for you. I've already spoken to Mr Ward about some grog. I knew you'd say "aye", and he's going to report back to me.'

✻ ✻ ✻

A meeting was called for the following evening and all the men who were not on duty stepped up to the call. Jim, who'd agreed to sing a shanty, arrived to report that Mr Ward had told the captain he thought 'spirits for spirits' were a good idea and that they should have their drink. The captain had agreed. Stag was relieved, since a dry do would not be a quarter the fun.

'What's that about spirits?' Tom asked Stag.

'Spirits to warm the insides and spirits to keep your spirits up, is what he means,' said Jim. 'Cooped up down here in steerage, you haven't got much cheer.'

Stag gave Jim a friendly slap on the back and thanked him. He was still grateful that he'd warned them away from the spot where they stacked the privy pot.

Owen frowned. 'Three bottles and twenty-three men. Not o'er generous. No need to worry about lasses.'

Stag also doubted it was enough, especially since once they'd had a taste they'd want more.

'We could invite the teacher and his wife and daughter. They're Irish – I'll wager they like a good get-together,' said Tom.

Stag thought it was an excellent idea then wondered if the McAvoys would come to a colliers' dance. Maybe they'd think it was too rowdy or not smart enough. He looked around. If they did come, there'd have to be a clean-up. He didn't think Mrs McAvoy would find it very wholesome.

Owen considered it. 'They might bring a bottle; they look like they can afford it. I'll ask Queenie to invite them.'

One of the Brierley Hill group asked, 'How can we dance in here?' He looked up at the ceiling. 'We'll be cracking our bonces if we forget and jump up.'

'You'll only do it once,' said Owen.

After the arrangements were confirmed and roles allocated, the meeting was formally closed. As the men dispersed, Jim held back and Stag saw him beckon to Owen to follow him up the ladder.

Owen reappeared five minutes later. 'Jim can help us with more grog,' he said, looking pleased with himself. 'Under the table, of course.'

'How much?' asked Stag.

'We've come to a trade-off,' said Owen.

'Under the table? What's that?' asked Tom.

Stag dug him in the ribs. 'Shhh, he means it's hush-hush. Not allowed. On the quiet.' He placed a finger over his lips.

Owen nodded. 'That's right, no blabbing. We'll lose it and Jim'll cop it.'

'I'm surprised we got those other bottles from the captain,' said Tom.

'Seems he does have a heart,' Owen replied.

Stag chuckled. 'More like he's looking forward to delivering one of his sermons on the evils of drink the morning after.'

* * *

Hannah was reading to the boys while Kate was gathering up laundry when they were interrupted by an intrusive knocking on their cabin door. A collier Hannah didn't recognise thrust a scrappy piece of paper into her hands and scurried off. It turned out to be an invitation to a dance in steerage the next day. Hannah handed it to Patrick and, after he had read it, he passed it to Kate.

Hannah was the first to speak.

'I know you want to get closer to the women, Kate, and you're young and would like to dance, but don't you think it better to show some reserve on this occasion? You're the schoolteacher, and for them to see you gadding about may not be wise.'

All Kate could think about was that her collier would be there. Yes, she would like a dance with him. She checked herself. He was 'Stag the collier', not 'her collier'. He had passed her twice on deck the previous day and smiled both times. This time, instead of looking away, she had smiled back. She looked to her father.

'I hear what you're saying, my love,' said Patrick. 'But I think a little fraternising could be a good thing. If we don't accept this invitation given in good faith, it will make us seem stand-offish. It's a long voyage and we don't want to cause any ill feeling. We can always leave early.'

Hannah frowned. 'Yes, I suppose you're right. I'm just

thinking how hot it's going to be down there, and with drink flowing it will probably be boisterous.'

'Like Pa says,' said Kate, 'You can leave early if it's not to your liking.'

To Kate's relief her mother smiled. 'Well, it will give us a chance to wear something a bit different, but only if we can find someone to look after the boys.'

'We'll sort something out,' said Patrick. 'First we must reply. Can you do that, Kate, and deliver it?'

She nodded. 'Of course, I'll see to it right away before it gets dark.' She quickly wrote out an acceptance and was hurrying along the deck when a voice rang out.

'Miss McAvoy, you're in a hurry.'

She turned round. She'd thought so – it was her collier. He was leaning against the rail. He must have been watching her scurrying along.

'I've an errand to run. We've been invited to the dance tomorrow.'

'Are you coming? I'll be playing for the dancing.'

'Yes,' she said. A smile broke out on Stag's face. Then she quickly corrected herself. 'Well, that is to say we will if we can get someone to sit with Seamus and Bartley. They're too young to come and too small to leave on their own. If we can't, then I guess I'll have to do it.'

A flicker of disappointment swept over his face. 'I think the women are looking forward to seeing you. They like you and will be sorry if you can't come.'

He was looking right into Kate's eyes. She wasn't sure if it was the movement of the ship or his scrutiny that made her feel a little giddy. 'I must go.'

She had walked on when she heard him call out.

'Wait. Miss McAvoy, wait.'

She turned. He was brushing his hair back from his forehead as he strode towards her.

'Yes?'

'I have an idea. You teach Evie, don't you?'

'Yes, I do.'

'I think the dance is going to be too much for her. The noise and the heat. What if you ask Evie to sit with the boys? It would help everyone. That is, if you think Mr and Mrs McAvoy won't mind her being in your cabin. I'm sure she's honest and would look after the boys really well.'

Kate could have kissed him there and then for finding such a practical solution to their problem, and for helping Evie too. 'That's a wonderful idea. Do you think she will agree?'

'I'm sure she will.' He was beaming from ear to ear. 'I'll ask her. Will you ask your father and mother?'

'Yes, and I think I can safely say they will be very happy with that arrangement.' Kate wasn't actually so sure about her mother, but they would bring her round to the idea, and the boys would be delighted with someone new to talk to. 'I'll be teaching tomorrow. We can confirm.'

Stag nodded. 'Until tomorrow.'

As she began making her way to steerage again, she thought she heard 'Save a dance for me' – but then perhaps she'd imagined it.

❊ ❊ ❊

The evening of the dance, Kate had only got as far as the bottom of the ladder into steerage, and was just noticing how everything had been tidied up to create a large space, when Queenie rushed forward to greet her.

'We're so pleased you've come.' She registered there was no one following Kate down the ladder. 'Mr and Mrs McAvoy? Are they coming too?'

'Yes, they're just settling the boys. They'll be here in a moment.'

'And Evie's looking after them. I think that's a fine idea, don't you?'

Kate nodded. She was conscious that the women were looking at her clothes. She was wearing a dress they hadn't seen before. It was a blue summer one with pale yellow muslin sleeves. She'd been saving it for the warmer weather and thought it would be a good choice to combat the heat of a steerage dance. The women were wearing dresses she had seen before, but each one had made an effort with a ribbon or a piece of lace. The atmosphere was jolly and everyone seemed in good spirits.

She spotted Stag chatting with his friends. He was rolling his mouth organ round in his hands and looked keen to get going. He was wearing a new necktie – a bright red one with a paisley scroll design – and a white shirt. It was the first time she'd seen him close to without a waistcoat or jacket, and she could make out the outline of his broad shoulders. Kate had often wondered how the people in steerage managed to keep up with the washing that was required. Stag's shirt looked so fresh and clean, she guessed it was one he'd kept back for a special occasion. Certainly, this evening was special for them all.

People were looking behind her. Kate turned. Her parents had arrived and all eyes were now upon them. A hush fell on the room, which made it seem as if they were making a grand entrance, almost as if they were the royalty on the ship. They did make a handsome pair: her father in his best jacket, waistcoat, and trousers and her mother in a green and white tartan dress. Tied tightly around her throat was a black choker from which fell a single pearl. Her father was holding a bottle which Jim rushed up to collect from him.

Owen took the McAvoys' arrival as a signal for the dance to begin.

'Welcome one and all.' He nodded to the McAvoys before blowing his whistle. 'Gather round. There's no grog 'til I'm done. This evening's programme is a concert of music and song, followed by recitation and dancing. It's an opportunity for us to get to enjoy ourselves now we've all got our sea legs. It's taken a month and here we are. Our first Whitehaven and Brierley Hill folk get-together.'

'What about the Liverpool folk?' interrupted Tom, pointing to the McAvoys.

'Aye, apologies, Mr and Mrs McAvoy, Liverpool folk and any others,' said Owen.

Sam Gray shouted out, 'Come on, Owen, hurry to it. We're parched for a drop of something. We can hear your voice any time, let's get to the drinking part.' A smattering of applause followed the comment.

'All right, all right, all right. Like I say, we've been on board one month. We can manage the rest, God willing. Grog's over there.' He pointed to the liquor. 'It just leaves me to wish you all more luck and less trouble. Now, let the music begin.'

Despite the movement of the ship, the fiddler played in lively fashion and his daughter, to good-natured applause, managed a complicated clog dance that Kate knew was the result of much practice, as she'd seen her rehearsing.

This was followed by Tom reciting his party piece ballad in broad Cumbrian dialect, to the bafflement of those unfamiliar with it. It didn't matter, as the musicality of the dialect was entertainment in itself.

A small group of off-duty crewmen joined them for the entertainment, making the area even more cramped than usual. There were six of them – big men, with tattoos all the way up their arms, and gold earrings. One had a snake tattoo that swirled up around his neck, with its open mouth, complete with fangs, appearing from behind his ear, and a forked tongue coming to rest across his cheek. Kate could see the men would be frightening if they were strangers encountered on shore, but they were laughing and smiling. They took up a lot of space and the fiddler's daughter had to retreat into her mother's skirt folds. It was not as if they had not seen the men before, but so many, and so close you could smell the protective animal grease they put on their bodies, made them both exotic and scary at the same time.

Owen banged his fist on the nearest bench and signalled to the fiddler to lay aside his instrument. 'Silence. Silence.' With much shushing and nudging of elbows, eventually there was an expectant quiet. 'Thank you. Now please give your full attention to Seaman Jim and the crew, who'll sing for us the well-known ballad, *The Rambling Royal*.'

All attention was now upon Jim, who took off his cap and stuffed it in his pocket as he stepped forward. After clearing his throat and putting one hand flat against his ear in true Jack Tar fashion, he began singing, and the others came in for the chorus:

'*I am a rambling Royal, from Liverpool I come,*
And to my sad misfortune, I enlisted in the Marines...'

Kate knew the song well, for it was a popular one on Liverpool's streets. Standing directly across from her, Stag, looking confident, was still fidgeting with his mouth organ, as if now he was impatient to try this new melody. He saw Kate looking at him and smiled across at her. It was a broad smile that began tentatively, then lit up his whole face. She smiled back and a flush of embarrassment spread across her complexion. She could see he was happy. She tried to look anywhere apart from his direction, but he was exactly opposite her line of vision in the circle surrounding Jim and the crewmen. After a few difficult minutes, she couldn't stop herself checking to see if he was still looking at her, but to her disappointment he'd turned his attention back to the ballad and its singer. As the song drew to a sad close, amidst cheering and stomping of feet, Kate turned round to find herself under what appeared to be critical appraisal from Lavinia. She smiled at the woman, but since nothing was reciprocated, she looked away.

Hannah McAvoy wiped away a tear. 'I'm loving a good weep,' she said, laughing and dabbing her eyes with the corner of her handkerchief. Kate was relieved to see her mother was enjoying herself. Perhaps she wouldn't leave early.

'Don't we all love a good weep?' said Queenie, searching in vain for something with which to dab. 'Is Stag going to play now?' She nudged Hannah gently on the arm. 'He's very good, can play almost anything.' She beamed as Stag sauntered forward, as if without a care in the world. Then, in what seemed an afterthought, she added, 'He's a very good friend of my daughter's husband, Tom. Did you know that?'

Hannah said she didn't and smiled politely.

When the applause that heralded his appearance had died down, Stag began to play. He started with some well-known melodies which were gathered up keenly by the impatient dancers. Space was tight and the ceiling did prove to be too low, but spirits were high. After several tunes, Stag stopped for breath, then announced, 'Here's an Irish jig for Mr and Mrs McAvoy.'

Patrick took Hannah by the hand and led her onto the floor and everyone began clapping. The onlookers moved back to create a space big enough for them to dance. With a huge grin on his face, Patrick turned Hannah first one way and then the other as the music gathered momentum. The onlookers began clapping in time and Patrick beckoned to others to join in. Kate surveyed the gathered crowd; they were all laughing and smiling. They appeared to be uplifted by the sight of the usually rather sombre schoolteacher relaxing in good heart.

Stag's playing seemed effortless. Queenie was right, he played with flair. He'd looked in her direction several times and raised his eyebrows. When the jig came to an end, everyone cheered and Patrick bowed extravagantly. Hannah took his cue and made an over-deep curtsey. Kate felt a burst of pride that both her parents had entered into the spirit of the occasion.

After half an hour, Stag begged to be allowed to stop. 'I'm as dry as the Red Sea bed,' he said, putting his mouth organ in his pocket and patting it. 'You'll not begrudge me something to wet my whistle, will you? Anyway, I want a dance myself.'

The dancers moved aside to let him join his mates gathered around the beverages. Tongues had been loosened by the grog and there was much laughter and some ribaldry.

'Right, lads,' said Sam, handing Stag a double tot of rum. Sam was an obvious choice to be put in charge of the drink since, Evie being with the McAvoy boys, he had no wife to dance with. Sam spoke to Tom who put his measure down and looked around. Kate hoped he had told him to find his wife. Lavinia was sitting with her mother near Kate. Even though she was now well-swollen with child, she was swaying in her seat to the music. She would probably welcome a gentle turn around the dance floor. Kate watched Stag down his rum in one go and wipe his lips with the back of his hand. He helped himself to a large glass of the sweetened water laid out for the women and the Pledgers, then looked to Owen for a refill before following Tom. They began making their way over to the women.

'Do you know my son-in-law, Tom?' Queenie asked Kate and Hannah with pride. 'He's Stag's marrer. You know Stag, don't you? You've just been listening to him, haven't you?' As was her habit, she didn't waste time waiting for a reply to her many questions. 'Well, I s'pose you young ones'll be wanting to dance, won't you?' Queenie nudged Tom, while looking at Stag.

Tom took Lavinia by the hand and they were quickly swallowed up by the other dancers. Stag hesitated, then looked at Kate. It was obvious from her expression that Queenie was expecting him to invite her to dance.

Kate opened her mouth to make an excuse, but Queenie was not to be outdone. She turned to Hannah. 'It's so pleasing to see the young ones dancing, isn't it, Mrs McAvoy? My Jefferson and I used to love it in our younger days. Did you? I'll wager your Kate here likes to dance? Doesn't she? Yes, I think I'm right on this, aren't I?'

'I –' began Kate.

'It's dancing Kate loves,' said Hannah. 'It's in my husband's family. There's nothing a Dubliner likes better than an evening spent dancing.'

Kate glowered at her mother. How could she be so insensitive? Stag would have to ask her to dance now. She wanted to, it was just that she felt unexpectedly shy being so close to him. Then she was struck by the embarrassing thought that after all this prompting he might fail to ask her. That was worse than dancing with him, so she gave him an encouraging smile and when he offered his hand, took it with relief.

She was surprised at his touch; she'd expected a collier's hand to be rougher, pitted, maybe even stiff. Then she remembered he'd not been in a mine for some time.

It was still a working man's hand, but it was welcoming, firm and strong, and most of all it was one with which she felt comfortable. He adjusted his grip so their fingers became entwined and they merged themselves with the other dancers.

It was a quick dance and for such a strong, well-built man Stag was nimble and light on his feet. Kate didn't know why this was a surprise too, for she knew he was musical. When she thought about it he had probably been to a lot more dances than she had. They were keen dancers in Cumbria. It was exciting and Kate felt her spirits soar. Maybe leaving Liverpool was going to turn out not to be the disaster she had been thinking. She didn't want the dance to end, but end it did, and all too soon.

When the music stopped Kate didn't know what to do, so she made as if to leave, but Stag put a light hand upon her arm. 'Don't be going yet, lass. It's only just starting to liven up a bit. Don't you like to dance? You look as if you do.'

'I like it very much. I thought you might like a rest.' She tucked some curls behind her ears that had worked their way loose. Kate noticed again how extraordinarily blue his eyes were. It was noticeable even in steerage's strange light. Also, how he flexed the corners of his mouth slightly before breaking into a full smile.

'Me? Not want to dance? Why it's a sure thing you don't know me and my ways.' He threw back his head and a rich laugh came from deep within his throat. It was stirring to hear and several people looked round in search of its source. 'Nay, I live to dance.' His eyes travelled over her face. 'Unless you don't want to?'

By way of answer Kate turned to him and made ready. Owen had taken charge and the dancers were positioned in two lines facing each other. After each verse the women moved to the right, leaving their original partners and, in high spirits, greeting their new partners with welcoming smiles and open arms. When she and Stag finally met up again, Kate was radiant. Even though he was sweating with the effort of the dance, Stag still had not had enough and whisked her off for another bout. At each end of the line turn, Kate noticed Lavinia was sitting with a frown on her face. She wondered why.

The heat in steerage was stifling and with the excitement she suddenly felt dizzy. 'You'll have to excuse me,' she mouthed to Stag above the general din. 'I'll have to sit down.' She began fanning herself with her hand.

Stag pointed in the direction of the ladder leading to the open hatch. 'You'd better go on deck for some fresh air.' Kate hesitated as he made to follow her. 'It's all right, we'll not be alone. I'll bet there's plenty up there already for the same reason.'

The air on deck, although sharp, was much sweeter than the scent of the sweaty bodies below. The canvas sails flapped overhead and the ropes, caught in the wind, cracked against the masts. Now they were alone the atmosphere was different, more intimate. Kate had lots of questions she wanted to ask, but out in the open, away from the hustle and bustle below, she felt awkward. They stood in silence by the rail and listened to the noises of the ship against the background of the music below and the seamen's bare feet slapping on the boards as they hurried by. Kate peered over the side into the blackness, but there was nothing to see except the white foamy waves thrown up as the passage of the ship parted the water. She was acutely conscious of Stag being alongside her, his hands on the rail so close to her own. She breathed in deeply and she could smell not just the liquor and the heat emanating from his body, but also, she sensed, his actual essence, and it frightened and attracted her in equal measures. She took a few paces along the rail, all the while looking out into the darkness of the horizon. She wondered, had she been a collier girl, would he have put an arm round her?

Stag broke the silence. 'We've a way to go on this journey.'

Kate turned away from the rail to face him. 'I wonder if it'll live up to my parents' hopes of a Promised Land?'

'You sound as if you didn't want to leave Liverpool.'

'No, I didn't. Did you want to leave your home?'

'Whitehaven? Nay. I had to. If I'd stayed, I know I'd never be anything other than a collier.' He laughed. 'I'd been saying that for years and not done anything. It was hearing about this opportunity that spurred me on.'

Kate wanted to ask him about Whitehaven and his family, and a world so different from her own. She couldn't imagine what it was like to work inside the earth, but she knew it wasn't the right time to be questioning him about his past. It would only emphasise what different backgrounds they'd come from. A sobering thought crossed her mind: perhaps the gulf between their worlds was too great and always would be.

An uneasy silence followed. Kate shivered; the heat she'd been suffering from had vanished. She should return below.

'You're cold, lass.' Stag went to put his arm around her, then seemed to think better of it. She had already sidestepped. It wasn't that she was afraid of him, for he was right – there were plenty about who would have come running if she had chanced to shout. It was that she found his attractiveness overwhelming, and she wasn't yet sure whether this was something special to grasp with both hands, or something dangerous to be avoided at all costs.

❊ ❊ ❊

Kate and her parents found Seamus and Bartley fast asleep when they returned from the dance.

'They're lovely boys,' said Evie. 'They didn't play me up at all. I was able to read one of their stories, Miss McAvoy. I've really come on with my reading. Thank you.'

Out of the corner of her eye, Kate saw her father nod approvingly.

'Did you have a nice time?' asked Evie, gathering up her bonnet.

'Oh, yes,' said Hannah. 'They'll tell you all about our dancing, I'm sure of that.'

'I'm wondering, if the boys say they were happy with me in the morning, if you'd like me to look after them another time. I'd be happy to. I love children.'

The few hours Evie had had on her own seemed to have done her the world of good, and Kate made a note to look out for her in the future. She'd already repaid her by being an attentive pupil, and she liked her.

Patrick left to escort Evie back to steerage.

Hannah yawned. 'I'm glad now that we went. Everyone

was very welcoming to us. Don't you wonder how people manage in steerage, living so close all the time?'

'I think they get used to it, and it was a lot more crowded this evening than it usually is,' said Kate. 'People seem to get by. Also, we don't know the kind of conditions they've left behind. You have to ask yourself, would they be leaving if their lives in Whitehaven and Brierley Hill were satisfactory?'

Hannah sat on her bunk. 'I'm ashamed to say this, but I don't think I could stand it down there, especially if Queenie Jefferson was at my side all day asking questions like she does. She's friendly enough, it's just that –'

'You're travellers on the same journey, but you're on different decks.'

'Yes, that's it. That's it exactly.'

CHAPTER ELEVEN

Evie's labour began three days after the dance, and having retained her newfound attachment to Queenie and Kate, she asked them to stay with her. When the pains began, she was at first stoical, but gradually Kate saw them take hold, the pain showing itself in her face while she clenched and unclenched her hands. Even between contractions she was tense, waiting for the next one. Queenie and Kate put up a sheet to give her some privacy. There was some murmuring from the other women, who said they had more experience in delivering bairns, but Queenie paid no attention. She wasted no time in sending Sam packing.

As the pains grew ever stronger, and the gap between them ever shorter, Evie muttered about being back in Whitehaven, walking along Lowther Street in her best frock and red clogs. She seemed to be greeting friends and talking to passers-by on a harbour wall, but it soon became obvious to Kate that the relentless rhythm of the contractions was becoming too great to allow her to drift from reality for long.

They were well into the afternoon when Evie said she felt as if her insides were turning over.

'You're ready to push,' said Queenie.

'I can't. I'm too tired and thirsty.'

'Now, child, I know you're exhausted, but that's your body wanting to push the baby out.' Queenie stroked Evie's hair. 'Push down long and hard and it'll soon all be over with.'

Kate caught Queenie's eye and the older woman nodded at her unspoken question before calling the fiddler's wife, who was on sentry duty on the other side of the curtain. 'Fetch Dr MacDonald.'

No matter how hard they tried, it was impossible for those within earshot to blot out the sounds of Evie's agonisingly slow progress. When Dr MacDonald arrived, Kate left to join the women to give him more space. Some of the women were reliving their own birthing experiences, in hushed tones. Kate was shocked to see Lavinia in distress, plucking at her skirt sides with agitated fingers. Suddenly she rose and began pacing up and down, her hands draped protectively over her as yet unborn child. Kate called Queenie to tend her daughter, leaving Evie alone with the doctor.

With everyone looking at her, wondering what to do, Lavinia spoke. 'I won't have my bairn here, I won't.' She looked from face to face as the others regarded her with undisguised alarm.

Queenie tried to pacify her. 'Hush now, lass, it sounds

much worse than it is.' But her words of comfort served only to fuel Lavinia's hysteria.

'That's the point! Can't you see that's the point? Everyone sitting here listening to it all. It'll be like that for me. Must I submit myself to such a public ordeal? I won't do it.' She began backing away from the women as if she thought they were in some way responsible for her distress.

'Come and sit with me, lass,' said her mother, rising to take her hand. Lavinia shied away as if from a flame.

'Why don't you take her up top?' suggested one of the women, voicing everyone's thoughts. 'Kate can help if the doctor needs someone else.'

Lavinia was clenching her teeth and staring out like some wild woman who'd escaped from an asylum. No one wanted to approach her.

'Fetch Tom back,' said Queenie, not daring to look away from her daughter. 'He might be able to calm her.'

Owen went off in search of him.

After a while, Lavinia's distress appeared to have reached a plateau, and she grew quiet. However, catching sight of Tom descending the ladder into steerage only fuelled her distress, and she began shouting out again. Dr MacDonald pulled back the curtain with a bloodied hand and bellowed, 'Silence that woman immediately by any means necessary.' He panned the room before letting his gaze fall on Kate. He raised his eyebrows to her. She interpreted his gaze as asking her to step in to alleviate the situation.

The sight of blood on the doctor's hands cut through the last reins of control and Lavinia opened her mouth to draw in the breath needed to fuel a drawn-out scream. Kate stepped forward and slapped her hard across the face. Lavinia flinched as she felt the unexpected blow. The imprint of Kate's hand could be seen on her cheek. A red welt began rising, in livid contrast to the paleness of the surrounding skin. Silence was immediate, and by the narrowing of Lavinia's eyes Kate knew she had made an enemy.

It was not long before the doctor moved the curtain aside to reveal Sam, holding his dead son. He'd been swaddled in sheeting and from a distance it looked as if he was only sleeping. The faces of his parents, however, told a different story. Kate looked away as the doctor put out his arms to take the swaddled bundle. The pain on Sam and Evie's faces was too much. It was not a time to stand and stare.

As the doctor came out from behind the curtain, carrying the baby, his eyes sought Kate and Queenie. 'I've to make my report to the captain. Thank you both for your help.'

He then saw Tom.

'Call me immediately your wife feels anything. I suspect hers will be a difficult labour.' Tom's face registered alarm. 'Not because of physical problems – she seems healthy enough – but I fear she will fall into distress again.'

'You want me there when she has the baby?' asked Tom, trying not to look at the sheeted parcel in the doctor's arms.

'No, I'm talking of the next few weeks. She'll need reassurance that all will be well, as I expect it to be.'

Kate wondered how the doctor managed to go about his work when it was so sad.

✻ ✻ ✻

After the doctor had left, Queenie offered to bring hot water for Evie. Stag, seeing Sam had been asked to leave, suggested they go up on deck to take some air.

'He was perfect, Stag. I could see nothing wrong with him. It was just as if he was only sleeping.'

'This is a hard thing to bear, Sam.' Stag put an arm around his friend's shoulders. 'We're all so sorry.'

'We knew the bairn was dead, but, you know, I think we thought maybe the doctor was wrong. Maybe he just slept a lot. Does that sound wrong?'

'No, not at all,' said Stag. 'We always hope for the best.'

'When the doctor went to cover the baby's face, I wanted to cry out and stop him. He was like one of those wax dolls I've seen in toy shop windows. I shall never be able to see a wax doll now without thinking of him.'

Stag hoped the sympathy he was feeling for Sam was showing on his face, for he could think of nothing to say to ease Sam's grief.

'Will you think me simple in the head if I tell you it was his limpness, like a doll, that drew me to keep looking at him? And yet it was the stillness and silence that was the very reason my son was being taken away so quickly and quietly.'

'I can understand that. You were looking for movement, for a glimmer of life.'

'Yes, I think you're right.'

✻ ✻ ✻

Later that evening, Sam pleaded he dare not leave his wife's side and he asked Stag to ask Captain Fleming about the committal arrangements. It took some persuasion, but Mr Ward eventually said he would accompany Stag to facilitate an interview with the captain.

Captain Fleming was studying some large charts on his desk. He frowned when Stag and Mr Ward entered.

Stag paused at the entrance to the captain's saloon and stared. Trophies and souvenirs from earlier voyages were scattered around it. Beaver pelts were strewn on the floor and a long native Indian pipe had been strung from the ceiling by its feather ornamentation, leaving it free to sway from side to side in tandem with the pitching of the ship. A large bleached seashell with wavy edges had been placed to one side of the desk to act as a spittoon. Strangely decorated blankets were piled on a wooden chest, and by its side was a large woven basket, decorated with stylised fish. Inside the bunk space was a small wooden shelf with a brass holding rail across its front. The shelf contained three books which looked like bibles or prayer books. Stag had never considered what a captain's cabin would look like and, despite the sadness of the occasion of his visit, he found it fascinating.

'Well?' The captain had waited while Stag looked around as if he appreciated the effect his cabin was having on his visitor.

'Stag Liddell requesting an interview, cap'n,' said Mr Ward.

Stag cleared his throat unnecessarily. 'I've come about the Gray's bairn. The stillborn bairn.'

The captain turned to study Stag. 'What about it?'

'The funeral arrangements, cap'n. Sam Gray, the bairn's pa, thinks it'll help soothe his wife's grief if we can have the service soon.'

Captain Fleming pursed his lips. 'There'll be no funeral.' He returned his attention to the charts laid out in front of him and Mr Ward made as if to retire.

Stag was confused. He'd expected the captain to be sympathetic, being such a God-fearing man. Perhaps he was a little awkward at a death on his ship, especially a bairn's death. There must be a mistake. 'Has the funeral already been?' he asked.

Captain Fleming looked up from his charts. 'There has not been, and will not be, a funeral. A stillborn child is a devil's child, judged unfit for this life by Our Lord.' There was a slight pause before he added, 'I threw it overboard. Any objections?'

Stag had a thousand objections. And what was he going to tell Evie and Sam? How could he tell them their baby had been thrown out with the rubbish? He wondered if he could lie and say the captain had said some prayers. He would do that and hope they never found out otherwise. It was a lie, but a necessary one.

CHAPTER TWELVE

Under a sky speckled with angry, fast moving clouds Stag, Owen, and Tom were working on deck, lining up water casks. They were well-accustomed to the pitching of the ship and the daily routine, but these were larger barrels than they'd previously had to move.

Stag took off his neckerchief and wiped his brow. 'We're not used to this sort of slog.'

'Aye, I've got out of the habit of lugging things.' Owen cast a glance around. 'These casks are worse than the corves at the mine. Reckon it's my age catching up.'

Stag inspected his hands. 'They've got slivers that'll jab you as soon as you lay a hand on 'em. Sling me that chisel.'

Stag applied the chisel to the cask top, and it jumped open. As it did so, both men sprang back, their noses wrinkling.

'Strewth,' said Owen, protecting his nose with a cupped hand. 'It's worse than the back wall of the Queen's Head on a holiday eve.' They peered into the casks. 'Ugh, looks the same too.'

'Let's try another.' Stag laid into a second with the same result. 'We can't drink this, it stinks.' As he was attempting to open a third barrel, Hooker, who'd been supervising men painting aloft, shouted out and came running over, his bare feet slapping the deck as he sprinted forward.

'Stop that, water's not easy to come by this trip.'

'This ain't water,' said Owen. 'It's cat's piss. Dead cat's piss and all.'

Hooker sniffed the barrels and cursed. 'There's nowt wrong with this water, it's the barrels. They've fobbed us off with old wine barrels. Turns the water into vinegar.'

'We can't sup this, it isn't fit,' said Tom.

'We'll have to.' Hooker scratched his beard with the end of his hook. 'There ain't no other.'

'You're pulling my leg,' said Owen, starting to laugh. 'You'll not pull any wool over me.' He rocked on his heels and slapped Hooker on the back.

Stag looked at Hooker's face and realised he was telling the truth.

'I'm not pulling any legs, arms, or arses for that matter. There's nowt wrong with that water, except for its pong. It'll do you no harm, except it can make you even thirstier if you drink too much. Plenty good enough for cooking and washing clothes.'

Owen's jaw dropped. 'What about drinking?'

Hooker looked up at the sky. 'That'll be rainwater from now on. We've no other, 'til we get to Honolulu.'

'The lasses'll not be happy about this,' said Tom. 'My

Lavinia especially. They'll kick up a dust about it. We're entitled to three quarts per person per day.'

'What about the bairns?' said Owen. 'There'll be a mutiny.'

Stag cringed and wasn't surprised when Hooker's face clouded over and he flourished his hook. 'Don't be using words like that on board, not even in jest. It's calling on the worst of luck, any old salt'll tell you that.'

The catastrophe sent the men hurrying below to share the news and soon a whole crowd of men were on deck, holding their noses, looking into the reeking casks. Hooker and the rest of the crew eyed them with amusement from a distance.

'I reckon we'd best see Mr Ward about this,' said Stag.

'Aye,' said Tom. 'Better to see Cap'n Fleming. He's the boss.'

'That's a half-baked idea,' said Owen. 'He'll not thank you for bothering him.'

Stag wasn't warming to the idea of a confrontation with the captain, but he could see they had to do something. 'It's my way of thinking they'll have other casks, at least for the bairns. The cap'n can at least register a complaint for the ship's log.' He set off to find Mr Ward, with three of the others. Owen and Sam lingered. Stag turned back and looked at them. 'Come on, lads, let's get this job settled. You won't let us go alone will you?' He looked directly to Owen. 'Damn it, you're a manager.'

Owen made one last effort to dissuade him. 'I still think we're asking for trouble if we bother the cap'n. He only issues orders via Mr Ward. He doesn't even talk to his crew.'

'He spoke to me,' said Stag.

'Well, you're the lucky one,' said Owen.

'That water stinks,' piped up one of the Brierley Hill colliers. 'It's no better than a cesspit. Would you drink that? Would you swim in it? Tom's right, we should go straight to the gaffer, the cap'n.'

Owen shook his head. 'Stag's already had words with him, remember? Over Sam's bairn. He paid no heed to owt he had to say then – why should this be any different? The cap'n won't welcome being told his water's like piss if he doesn't know already, which he probably does, and he can't do much about it either way.'

''Appen not, but like I say we've a duty to register a complaint and make sure it's recorded in the ship's log. It's the official Company record, it must mean something.' Stag looked around for support and was encouraged when he saw several of the men nodding. 'If we all go it'll make him listen.'

'Hold off a minute,' Owen went on. 'Last thing the cap'n wants is a record in the log about rotten supplies. Reflects on him.'

'What do you want then? To say nothing?' Stag turned to Owen 'You're mine manager level. What say you?'

Owen sighed. 'I'll come with you if you all reckon it's reet. Only seeing as how I'm mine manager level.'

Hooker looked at the six men's retreating backs. Stag heard him say, 'They're brave. They'll get more from the cap'n than they've bargained for.'

When they reached the captain's saloon, Stag and Owen found themselves manoeuvred to the front, as if heading the deputation. The men, who had been muttering amongst themselves as they walked along, fell silent in front of the closed door. Stag stepped forward and knocked.

He doffed his cap on hearing the captain's 'come,' and opened the door. The captain was sitting behind his desk. He looked at the men standing there as if he was bored by their presence. It was obvious to Stag he had heard their muttering voices and correctly judged them angry, since he'd placed a pistol on the polished desktop, its barrel pointing towards the door. It was the first thing Stag saw. He was shocked.

'You're the one known as Stag, aren't you?'

Stag nodded, looking straight at the captain, refusing to allow his gaze to wander back to the pistol.

'Well?' The captain's eyes were cold. He'd placed an elbow on his desk and was resting his chin on his closed fist, the knuckles pressing deep into his cheek. He couldn't have looked more bored by their presence than if he had been staring at a blank wall for the previous fifteen minutes.

'Cap'n, sir,' began Stag, his voice strong and steady. 'There's a problem with the water.'

'A problem? What problem?' The captain fixed on Stag as if he was the only person present. 'Tell me, is that your problem or mine?'

'Everyone's sir. The water's gone off.'

The captain sat up straight in his chair and squared his shoulders. 'Gone off? Gone off where? This is a surprise.' He laughed. 'Do you think it'll be back in time for me to sup this evening?'

'Only if you're planning on replacing your wine with vinegar, sir,' said Stag, regretting the words as soon as they left his mouth. It was not his intention to antagonise the captain.

A half-suppressed titter came from behind him.

Captain Fleming stood up. 'Water on this ship does not go off.'

'We can show you,' said Stag, turning to face the others. 'Make way and we'll show the cap'n.' He went as if to break through the small group of men, but the captain's voice thundered out, stopping him in his tracks.

'Remain where you are.'

Stag turned to face him.

'Are you telling me that because the water isn't perfumed to your liking, you're not happy?'

Stag registered the same expression he'd seen flash across the captain's face when they'd discussed the Gray baby's committal. It was a look of contempt, not just for Stag, but for all men. He guessed the captain considered himself to be rare amongst men, his strong faith setting him apart, bringing him to closer communion with his God, elevating him above other mortals.

Stag experienced a rush of blood. How dare he look at them with such insolence? 'No. We're not happy,' he said. 'We're saying the water stinks. It's your responsibility, you're the gaffer. What are you going to do about it?' Stag folded his arms over his chest. He needed to rouse the captain, to strike a sympathetic nerve, to shame him into some kind of emotional response, but his expression remained cold. 'Call yourself a God-fearing man. You've as much compassion for us as you had for the Gray baby. That bairn went overboard as if it was no more than a dead cat. Is that how you look upon us? Animals to be fed and watered with second-rate rations at your convenience?'

Owen put a hand on Stag's arm. 'Hush, Stag, you've said enough. Sam's here.'

Stag shrugged his hand off then glanced over at Sam to see he had blanched, but he could not stop. 'Well, what are you going to do about it?' He paused to take a deep breath. His emotions were so roused, they were causing him breathlessness.

After what seemed a long time, but was probably less than a minute, the captain gave a half-smile. 'Your wild ways may be all right when you're with your collier friends acting out your name – fighting and rutting – but here I am, as you so rightly say, 'the gaffer'. If you were a full member of my crew, I'd have you seized and punished with twenty-four cuts of the birch.' He waited for his words to sink in. 'So, it's water and compassion you're wanting is it? All right, I'll put you where you can reflect on your quick temper.' He called to Mr Ward, who'd been standing behind the group, watching and listening.

'Mr Ward, take these two.' He pointed at Stag and Owen. 'Clap them in irons. I'm being generous. I'm putting their hot-headedness down to ignorance of the ways of the sea and I'm showing compassion by not clapping them all in irons.'

As they were led away, Captain Fleming shouted after them, 'Make sure they've plenty of water to drink.' The retreating group could hear him laughing in the distance.

CHAPTER THIRTEEN

It was only when he felt the cold iron close around his wrists and ankles that Stag's anger began to evaporate, to be replaced by self-reproach.

'You were right, I shouldn't have pushed for complaining. The captain's made mugs of us.'

'Aye, he's taken us both by the scruff of the neck,' said Owen. 'For me, it's turned out just as I thought it would – in shackles, open to the wind and rain.'

'You've a right to be angry with me.'

Stag was sorry he'd allowed Owen to come with them – they were all young, and he was middle-aged. But it had never occurred to Stag they would end up in irons. The captain was right: he didn't know much about the ways of the sea. He turned his head so he could see Owen. 'I'm sorry, I really am.'

'Listen to me, lad, you've a lot to learn about gaffers. We are where we are because you wanted a record made in the log. Now there's a record all right – you and I slapped in irons, marked out as troublemakers. That's not the record you wanted to be made. I've had years dealing with trouble in pits, and going at gaffers shouting and making a fuss is not the way. Negotiation and discussion are the key. If you're clever enough you can put forward an idea, talk around it and get them to think it was their idea in the first place. Then they agree with what they think is their own idea and everyone's happy.'

'I was just trying to do what's right by us.'

Although they'd reached warmer climes with fewer clouds, a warm wind and more sun, the weather was still erratic, and there was no certainty it would hold. Stag remained angry with himself for losing his temper when nothing, on reflection, was to be gained by it. Owen remained silent. An hour passed and they lost their curiosity value for the crew, who had been walking past looking at them – some with sympathy, others with amusement. Lavinia and Queenie were summoned to feed the two men.

Lavinia went straight to Stag. 'Stag Liddell, how'd you get yourself and my pa in such a mess?' There was pride in her voice. 'You're a hero, standing up to that evil man for everyone.'

'He's not a hero with us ending up here like this,' said Owen.

Lavinia began feeding Stag. Casting a sideways glance at her parents, and seeing they were deep in conversation, she tentatively put out a hand to touch Stag's fingers. He started at the show of affection from another's wife.

'How's Tom?' he asked, attempting to cover his embarrassment.

She put her hand back on her lap. 'He and Sam've been put on extra duties to make up for your lost crew hours.'

'They'll not be pleased with me.'

'They ain't complaining. Truly, you're quite the hero.'

'Don't underestimate your father's role. He was right there at the front, by my side.' Stag turned to acknowledge him.

'We don't,' said Queenie, who'd been eavesdropping. 'We think it's just wicked the cap'n treating you both like this, don't we? My Jefferson's not of an age for sitting trussed up like a heifer at market, is he? If I wasn't a weak woman I'd go and tell the cap'n so, aye indeed I would, wouldn't I?'

'It was my decision to go with Stag,' said Owen. 'I've got a mind of my own. I wasn't afraid to say no. I thought he needed support from an older man.'

Over Lavinia's shoulder, Stag could see Kate helping her mother hang clothes out to dry in the small area on deck reserved for emigrant chores. There was a calmness and maturity in her bearing which, for her age, he found intriguing. He wondered what she was thinking now as she saw him in irons. Probably that he was a complete fool. But seeing her cheered his mood, and he was sorry when she gathered up the scrubbing brush and soap and made ready to leave. Before she left, she looked over at him and waved.

Stag turned to face Lavinia, and she changed her expression quickly, but not quickly enough. To his surprise, he thought he detected malice in her eyes, then quickly dismissed the thought as ridiculous.

That which Stag and Owen feared came about when a heavy squall rose from the south east. It came upon them with little warning, the blue of the sky turning to black in a matter of minutes. The darkening sky brought with it a short, passing period of eerie light, and everything became still. Even the crew's footsteps as they passed by seemed muted. Despite knowing they were in for a bad time, Stag couldn't help but admire the strange light, which exaggerated some hues and dampened the tones of others. There was a rare beauty to it all. Then came the wind – not one of the cheery temperate breezes they'd recently been enjoying, but a sullen force, promising worse to come. All those who could do so went below, whilst Stag and Owen were forced to remain above to endure what was to come. When the rain finally came it crashed down in sheets, each drop like a sharp knife being tossed at them. Hailstones attacked them from all sides, ricocheting off the hard wood of the deck onto their legs and arms, stinging and irritating skin that was already raw. The noise was relentless, Stag and Owen were well-used to a bit of damp down the mine and would have scoffed at anybody complaining of a bit of water, but such a thorough wetting was completely alien to them.

After two hours, the worst of the squall had passed, leaving drizzly rain. Owen and Stag were startled to see Captain Fleming make his way along the rail. He stood tall and straight in front of them to survey their sorry state.

'If it's water you wanted, you've had your fair share. The Lord's seen fit to provide what you asked for.' He passed on without making further comment.

CHAPTER FOURTEEN

'How's the proud pa then?' asked Stag.

Tom was beaming from ear to ear. 'Everyone said it was a really easy labour. The women can't believe it after all that fuss she made when Evie had her baby. I've been prepared for the worst, and then she pops him out like a pea from a pod.'

'It's what you've hoped for, isn't it? Another Kennedy male child.'

'Aye, and a big one too. A good strong Kennedy baby. Believe me he's got a really strong kick already, and he's lacking nothing in the gentleman's department either.'

'I'll take your word for that,' said Stag, smiling.

Tom lifted his son up for his friend to admire. 'Look at those tiny fingers. We put a coin in his hand almost straight away and he grabbed on to it really tight. He's going to have riches and not want for anything.'

Stag laughed one of his rich laughs. 'All babies do that, you idiot.'

'Well, my son will certainly want for nothing.'

'I'd say it's a very worthy sentiment for a father to express on his son's day of birth.'

'Remember, if anything happens to me, you'll honour our pact, won't you? It's always been the bond between us, but now I have a family, you'll see to them if anything happens to me, won't you?'

'You have to ask me that, today of all days?'

'Today is the day when I most need to ask you if you remember.'

'Of course, I remember and yes, I'll see to your family, but it won't come to that. It's the bond that's held us together all these years and will do so for all the years to come.'

Stag had never seen a baby almost immediately after its birth and he was fascinated. He couldn't take his eyes off the little boy, the erratic flailing around of the tiny arms, and was entranced by the opening and closing of the eyes in his screwed-up face whose instinct was urging him to open them. Yet when he did so, even the dim steerage light proved to be too bright. And then Stag saw it. The cleft in the chin. He was taken right back to his childhood, a windy day high up on the cliffs overlooking Whitehaven.

'Speaking of the pact, you've seen it, haven't you? I can tell by the look on your face.'

'Yes,' said Stag. 'I've just seen it. He looks like your brother Ruari.'

'He's the spitting picture, isn't he?'

As they were both staring intensely at the baby, Lavinia returned. 'Have you asked him yet, Tom?'

'Not yet.'

'What?'

'Will you be godfather to our son?'

'I'd be delighted, but first tell me, does this new Kennedy child, firstborn son of Tom and Lavinia, have a name?'

'Albert,' said Tom.

'Oh, no,' said Lavinia. 'We're not calling him that.'

Tom's eyes widened. 'It's our family name. I thought we'd decided. I'm Thomas Albert, my father was Albert Thomas.'

'I've changed my mind. I want to call him Jonty.'

'Jonty? Where'd you get that from?'

'That's the name of the eldest son at the big house.'

'You mean the bank manager's back in Whitehaven?'

'Aye, it's a name people won't forget. He's a very special child and deserves a very special name. One with class.' She looked down at her son in his father's arms, her gaze expressing admiration for what she'd created. 'He's perfect in every way.'

'Oh, you mean it's "refined". But what about Albert? He must have that as his middle name.'

'He can't, otherwise he'll be J. A. K., Jonty Albert Kennedy.'

'What's wrong with that?'

'Jak, that's what wrong. He'll be called Jak and I'm not having that. It reminds me of "Jack the Lad". What do you think, Stag?'

'I'm not saying anything. This is between you two.'

'It's a grand nickname,'

'To you, maybe, but not to me.'

'It's either Albert as his first name or as his second. There's an end to it. Which is it to be?'

'After all I've just been through to bring our son into this world and all you can do is speak unkindly to me.'

Stag looked down at his hands and inspected his nails. 'Jonty Albert, or Albert Jonty? Which?'

Lavinia looked away and took in a deep breath. 'All right, you win. Albert Jonty, but only because of the J. A. K.'

'You've done the right thing. He reminds me of my brother Ruari. He's got the same chin. It's a Kennedy thing. A dip in the middle of the chin. I didn't get it, but my father had it.'

'Your brother that died?'

'Aye, so it's right he should have our family name first. Albert Jonty Kennedy. That's a fine name for a man to have. Ruari Albert Kennedy, that was a fine name too, God bless his soul. Isn't that right, Stag?'

'A fine name, Tom, and he was a fine brother to you. Aye.'

Afterwards, when they were alone, Tom said to Stag, 'I let her have her own way because I want her to be happy, but it's a fine thing when a man can't name his own son in the tradition of his family. This "refined" business is getting out of hand. She's been like this ever since she worked for the banker. She was only a scullery maid. We're colliers, not moneyed folk like those in big houses. Their ways aren't our ways and never will be, no matter how "refined" she tries to be.'

Stag didn't say anything. Tom had taken on quite a

handful when he'd married Lavinia. *She's a nice-looking young woman, but my, she's a tongue on her*, he thought.

✷ ✷ ✷

It was mid-morning when Stag saw Kate making her way along the deck. He put his hammer down and made ready to step out into her path. He was sweaty from the efforts of the good honest labour Mr Ward always insisted upon from his steerage crew, but that was nothing to be ashamed of. *There's nowt wrong with sweating over hard work*, he told himself.

He greeted Kate with a smile. 'Can we talk?'

Kate returned his smile, her generous lips opening to show evenly spaced white teeth. He'd noticed them before, but in the sunshine on deck, they seemed even whiter than he remembered.

'I've a short while, as my brothers are reading.'

'This'll sound odd coming from me, as a collier. You'll hear me out?'

Kate smiled and nodded.

'I'm asking for your help.'

'How?'

'I can read well enough, and after years filling corves with coal and weighing, I'd say my totting-ups better than most.'

'Corves?'

'The baskets we carry coal in. Thick strips of wicker woven to make tubs.' He made circular movements with his arms to indicate their size and shape. 'I keep forgetting you don't know our work.'

'I'm learning.'

'My weakness is my writing and spelling. I'd like to improve it, make it better. Ma was devoted to my learning, but she died when I was twelve. I'm hoping maybe you can help me.' He hadn't meant to say quite so much, it'd just poured out.

'This is an agreeable surprise. I'm flattered you've sought me out, although I'm not sure I'm suitable. My father is the official teacher and I help. I don't think the women will like it.'

'It'll give them something to talk about.' He realised by the look on her face this was exactly what she didn't want – to be talked about. He corrected himself. 'What I mean is, they'll like it even less if I join their classes. One man amongst the women.'

'I'd like to help you and every teacher wants a willing pupil.'

'I'm willing.'

'I'll speak with my father. He may wish to teach you himself.'

'Please do, but be minded I would prefer you.'

'I feel we owe you something for taking on the captain like you did over the water.'

'That was nothing,' he said, pleased she'd noticed his efforts on their behalf. 'I need to improve my writing and spelling if I'm to make a go of things when my contract is served. That'll be in five years and then I'll be ready to go into business.' He found he couldn't stop talking. He wanted her to know all about him.

'Business? What kind of business?'

'My mother grew up in a shop – a general shop, vegetables, bread, meats, dry goods, drapery, that kind of thing. Her family had a good business in Whitehaven, and it would have passed down to her if her pa hadn't taken to drink. One way or another, he lost everything, and his family got nothing. She married my pa as a love match and her dream was for us to open a shop, which was the sort of business she knew.'

'General store?'

'Aye. Ma always thought a man could pick himself up if he worked hard and didn't turn to drink. That's why she read to me and made me look at maps of the world and pictures. So, I can read quite well thanks to her. I just need to be better at it.'

'I see you've got plans. So, your father, he opened a shop?'

'No. Ma died and Gran came to live with us to bring me up, and Pa never had the means to get out of the mine without a second wage. Gran took in sewing and did alterations to help out a bit, but with Ma gone, the dream died too.'

'And you can see a way out? You can still see the dream?'

'Aye, if I work hard. Why not? I've a brain and I'm a good worker. It'd make my ma happy if she's looking down on me, and bring me up in the world.'

'I'll speak with my father. It'll tell him you've got an inner force driving you along.'

He'd opened his heart to her. She probably thought he was cracked in the head, a collier wanting to open a shop.

Maybe she was right – maybe he was driven by an inner force. Certainly something was pushing him and driving him along.

* * *

Kate found her father reading *Nicholas Nickleby* to Hannah and the boys. She sat and waited until he'd finished.

'Dotheboys Hall is so dreadful,' said Hannah. 'I can't bear to think of those poor boys being sent there.'

'Will they have schools like that where we're going?' asked Bartley.

'Will they beat us too?' asked Seamus, with fear in his voice.

'No, no, nothing like that. It's only a story. You'll be in your father's school and you know how compassionate and generous he is with boys in his care.'

'And girls,' said Kate. 'Speaking of teaching, I saw Stag just now and he's asked me to help with his reading.'

A glance passed between Patrick and Hannah. 'Has he indeed? Why is that?' said Patrick.

'He wants to better himself. He says after his five years he wants to do something different. Some sort of business and he's serious about it.'

'That's admirable. Any man that wants to better himself through education earns my respect. I'll be happy to tutor him.'

'My dear, I think Kate said he asked *her* to teach him,' said Hannah.

'Oh no, that won't do. It's not seemly. You must tell

him I will teach him when he has free time. Send him a note, Kate.'

The note was written, and Bartley despatched to deliver it. Hannah sent Kate to Dr MacDonald with a request for headache tonic. When she'd gone, she turned to Patrick. 'Why did you not let Kate do it?'

'Because I want to see if he's serious about learning or whether he just wants to spend time with our lovely daughter.'

❊ ❊ ❊

Stag was sawing wooden planks with Tom to repair the crew's quarters prior to their arrival at the Horn when Bartley came rushing up, puffing, and panting.

'Now then, lad, you're all of a twitter. What's up?' said Stag.

'I've this for you,' said Bartley, handing over a folded piece of paper.

Stag felt a rush of excitement when he saw who it was from. Then his expression changed from excited expectation to disappointment as he read the words. He was going to be able to improve himself, that was good, but Kate wasn't going to teach him, which was not so good.

'Tell your pa I'll come and see him later,' he said to Bartley, who was standing by. He folded the note carefully before putting it in his breeches pocket.

'Bad news?' asked Tom.

'Nay, it's about having lessons from the teacher.'

'Whatever for? You're better than most colliers for reading. I thought you'd enough of book learning.'

'I can really only get by, Tom, no more. It seems silly to waste the opportunity. It may come in handy.'

'You can't read down a mine.'

'True, but remember, I don't intend to be down a mine for the rest of my life. I hesitated for years; I've got the wind in my sails now, since leaving Whitehaven.'

'Sounds a bit hare-brained to me, but I can see you making sense of it.' Tom ran his fingers lightly over his saw's teeth, testing the blade. 'I'd join you to pass the time, but with Lavinia and the bairn I don't have two minutes to myself these days, even with Queenie's help. Our Albert is a handful already, and barely three weeks old.'

'You sound as if you envy me my freedom, Tom.'

'Aye, maybe I do sometimes.' He winked and tapped the side of his nose with his finger. 'Don't tell Lavinia.'

'Wouldn't dream of it,' said Stag, returning the wink.

'Speaking of dreams, are you still having the falling-over-the-cliff nightmares?'

'Occasionally. I think I'll always have them. The robbery hasn't helped me sleep soundly.'

'You're still mithering over it after all these weeks? You mustn't.'

'After we first talked on it when we left Liverpool, I put thoughts of it aside. It wasn't difficult. Being on a ship, working alongside the crew, everything being new, my mind was busy. As I've got more used to everything, I've more time to think back, and there's one thing keeps simmering in my mind and it rises up and pesters me.'

'What's that? Donal Little?'

'No, but I hope he's going to be all right. I suspect for

no better reason than I laughed at their scheme, Stevens wanted to lay some blame on me, or he wouldn't have left the bait tin for the constable to find. What if the three of them've been caught by the police and they carry out their threat to say I was in on it? All they'd need to do was say it was my idea, I organised it and made plans to collect the money, and I hid out in Liverpool while they carried it out. Or that I wasn't really in Liverpool, I was waiting in Barrow or Cockermu'th or somewhere, so they had someone to drop the money off with. I mean, they'd have to stash it somewhere.'

'Look, Stag, as your marrer you know I'll always look out for you, and I'm telling you now, I don't think this robbery is going to affect your life in any way. Put it out of your mind, roll up that fleece and bury it. Maybe then you'll sleep better. Apart from anything else, there's nothing you can do. Concentrate on your learning. That'll keep your mind busy and your dreams sweet. Maybe you'll stop falling off a cliff and start falling in love.' Tom laughed.

'What's that supposed to mean?'

'Kate McAvoy, that's what it means.' Tom's face creased up in a wide grin. 'I might not be as good as you at reading books, but I can read you all right. Following her with your eyes, your face lighting up whenever she's nearby. She's sweet to the eyes, I'll give you that. You've got good taste.'

Stag laughed.

'Don't go denying it. You're as soft as a frosted turnip when you see her.'

CHAPTER FIFTEEN

Hooker addressed the collier crewmen.

'We're fast approaching the Horn, as you know. It may be August, but it's mid-winter there. We'll sail southwest, making as much westerly as we can, then change to port tack, heading northwest or north. It's important we don't head too far south or we may hit icebergs. Captain Fleming's playing it safe. Normally, we only have crew and cargo, but this time we've women and children to consider.'

'That makes a difference, does it?' asked Sam.

'It does. We've enjoyed good weather so far. The Lord seems to be with us. I'm warning you that we could run into trouble. Now, rather than warn the women, I think it's better that we leave it so they don't worry. Are you all in favour with me over this?'

Stag spoke up. 'Perhaps just suggest it could be a bit rocky and noisy.'

'That's best, trust me. If things get rough there's

nothing we can do. They'll have to stay battened down in steerage.'

'What about us as civilian crew?' asked Tom.

'We're going to need all hands, especially for the pumps. I think it's fair to say that some of you may get bumped around so we're asking the doctor to prepare. We always have some injuries. He's done this before – he knows what's what.'

'What about meals?' asked one of the Brierley Hill men.

'We'll be sending instructions when to dowse the galley stove. Then it's cold food only, no matter how bad the weather. Captain Fleming suggests you all pay special attention to your prayers. One time the Good Lord's attention is going to be elsewhere when we need him. I just hope it isn't going to be this time, with so many women and children under our care. Prayer and praise, that's the answer.'

Hooker left and the men began talking amongst themselves. Stag realised someone would have to pass the information on to the McAvoys. He went straight to their cabin. To his disappointment, only Mr McAvoy was there. Patrick frowned when Stag told him, but he agreed it was best not to worry the women over rough conditions they might not encounter.

As it was, things held well until after they'd passed the Horn. Then the barometer and temperature began dropping and continued to do so for several hours. Stag, on the pumps, watched Captain Fleming as he went about his business, ordering Mr Ward to see to the sails to reduce the increasing pressure on the masts. The sails were hard as iron and the men clawed and swore at the unbending canvas. Stag couldn't imagine what it was like up there. One false step and they'd fall and hit the deck. Drenched and half-blinded, they clung on, balancing precariously on the jiggling foot ropes, with one hand scrabbling for the sail and the other clinging to the ship.

Mr Ward came and stood by the pumps and shouted to Hooker against the defiant wind. 'Seventy to eighty knots of wind, I reckon!'

Hooker reported back. 'Mizzen lower topsail furled!'

'Keep the bow to the wind!'

'We're being forced back!' came a voice from above.

Stag turned away and looked at the sea. It was heavy and confused and they could all taste and smell it. The noise was deafening and continuous. By noon they were back east of the Horn and, with no let up, all the crewmen were exhausted. Despite all their efforts the ship was being pushed southwards into the Antarctic winter. Stag saw Mr Ward look out over the swirling waters, mouth a prayer and cross himself.

✳ ✳ ✳

Kate wondered how they were coping in steerage. Maybe she could help them in some way by entertaining some of the children. Against her mother's advice, she ventured forth.

'Are you sure you want to go down there?' said a passing crewman, when she asked him to open the hatch for her.

'I don't want them to think I've abandoned them.'

'Your choice. How long do you want? I'll come back for you. You won't want to stay.'

'An hour?'

'In my opinion that's plenty long enough. They'll be surprised to see you, that's for sure. I'll be back in an hour, then.'

As soon as the crewman lifted the hatch for her, Kate realised she had made a mistake. However, it was too late. She would have to descend the ladder, as some of the women had seen her.

The emigrants were huddled together in the semi-darkness, pale and fearful. The early battening of the hatches hadn't held tight and water had seeped in. Six inches was now covering the floor, slopping forward and back with each roll of the ship. Kate could see every sudden unexpected lurch, of which there were many, was loosening the ties holding their belongings together.

Of them all, only Evie Gray appeared calm, sitting on her own. Kate took off her shoes, lifted her skirt and made her way over to her.

'Are you all right?' she asked, putting her arm around her.

'Listen to them all crying out to their God. I don't know why they bother. He's forsaken us.'

'Don't say that, Evie, it's not true.'

'For them maybe, but not for me. I'm preparing myself for a watery grave and a reunion with my bairn.' She looked around. 'They told us to lift our belongings up from the floor.'

Kate followed her gaze. They hadn't raised their

belongings high enough and the floor was strewn with haphazard articles floating around. Having broken free, there was nowhere for them to go except back and forth in the water with the motion of the ship.

Kate had never seen such misery in her life. Lavinia and Queenie sat with their arms around each other, sheltering Arthur between them. Queenie was ashen. The women's screams and cries of despair mingled with the noise of the waves slapping against the ship's hull. It seemed the sides of the ship would collapse with the pounding, but worst of all was the knowledge, which Kate assumed was common to all, that there was no escape.

She stayed for the hour, even though there was nothing she could do, but she felt she was at least there with them, sharing their misery. The difference was that she had somewhere else she could go.

The hatch opened and the crewman's head appeared.

'I'll have to go now, Evie. Mother will be worried.'

'You go,' said Evie. 'I appreciate you coming down here. We all know you didn't have to.'

Kate began climbing the ladder. Before she reached the top she looked back. *This must be what hell looks and smells like*, she thought.

❊ ❊ ❊

All available hands manned the pumps on deck. They were ankle deep in swirling waters and their six hours of daylight were coming to an end. Patrick, although not technically required to be part of the crew, had volunteered his services. Unlike the others, he wasn't used to physical activity of any kind. At the best of times he didn't enjoy walking, and his body was that of a wordsmith.

'I can't go on,' he shouted to Stag over the noise. 'My arms are screaming at me. My fingers are numb.'

'Come on, Patrick, where's the Irish in you?' Stag shouted. 'You can't give up yet.'

Patrick was burdened with borrowed oilskins that were overlarge, and Stag could see they were chafing his wrists and ankles, wearing away the skin. Saltwater was sloshing into the new sores, making things worse.

'We're all wringing wet and suffering, but if we don't keep pumping, we'll drown.' It wasn't an encouraging thing to say, but it was true. Stag's muscles and sinews were begging for respite too.

Twenty minutes later, Mr Ward passed by and spoke to Patrick.

'Dr MacDonald needs help with the injured. I can't spare any of the men. What about your daughter? She's no children that need her right now and she looks as if she's a calm head about her.'

'It's no work for a gentlewoman like her,' said Patrick. 'What about one of the collier's wives?'

Hearing Kate's father refer to her as a gentlewoman brought Stag up sharp. He knew that he himself was no gentleman and probably would never be seen as such. His fears that he was aiming higher than his station returned.

'He's not asking for her to take up nursing as a career. Just to stand by, be alert and provide another pair of hands. Some of the seamen are getting knocked about a bit, losing their balance, crashing into rails, ropes flying about. That sort of thing. He's not lopping limbs off, just stitching up. Seeing her there will give some of them courage too.'

Patrick agreed to ask Kate if he would volunteer. Stag was left waterlogged and unhappy in the midst of the storm.

✳ ✳ ✳

In their cabin, Patrick found his family huddled together, squeezed onto one bunk. Hannah rushed forward to help him out of his wet clothes.

'You're completely drenched,' said Kate. Even though she'd known he would be, it was still a shock to see.

'Dr MacDonald asked if Kate might go and help him.'

'In what way?' asked Kate.

'In the sick berth.'

'Help him? She's far too young. I'll go,' said Hannah.

'No, the boys need their mama. Also, I think he's of a mind that when the men see Kate, it'll give them greater strength to face pain. They'll not want to look like babes in front of a mere lass. A pretty one at that.'

'And I'm too old?' said Hannah.

'He didn't mean that,' said Patrick. 'He's right about the men though, and Seamus and Bartley are better being with their mother right now.' He knelt beside his sons, bedraggled and fearful, sitting on their bunk. 'Cheer up, boys. You'll have a grand time telling your friends in the new country how you went round the Horn and how brave you were.' He tousled their hair.

Kate spoke up. 'Since you're talking about me in front

of me, do I have an opinion? If so, I'll do it. It can't be worse than sitting here listening to the ship's sides creaking and groaning. If I can be useful, then I'd like to be.'

'I'm worried what you'll see,' said Hannah. 'It might be frightening. There may be blood, and things that are inappropriate.'

'You needn't worry,' said Patrick. 'Mr Ward says it's just minor injuries. I'm sure Dr MacDonald will look after her.'

Hannah began pulling clothes out of a drawer. 'Here,' she said, handing Kate a heavy coat and hat. 'I've misgivings, I can tell you that. I'm not persuaded it's for the best. However, I'll make sure you wrap up warm against the cold outside on the way.'

'It's not far. I'll escort her safely.' Patrick put the oilskin back on.

'Once cold like this sets in your bones, it's the devil to get warm again. If she's going, she's going well wrapped up. I can't help it – once a mother, always a mother.'

With the ship lurching, father and daughter made their way through the sheet rain. A loud thunderclap caused Kate to jump. The accompanying lightning gave off an eerie half-light that bathed them both as it lit up the sky, and Kate wondered if she'd been hasty in volunteering her services. Her mother was right – it was bitter, and she was glad of the extra clothing.

When they arrived at the sick berth, Dr MacDonald looked up.

'At last.' He turned back to the seaman whose leg he was attending. 'You'll walk again. Off you go.'

Patrick kissed Kate on the cheek, squeezed her arm and took his leave.

There was a clinking sound of light metal banging together. Kate traced it to a set of strange metal implements in a box by the doctor's side. She looked at the men waiting patiently for his services, their discomfort showing in tight, hunched shoulders. Dr MacDonald wiped his table with a grubby rag and she watched as what she imagined to be human detritus fell onto the sanded floor. She wondered why it was sanded, then realised it was to soak up blood. She hadn't thought it would be like this and her resolve faltered. Although the doctor wore an apron, he'd wiped his hands and instruments on it so many times there was not one clean spot.

'It's as if we're at war,' said Kate under her breath.

'We are,' said Dr MacDonald. 'It's us against the forces of nature.' He handed Kate an apron covered in brown stains. She was about to refuse it when she realised the stains were old ones that were well washed in. It was as clean an apron as she was going to be offered. She tied it around her neck and rolled up her sleeves as best she could, thankful she was not wearing a dress with wide sleeves. As she stood by the doctor's side, concentrating on keeping her balance while the ship rose and fell, she was once again aware of the water pounding against the ship's sides, lifting and then tossing them from side to side. It was as if the ship was just a bottle, so easily was it thrown around by the waves. She was thankful she was able to hold her footing, and that she'd been at sea long enough to be able to steady herself without consciously thinking about it all the time.

Kate helped tend two of the waiting seamen, who were soon swabbed and stitched up. Besides cuts, the injuries were mostly the result of knocks and bangs against the rigging as the ship bounced around in the wintry sea.

As the foul weather continued, Kate discovered how easy it was to lie convincingly when necessary. She managed to smile and joke outwardly, whilst inside registering horror and sympathy for the broken bodies that were revealed before her. Her father was right: the men were finding courage came more easily in the presence of a young woman. Kate was embarrassed to admit to herself that as each new casualty appeared, she was always relieved it wasn't Stag.

When Stag did appear at the door, Kate froze, feeling her fears were going to be realised, even though she couldn't see anything immediately wrong with him. Then she saw Tom was with him, blood dripping from a gash on his face and she had a shameful moment, feeling glad it was he and not Stag who needed attention.

'Tom tripped on a pile of ratlinns that've come loose and fallen on deck.'

'My feet just gave way and down I went,' said Tom.

'Aye,' said Stag. 'He didn't have time to put his hands out and he went straight down like a lead weight with his head on an iron ringbolt.'

Dr MacDonald thanked Stag for accompanying his friend.

'He'd never have made it on his own,' said Stag. 'Anyway, there's more binds us together than just friendship, isn't there, Tom?'

Tom nodded and Kate heard him say under his breath, 'Aye, the pact.'

Dr Macdonald either didn't hear or was too busy to enquire further and Kate gave no indication she had heard.

Tom swayed and Stag put out an arm to steady him. Kate wondered if thinking about the accident had made him feel giddy, but when Dr MacDonald moved Tom into a better light, she gasped. Blood was pouring from a huge gash just under his left eye. His lip had been split on the same side and a shiny purple swelling was beginning to rise up on his forehead. Thick red blood was running down his face, its warmth causing the icicles on his moustache to melt. From there, paler drips joined together to form sluggish rivulets that ran onto his shirt.

'Lie down,' said Dr MacDonald, pointing to a sturdy trestle table. 'Put your arms under your head, lad. If I move quickly, we can get you sewn up while the skin flaps are still numb. You'll not feel it.' He spoke to Stag. 'Keep a good hold on him.' Then he put a small pile of clean swabs on the table, before handing Kate a small lamp. 'Come close to me and keep the light on his wound. It's a nasty one.'

Stag positioned himself at the top of the table behind Tom's head, where he could support his elbows and be ready to exert more force if need be. After pouring spirit into the open, but still partly frozen, wound and mopping up as much of the blood as he could, the doctor began probing amongst the broken flaps of skin. The warmth of the flowing blood was arousing the surrounding area and as the stitching continued, every twist of the needle began to cause Tom to flinch. With the rolling of the ship in the storm winds and Tom's twitching, it became obvious there was a real danger the doctor might stab his needle in Tom's eye. Stag was forced to climb onto the table himself and immobilise Tom's head vice-like between his knees, while holding his arms. Every time the needle came into his line of vision, Tom tracked it and Kate saw him tense up in anticipation of its assault. She thought it would have been more humane if Tom had been able to hold and squeeze someone's hand. She would have offered her own, but knew it would be refused, since holding the light was more important.

'I'm almost finished. It looks a mess, but the face always bleeds more than you'd expect.' Then, in a matter-of-fact manner, the doctor paused to cast a critical eye over his handiwork. 'Just this last corner.' He signalled to Stag he was going to apply more spirit. As the steady stream of fluid entered the now fully thawed side of the cheek wound, Stag braced his knees. This time Tom might thrash out and jerk wildly as the liquid ran searchingly into every outraged crevice. Tom wriggled his hands as soon as he felt Stag's knees tense, but he was unable to free himself, and was forced to ease the pain by screaming out, 'I can't stand it.'

Lord, give him strength, release him from this pain, were the words repeating in Kate's head. Stag too seemed to be mouthing a prayer. Tom stubbornly clung to consciousness.

Kate marvelled at the doctor's skill, noting how quickly and expertly he worked, how he twisted the thread to make the stitches, seemingly removed from the pandemonium both within and outside his cabin. He was focused solely upon his patient.

When he'd finished, Dr MacDonald instructed Stag to take Tom back to steerage. 'He'd better get some rest in case he's needed again to man the pumps. Doctor's orders, at least three hours. The shock'll wear off soon and he'll feel greater pain. Get his wife to tend him, and be careful – there's snow out there.'

After Tom and Stag had left, Dr Macdonald turned to Kate and said, 'Now it's just the two of us again.'

Kate pursed her lips and nodded. 'I'll do my best. I know these men are working to save our lives.'

CHAPTER SIXTEEN

Lavinia looked up and screamed when she saw Tom's swollen, bloodied face and shirt.

'Give me that cloth,' shouted Queenie, pointing to a piece of red flannel they'd been using as a baby comforter. 'We'll clean Tom up a bit with it.'

'You ninny,' cried Lavinia. 'We should never have left Whitehaven. You and my pa and your wild schemes.'

Queenie turned to Owen. 'She's right.' She banged her boot against the hull. 'These planks are all that's between us and drowning.'

'Don't worry, Queenie,' said Stag. 'The hull is sound and the pumps are working well. We're safe.'

Lavinia cuddled Albert then held him out towards Tom as if presenting a trophy. 'And what about our son? You never gave a thought to him when you decided on this stupid plan, did you?'

'We thought the decision was the right one at the time,' said Tom, with a defeated edge to his voice. 'Now is not the time to talk this way.'

'Dr MacDonald says Tom needs rest,' said Stag, thinking Lavinia could show more care.

Lavinia ignored him. 'Thought it was right at the time, did you? Well, what do you think of it now?'

Tom closed his eyes. 'Lavinia, for the Lord's sake, not now, we've enough noise without you complaining.'

'Aye,' said Owen. 'Leave the lad alone. It's a fair shame to speak to your husband in that way when he's sick. We've left snow eight inches deep on the deck houses. He's only got a few hours' rest – leave him be to spend it in what peace he can get. It's plain as a pikestaff he's in a lot of pain. You can argue all you like when the wind drops.'

'There's sense in your pa's words,' said Stag.

Queenie put her hand on Lavinia's arm. 'Look to your husband. Rub his arms and legs. He's blue with cold.' In an aside to Stag she said, 'She needs something to keep her mind off things. All she ever thinks about is the bairn.'

Lavinia, with a dour face, turned her back on them all in a deliberate movement and began rocking her son. 'My son needs me more than my husband.' Tom seemed in too much pain to care. Shrugging off his mother-in-law's help, he climbed onto his damp berth to cradle his throbbing head in his hands. Not for the first time Stag wondered how Tom was going to cope with life with Lavinia.

✳ ✳ ✳

Despite the tremors of the storm raging about them, time passed quickly for Dr MacDonald and Kate.

Dr MacDonald passed Kate a flask. 'Here, take a nip.'

She placed her nose gingerly to the flask nozzle and recognised it at once as brandy. She took a small sip and handed it back.

The height of the storm was marked by three terrific claps of thunder which seemed to explode directly over the ship. So used was Kate now to the continual noise and pitching that she only realised the storm had passed over when the doctor sat down and wiped his brow. She'd no idea how long they'd been working, only that a steady stream of men had made their way through the doors of the sick room. Some had been patched up only to reappear later with further lacerations.

The doctor looked as if he was too tired to remain in another's company for a second longer than necessary. He was sitting down for the first time in twelve hours. He dismissed Kate with a weary wave of his hand, and his mumbled thanks ceased in mid-flow as his head fell forward onto his chest. Kate draped a blanket across him and left.

CHAPTER SEVENTEEN

'Can you smell the trade winds?' asked Hooker, as he and Stag were storing the men's oilskins.

'I'd like to say aye, but I can't,' said Stag.

'We're still meeting head winds. However, I think we can safely say we're round the Horn once again. Mr Ward says the captain's made the "all immediate danger now passed" entry in the ship's log.'

'Is that the danger from the weather?'

'The weather, and also to note all the rigging is back in order and fit for purpose. The temperatures are still low; after all, it's only mid-September, but they'll rise soon enough.'

'This is good news. We're still very damp in steerage.'

'No need to worry. The good weather'll dry everything out soon enough. How's that mate of yours, Tom?'

'The cheek wound still has to be opened, packed with gauze and cleaned out every day. The skin around it is stretched and shiny. It's close to his eye and the bruise on his forehead is still angry and swollen.'

'Sounds nasty. As long as it doesn't stink, then he's all right.'

Stag stopped folding an oilskin and looked at Hooker. 'What do you mean? Dr MacDonald's looking after it.'

'I mean if there's a rotting smell, or purple blotches, then that's it. Once you've smelt the smell, you'll instantly recognise it another time.'

'I'll see him when I've finished. I'll report back for you.' Stag felt as if he was standing on ice. His whole body had gone cold. He'd smelt a strange smell on Tom that morning. A nasty, angry smell – an animal odour he had had to turn his nose away from.

Stag descended into steerage after his crew work to find a group of people surrounding a figure on the floor. As he drew near, he saw it was Tom. Lavinia was by his side, holding his hand. Tom's face was grey with the grim mask of impending death; it was a look Stag recognised immediately. He was gripped with despair – there was nothing that could be done to prevent the inevitable.

'Ah, it's my marrer,' said Tom. He gave a feeble child-like wave before bracing himself in response to a cramping spasm of pain.

Stag crouched on his heels and took Tom's other hand. He looked at Lavinia, searching her face for information. 'Who's gone for the doctor?'

'My Jefferson,' said Queenie, sobbing quietly.

A few minutes later the group huddled around Tom parted to allow Dr MacDonald to attend.

'Is it bad?' Lavinia asked him.

Seeing the purple patches and tell-tale signs of sepsis on Tom's arms, Stag knew he could answer her question just as well as the doctor; it was hopeless.

After placing a hand on Tom's brow as if in benediction, Dr MacDonald wiped the sweat off on his handkerchief before turning to Lavinia. 'I'm sorry,' he said.

Lavinia began to weep. Tom put out a trembling hand and began to speak in a voice just audible to those close to him.

'Don't cry,' he said, looking from Lavinia to Stag as if no others were present. 'I know I'm not long now. I can see it in your faces and I've seen the marks on my body.' He trembled as another spasm of pain passed through him. 'T'was God's will that sent you with us on this journey, Stag. Give me your word you'll see to Lavinia and the boy.' He paused for a moment before adding, 'Remember our pact. Look at my boy closely and remember.'

Stag, his throat closing with the effort of keeping his emotions in check, leant down to speak in Tom's ear. 'I give you my word I'll see to them.'

'And the pact, Stag, do you remember?' Tom's gaze was fixed unflinchingly on his friend. 'Swear to me you do.'

'I swear I remember the pact,' said Stag, returning his marrer's steady gaze.

'What pact?' asked Lavinia.

'Stag knows. It's between him and me,' said Tom.

As Tom lost his hold on life, Stag gave free rein to his emotions. Tears of anguish at the loss of a life so full of promise rolled down his cheeks. More tears followed:

tears for a life taken too soon, tears of rage at the finality of it all and tears of frustration that Tom would no longer be able to chase his dreams.

* * *

That evening, after Lavinia had changed into mourning dress, she sat quietly with her parents and Stag. Albert gurgled on her lap, trying to stuff tightly furled fists into his mouth.

'It's such a sad day,' said Queenie to break the silence. 'I can't believe it. He was pithy, he was strong.' She began to sob. 'You're a widow now with a bairn to look after.'

'You know, when he died, I felt a part of me go with him.'

'That's only natural, lass,' said Owen, 'He was the father of your bairn. Your husband. It would be queer if you hadn't.'

'I think it was because he gave me the most precious thing I will ever own in my life. My son. And now he's all mine. I've already decided I'm not going back to Whitehaven. I'm going to devote myself entirely to the raising of my son Jonty here.'

'Jonty? You mean Albert.'

'No, from now on he'll be known as Jonty Kennedy. J. K.'

'You can't change his name, it's in the ship's log.'

'I'll ask the captain to make a correction.'

'I don't think he can do that,' said Stag.

Queenie looked shocked. 'But what about Tom's memory? I don't think it's right.'

'It matters not. He's my son and that's how it's going to be. Stag, meet your godson, Jonty.'

Stag didn't know what to say. He couldn't believe what he was hearing and he put it down to shock over Tom's death.

While they were debating Jonty's new name, Dr MacDonald came to see them. He passed on the crew's condolences. 'I can only surmise some detritus from the fallen ratlines lodged deep in the wound and festered. The Company has surely lost a good man.'

Stag accompanied him as he left.

'I was there, Dr MacDonald. I saw you clean the wound. You were very thorough.'

'I've gone over and over it. I probed as deeply as I could at the time. A bit of rust from the ringbolt must have hidden itself in there. As I told you yesterday, when I saw him in the morning, I could smell death on him. I said nothing to the family. It would only have caused distress to no purpose.'

'Muck's strange stuff. It hides deep. I smelt it too, but I didn't know what it was.'

'You'll recognise it immediately another time.'

'I've asked the captain to make an entry in the ship's log. It will be a black-edged one to signify a death.'

CHAPTER EIGHTEEN

Captain Fleming's committal service for Tom was profoundly moving. It made his earlier reluctance to recognise the death of Sam and Evie's baby seem even more peculiar. All the passengers were present, except Evie who said she couldn't stand to be there so soon after her own loss. Stag wondered how many were attending to break their boredom rather than out of true respect for Tom, then quickly dismissed the thought as being uncharitable. Lavinia was the perfect widow, clutching Jonty, who was wearing a tiny black arm band on his jacket sleeve. Even the baby seemed to appreciate the solemnity of the occasion for, although alert and looking round with interest, he never uttered a sound.

As the roughly constructed weighted coffin was tipped over the side, Stag played a farewell to his marrer. It was a still day and the sound of the mouth organ hovered in the air. Lavinia handed Jonty to her mother and stepped forward to gaze at the spot where Tom had been accepted by the sea. She remained there for some time, just looking.

Tom's death sobered them all. Simple scratches and boils now held much greater threat. Few escaped skin infections and among the emigrants there was a universal upsurge in washing. The crew mocked their efforts.

'You're making a big mistake,' Hooker told Stag as he washed himself down with salt water.' You'll only make them boils worse.'

'So you keep telling us, but what do *you* do?' Stag was always respectful of Hooker's greater knowledge of the ways of the sea.

'We leaves the dirt on. I'd say even to rub it in. It makes a second layer to protect the skin.'

Stag was well used to coal dust invading every crevice, but the idea of leaving himself unwashed with a build-up of what he called "real" dirt was not appealing.

'Do as you like,' said Hooker, seeing Stag's reluctance to take his advice. 'But washing with sea water'll give you boils and then make 'em worse. I've told you many times. Anyways, we're not long afore Honolulu. We'll find plenty of water there.'

✾ ✾ ✾

'October 20th, Honolulu,' said Patrick, standing with Kate watching the ship draw near to the shore. 'That first step on dry land will be a glorious one, to be sure. It was hard sailing past Madeira, so close and not stopping. Especially when it was bathed in those shades of purple, gold and pink in the evening sunset.'

'Hard for everyone,' said Kate.

'I'm so happy I'd like to kneel down and kiss the

ground, and I would, but it's probably not the sort of thing a schoolteacher should do.'

As the ship drew near, everyone leaned against the rail to see land, something they had not seen close up since they left Liverpool. A warm breeze wafted out from the island carrying an unfamiliar, very welcome, sweet perfume. They watched people setting out tables that soon overflowed with produce to tempt the visitors. Disembarkation was a muddled affair with crew and passengers all keen to feel firm earth beneath their feet. Once on shore, Kate laughed along with her mother as Seamus and Bartley ran off as far and as fast as they could to exercise their now scrawny legs. Kate's smile, initially bright and carefree, became fixed when she saw Stag helping Lavinia with Jonty. She'd seen him a lot with Lavinia in the past few weeks. He appeared to have adopted a fatherly role towards the baby. She'd heard about Tom saying they had a pact and wondered if that meant Stag was going to have to marry her. It hadn't occurred to her he was capable of such tenderness, It was a side of his character she'd not seen before. She forced herself to turn her attention back to the boys, who were larking about playing tag with some of the other children from the ship. It was heart-warming to see them so excited, with such wonderful things to explore. Beautiful ivory-coloured shells, strange weavings, wooden carvings, the oddest fruits, the brilliantly coloured fish – all under a perfectly blue sky. Flowers everywhere in all colours with enticing perfumes. It was as if they had stopped off in Paradise on their way to the Promised Land.

Out of sight, the skeleton crew on duty were offloading verminous food supplies into the harbour to make room for fresh provisions. Everything was thrown over the side, with no heed taken of the mess building up alongside the dock. As Mr Ward made a point of saying to all who passed by, 'It'll all go out on the next tide.'

As a result of the vinegary water episode, as the crew were checking the water casks at random, to ascertain the purity of the water being taken on board. The cook was checking off supplies. Kate knew they were all looking forward to having a change of menu after having been reduced to eating rancid stringed pork for almost every meal in the last three weeks.

CHAPTER NINETEEN

With Vancouver Island seeming so much closer after they'd departed from Honolulu, Patrick took more than a little pleasure in planning his school.

'My contract says it will be a wooden building. Two rooms to start with and then maybe we can add what we need as the community expands. We've children of school age and there may be others already there.'

'Others will come along, of that I'm sure. Your excitement is showing,' said Hannah, laughing with him. 'It's good to see you so joyous.'

'We'll need plenty of books and slates. I'll need to convince the colliers this is money well spent, as it's up to them to provide these for each child. Do you think they'll resent this?'

'No, they'll be on a good wage and it's an investment in the settlement. They're all seeking a better future, so if you put it to them that way, they'll surely see the sense in it. At least that's what I'm thinking.'

Kate was listening in. 'And maybe you can arrange something to raise money from the community. Everyone contributing, so the cost doesn't fall only on those with children.'

'There'll be some who'll object to that, I'm sure, but yes, if I need to, I can appeal. I'm raising the next generation of workers. I can remind the Company of that too.'

'I'm thinking you can already hear that school bell ringing, Father, and see yourself assembling classes and dismissing everyone at the end of the day. You'll love it.'

'If I can teach in the bowels of this ship and still enjoy it, I can teach anywhere.'

Patrick began to change his clothes.

'Father, is it necessary to dress so formally still?'

'I've told you before, I always try to teach as correctly attired as I can, as an example to my pupils. I'll put on a thinner shirt, though.'

'It seems to me you think it's a bad day when it's too hot to wear your waistcoat,' said Hannah. 'I'm sure you can dispense with that now the weather is so much warmer.'

Patrick took off his top jacket and laid it carefully on his bunk. He loosened his shoulders; it was obvious to Kate he was enjoying the relief its removal gave him. He began looking in a pile of clean linen.

'The thinner ones are in the box up there,' said Hannah, pointing to a high shelf. 'Look in the one with the top on its side. I think they're in there.'

'I see. I can reach it.'

'Take it to the light,' said Hannah. 'You'll be able to see what's in there.'

'It's all right, I can already feel my blue shirt.' He began pulling. 'It's stuck,' he said, making a face. He put his hand in deeper. 'Oh my God,' he yelled. 'Rats!' He jerked his hand out of the box. A rat was hanging by its teeth in the soft flesh at the base of his thumb, its red eyes throwing out grim beams of hate at having been so roughly disturbed. Its little legs were dancing a hanging man's jig, struggling to gain a foothold, while finding only air.

Kate kept her head. 'Dash it against the bunk,' she said, throwing her own arm against the hard wood by way of illustration. The rat, caught unawares by the first impact, was momentarily stunned, but not enough to disengage its jaw. 'Again! Do it again.'

On the second attempt, the impact threw the rat off kilter, and it released its grip to fall upside down on the floor. In the two seconds it took to right itself, Hannah impaled it neatly on one of the cabin's rat hooks. It twitched twice before lying still in a pool of sticky blood that, as they looked, fanned out over the floor.

'Check inside,' said Hannah.

Kate lifted the box, which had tipped over onto its side in the melee, and peered in. She held it up to the light for a clearer view and saw four blind mewling baby rats scrabbling around. The boys, who had been watching the commotion from their bunk on the opposite side, came to life.

'Give them to me,' said Seamus. 'I want to do it.'

'I want one too,' shouted Bartley, with uncontrolled glee.

Patrick, a man normally intent on protecting animals, said, 'Two each and do it quickly.'

Each boy picked up one of the hapless babies by the tail in readiness to dash them against the bunk sides.

'No, stop it, put them down,' said Hannah quietly but firmly. 'I'll fetch a bucket, we'll drown them.'

'Oh, Ma, why can't we kill them like Pa did and mash them to death?' Despite being the younger child, Seamus was the least squeamish.

'Because it'll make a mess, that's why, and do you want to clean it up afterwards?'

The boys put the baby rats back. Kate fetched a bucket of water and they were summarily despatched.

When they were sure there were no other rats lurking in corners, Hannah wrapped Patrick's hand in a handkerchief and, as the passengers had been instructed, should they be bitten by a rat, they called on Dr MacDonald.

The doctor laid aside his book when he saw Hannah, Kate and Patrick at his door. 'A problem?'

'Rat bite.' Hannah pointed to her husband's hastily bandaged hand.

The doctor unwrapped the bandage and frowned. 'It is indeed. Nasty.'

'The bastard wouldn't let go,' said Patrick, his voice a mixture of anger and fear. 'But we got him, and the nest full.'

'That means it was a "she",' corrected the doctor, selecting a scalpel from his vast collection. Sucking in his breath, he swore softly as he examined the wound. Already the skin around it was red and puffy. He pressed gently, watching for the reaction in Patrick's face. 'I'm going to have to open this and cleanse it thoroughly. Look away.'

'Just do it. I can't get rid of seeing its nauseating eyes looking up at me. It was like it was challenging me. I know it's going to be painful, but I can't stand the thought of that rat's spittle in there. Clean it out, I can bear it.'

The line of incision passed neatly through the two puncture holes made by the rat's incisors. Dr MacDonald spread the sides of the wound.

Kate attempted, but failed, to think of her father as just another of the doctor's patients. It seemed a slow process as the doctor struggled to avoid the tendons and muscles in the thumb, and all the while Patrick was sweating with the effort of keeping his hand still.

'I'm sorry, Patrick,' said Dr MacDonald, as if reading Kate's thoughts. 'This is a longer job than I thought it was going to be. If I don't get it cleaned out now there's a danger of fever from the bite.' Patrick nodded. Kate remembered Tom's sepsis and a shiver run down her spine.

❖ ❖ ❖

After the shock of Tom's death, Stag tried to throw himself into his work on board and his lessons, but thoughts of Tom kept rising to the surface. He'd not realised until the very end that Tom was so ill. Over the years, many times he'd imagined them both entombed by a rock fall or caught up in chokedamp. Never had it occurred to him that either of them could die from illness. Young miners didn't die from being sick – they had accidents or got caught up in explosions. There were so many things he wished he'd said. Remembering the time they'd spent together as boys, Stag's thoughts went back to the pact. It was a pact of silence, a secret they'd shared for years. No, he'd not forgotten it. How could he? He'd do his best for Lavinia and the boy, keep a watchful eye.

Carrying these thoughts, Stag sought out Lavinia. He'd bought a wooden elephant from Billy Botcher that morning. He held it up for the baby to see.

'I know he's too young for it. I thought I'd buy it while I saw it. He can grow into it.'

'I'm sure he'll love it. How clever to make an elephant out of a scrap of old wood.'

'Billy's made all sort of toys. He's got more time now the weather's better. He makes horses, dogs, boats, all sorts of things. He told me on one voyage it was so uneventful, he had time to make a Noah's ark for his children and all the animals to go with it.'

'Have you thought of learning from the ship's workmen? Skills such as theirs will be valuable later.'

'I don't have time.'

'You could give up your learning. All that book reading takes a lot of time. It's not as if you can't read.'

'I've got my ma to thank for that.'

'You could make a bit of extra brass on the side, you know, helping people with repairs, that sort of thing, instead of wasting time reading.'

'It's not time wasted,' Stag replied sharply. 'Education is never wasted. And when we arrive in Colville I'll be working hard, helping set up the mine. There'll be no time for lessons.'

'I still think it's a good idea.'

'I disagree. To my mind, in a new town like Colville,

carpenters and builders will be ten a penny. I'm not going to stay in the mine for ever and I can pick up manual skills any time I feel the need. I'm better making use of the schoolteacher whilst he and I have time to draw on.'

Lavinia pouted, a ploy that had worked well with Tom, but was proving useless with Stag. 'It's just that... I thought you wanted to go up in the world.'

'I do. Education's the way, not manual work.'

'Maybe you're right. Anyways, I can see you'll not be put off.'

It was clear to Stag others on the ship were thinking his thirst for learning a bit peculiar. First Tom, now Lavinia.

✽ ✽ ✽

Three days later Kate made an announcement in steerage that her father would not be teaching that day.

'Why?' asked Lavinia.

'My father's not well.'

After a night of sweats, fever and severe muscle pain, Patrick woke with a rash. Kate fetched Dr MacDonald, who took one look at the rash and said, 'I want him out of your cabin and to the sick berth.'

Kate thought she heard him say, 'Not another so soon.'

Billy Botcher organised Patrick's transfer to the sick berth and was then despatched to fetch the captain, who came immediately. He acknowledged Kate and her mother, then turned to the doctor.

'I've bad news, Captain Fleming. A case of rat bite fever. Patrick suffered a rat bite shortly after we left Honolulu.'

The captain's whiskers twitched as he clenched his

jaw. 'The Lord protect the poor soul. This is tragic news for him, the family and for the Company.' He drummed his fingers on the table top. 'Why didn't you tell me this before?'

'If I reported every minor injury on this ship, you'd be seeing me four or five times a day, at the very least.'

'Humph,' was all the captain said. 'You're right, I suppose.'

Hannah spoke up. 'I understand you've had rat bites before.'

'Yes, all before Honolulu. My guess is we've new rats aboard from there.'

'I'll bide by that opinion,' said the captain. 'You deal with your patient, Dr MacDonald, and I'll deal with the rats. We lost two cats recently. Looks like it's made a difference.'

After the captain had left, the doctor asked Kate and her mother to sit down.

'You will have gathered from my conversation with the captain that the situation is poor. I apologise for giving you bad news in such a way. I will be quite frank with you both. All I can do is ease your husband's passing. The disease will take its course, no matter what I do. I'm very sorry. I tell you now because anything you wish to say to him you should say now. He will begin drifting in and out of consciousness.'

Kate began to cry. How could everything change so quickly?

Patrick began thrashing around in the throes of a muscular spasm.

'How long do we have?' asked Hannah.

'I wish I could relieve you of the relentlessness of the disease's course, but I cannot.' The doctor's voice was gentle. 'I've seen cases last more than a week on land. I wouldn't like to say in conditions like this. The motions of the ship are enough to complicate any serious illness –'

Hannah interrupted him. 'Have you ever seen anyone survive?'

'I'm afraid not, Mrs McAvoy. Not with the rash. I'm sorry.' He put a hand on her shoulder.

'Well then, we must make him comfortable,' said Hannah, fighting back tears. 'May I stay with him?'

'Of course.'

Hannah motioned to Kate to come near, hugged her and said, 'I need you to go and look after the boys. They must not know how sick your father is. We'll get through this. There'll be time aplenty later to mourn.'

Four days later, with his wife and daughter by his side, Patrick McAvoy passed away, not having reached the Promised Land he'd dreamed of. The last word he spoke was "blessed".

Hannah responded with, 'Truly, Patrick, my love, I have been blessed to have shared my life with such a loving husband as you.' She looked at Dr Macdonald. 'Did he hear me, do you think?'

'Most likely. It seems that people can hear right up to near the end.'

As her father drew his last laboured breath and passed away, Kate glanced at her mother. She looked different, older. With the second and third finger of her right hand, Hannah drew the lids down over her husband's eyes.

Mother and daughter came together, arms tight around each other. Kate realised, in that moment, their roles had reversed. She and her mother had often come together in hugs – loving, caring hugs. This time it was the unbearably painful hug of grief. It was not an equal hug, as all previous ones had been. No, this time Kate was hugging her mother. It was she who was providing the comfort, and she had a horror it was going to be ever thus. If she didn't accept the position of keeper of the flame for their little family it was going to fall apart. It was her job now to look after her mother and the boys.

They wept, their shoulders rising and falling with their sobs. When at last they drew apart, Kate saw her thoughts had been correct. Her mother's laughing eyes were dull; a light seemed to have left her. *Father's taken her with him in spirit*, Kate thought.

They stood in silence for a few minutes, looking at Patrick's body.

'Now is the time to grieve.' Hannah's voice was quiet, distant. 'I know, because I'm standing looking into a tunnel.'

'A tunnel?'

'Yes, a long dark tunnel. There's no light at the end of it and it's going down into the bowels of the earth. It's a tunnel of grief and it's going to take me right into its depths, so deep I will never be able to climb out.'

'Don't say that. Father wouldn't want you to feel this way. You're still young, you have a long life ahead of you.'

'It is not a journey I am choosing, Kate. It is just how things are.'

Kate wanted to say that the boys needed her to be a laughing mother, not an always sad and grieving one, and that she *would* laugh again. But it was too soon for such words. Instead, she sent a prayer asking God and the Lord Jesus to make sure the entrance door to this tunnel of grief would not close permanently behind her mother, and that she would one day turn around and see the life she had led beckoning to her to return. It would be an uphill climb, but she begged God and his Son to provide her mother with the strength to make the journey back to her and the boys.

* * *

'I've come to pay my condolences,' said Stag. 'I'm so sorry.'

Kate looked so fragile in her mourning dress, the black heightening the paleness of her face. Tears began escaping from her eyes. If he couldn't give her physical comfort at a time like this, then when could he, he asked himself? He stepped forward and put his arms around her. She leant into him and began sobbing. Stag was conscious she was at last in his arms. If only the circumstances were different. There was a fragrant scent about her. He breathed deeply into her hair to draw it in. After a few minutes, she stepped back and Stag released her.

'Thank you,' she said. 'I will pass your condolences on to my mother.'

Stag nodded. 'If there's anything I can do...'

'I will call upon you. Thank you again.'

He took his leave. How tragic she looked; it was a bitter blow for the family. He wondered how they would get over it, if ever.

CHAPTER TWENTY

A few days after her father passed away Kate was summoned to appear before Captain Fleming.

'I trust you and your family are praying for deliverance from the burden of grief. The passing of a loved one on their journey to the Lord's heaven should be a time of rejoicing. Too much mourning is self-indulgent.'

'It's a difficult time for us. You'll appreciate that, I'm sure,' said Kate.

'I have summoned you here to discuss the question of the schooling.' The captain leaned back in his chair. 'Since the unfortunate demise of your father we have, as you will appreciate, lost our schoolmaster. The Devil finds work for idle hands and minds and I intend to appoint a replacement immediately to take up his duties.'

He had a replacement already? How could anyone replace her father? He was so dedicated, so knowledgeable. The whole idea of replacement was offensive yet she could hardly voice such thoughts.

'I assume you have someone in mind?'

'I have indeed.' He placed the fingertips of each hand together to form a pyramid, then looked over it at her. 'You.'

'Me?' Kate's eyebrows shot up. 'I know I've done some teaching on board, but I don't think that's possible.'

Captain Fleming frowned. 'Why not?'

Kate knew he wasn't used to being questioned and certainly not by someone he probably regarded as a mere girl. He drummed his fingers on his desk.

'I'm in mourning,' said Kate. 'And besides, I don't think the Company would approve.'

'I would have thought, by now, you would have learned I am the master of this ship and the Hudson's Bay Company's representative when at sea. I can appoint whomsoever I wish and make a full report of the circumstances, should I be asked to do so, on arrival in Fort Victoria. However, I doubt very much such a circumstance will arise. As for being in mourning, you must remember you are a long way from Liverpool now. Your father is enjoying God's grace, of that I am sure, as he was a sound man. You and your mother must be prepared to change some of your customs and ways. Traditions fade quickly in North America.'

Kate considered his proposition. It was not unattractive to her. 'May I ask why you've chosen me?'

'Because you're your father's daughter and have his head on your shoulders. I have received pleasing reports from Dr MacDonald concerning your general demeanour and for a woman, you seem to have an unusual amount of common sense. Kindly use it now. Then there's the other factor.'

'What other factor?'

'Well, Miss McAvoy, I understand you are a trained teacher so, in my position, who would you appoint?'

To Kate's surprise, the captain was smiling – something she had never seen him do before.

'Yes, I attended the Miss Holland's College at Gateacre and I am certificated and, since you ask, I'd appoint myself.'

'Correct. In other words, you are the only one who has any hope of success in the role. The women and children already know you. I did consider your mother, but you have more experience. You are eminently suitable.' He rose to indicate the interview was at an end, adopting his previous business-like tone. 'I trust you will not scrimp on the religious aspects of your instruction. There will be a remuneration due to you, but only if I find you satisfactory. You may go now.'

Kate hadn't considered this aspect and it was a welcome surprise. There would be a widow's pension from the Company; however, it would not be enough to keep them as they were used to being kept.

Her position was announced officially and seemed to be warmly welcomed, so when the women failed to appear for their lessons, despite sending their children as before, Kate was puzzled. She approached each woman individually, only to receive the same embarrassed answer. They were near their journey's end, they had more to do and couldn't spare the time. Kate knew this to be untrue as they continued to sit in tight little circles gossiping amongst themselves, and there was over a month left at sea.

Later that week, Stag appeared. She dismissed her class early rather than have him stand there watching her.

'I've come for my lesson,' he said, holding out his reader. 'You're the official Company teacher now, aren't you?'

'Well, yes I am but...' She gathered up the slates the children had thrown down in their eagerness to get away.

'Well, then, I'm your pupil. Teach me.'

He's laying down the gauntlet, she thought, remembering the discussion she'd had with her parents, when her father had said it wasn't seemly for her to teach him. But things were very different now.

'If you're happy for me to tutor you, then I'm happy to take you on. Please sit next to me here.' She gestured to the end of the bench and soon she and Stag were bent eagerly over his reading book. Her father had been right when he'd told her that, for a collier, Stag read well. Kate had to admit to herself he had courage just by coming to the lessons, and it was obvious he'd really come to learn, not to just sit with her, since there was no conversation that didn't relate to the task in hand.

❖ ❖ ❖

Rather than passing quickly, as their destination came ever nearer, the last weeks seemed stretched. Excitement grew, and there was much talk of Colville and what people expected to find there.

Kate's mother sank into the grief tunnel she'd spoken

of. The boys became listless and began behaving badly. One day Seamus threw a ball at one of the ship's cats. When she reprimanded him about it, he said he'd thrown to miss, but she knew he hadn't. The boys had begun bickering between themselves almost immediately after the committal. Kate knew it was their grief that was making them behave out of character, and she had every sympathy for them, but she wasn't going to let it pass.

Kate was delighted when a few of the women came forward, including Evie, asking for lessons which gave her something to keep herself occupied with.

When at last Vancouver Island was in sight, Kate experienced mixed emotions. Excitement that their journey was almost over after so many months was tinged with immense sadness at the passing of her father. Yet her family was not the only one to have suffered bereavement and many on board had endured much worse conditions. She straightened her back and looked out at the fast-approaching land. She made a vow to herself: she would do all she could to keep the family safe and make their move a successful one.

PART TWO

CHAPTER TWENTY-ONE

Esquimalt, Fort Victoria,
Late November, 1854

As the *Princess Rose* drew ever closer to land, the last half hour of her journey seemed to stretch on endlessly, despite there being much to entertain onlookers both on and off shore. Stag heard a gun salute and saw smoke rising from the fort's guns as the ship passed by on its way to its berth at Esquimalt. Gradually the figures on the dock and on the boat became clearer to each other. Some of the crew, hanging off the rigging, whooped and waved. Hooker had explained to Stag the previous night that, as the ship's draught was too deep for the harbour at Fort Victoria, she had to sail on to Esquimalt, just under three miles to the north.

At last, the *Princess Rose* dropped anchor and lay still. For the last three days, almost in sight of her destination, she'd fought storms in the Jean de Fuca Strait, and was now able to rest.

Captain Fleming presided over their arrival with the same unsmiling detachment he'd displayed in Liverpool while the ship was being provisioned. If he felt any of his crew's or passengers' excitement, it was not betrayed by his countenance. Stag imagined him preparing to instruct Mr Ward to order the stripping of the bunks and tables in steerage, in preparation for the return voyage. The *Princess Rose*'s belly would soon be filled with fresh timber and furs. Stag was experiencing mixed emotions: he was overjoyed to be in North America at last, but the journey had been grim and he'd lost his best friend. He was not the same man who had left Whitehaven. He'd experienced great loss, coupled with an awakening of his emotions.

Lavinia broke into his thoughts. 'Look, Stag,' she said, pointing at the crowds gathered on the quay. He followed her outstretched arm with his gaze. 'Look, it's someone important come to welcome us.' Her face was bright with excitement. 'He's rather dashing.'

An official deputation boarded a long boat. Everyone watched as it made its way through the water. On arrival, a tall, youngish man in a buckskin jacket with fringed sleeves climbed onboard and addressed the emigrants. Apart from a small moustache, which added a slightly jaunty air to his appearance, he was clean-shaven. He looked fit and well and walked with confidence.

'Ladies and gentlemen, may I, Charles Hollett, the Company Island Liaison Officer, welcome you to Vancouver Island as settlers and miners in Colville. We are delighted to see you safe and well after your long journey and we welcome you all. I would ask for your full attention for the next few minutes, whilst I outline the final part of your journey.'

'Seems we're settlers and miners now,' Owen whispered to Stag. 'No longer emigrants and colliers.'

'You'll be spending one night at Fort Victoria,' Mr Hollett continued, 'before beginning the final part of your journey up island in the steamship *Beaver*. You'll see her in the smaller harbour below the fort. Our Company flagship since 1835.'

'Will we have beds?' Bartley asked his mother in a loud voice.

'I don't know. Ssh, now, the gentleman's speaking.'

'Is he important?'

'Yes, be quiet.'

'In Colville, Mr Wilson, the mine manager, will welcome you. We've sent word and they're expecting you tomorrow. There are, of course, a few formalities that must be undertaken first, and I would ask you to form an orderly line. Please have your contract to hand. After these preliminaries have been dispensed with, His Excellency the Governor, James Douglas, will officially welcome you at the quayside.' He indicated the dock, where men were hastily erecting a dais and hanging flags. However, there seemed as yet to be no one of great importance waiting. 'Please form an orderly line so we can proceed as rapidly as possible.'

Stag left Lavinia to join the general mêlée as the men disappeared to locate their contracts. He sighed. Captain Fleming should have warned them. They hadn't expected such rigid checking of their status, and it was not a good start.

* * *

Kate waited until most of the men had returned before retrieving her father's contract from their luggage. Unrolling it, she looked at his signature and smiled. He'd added a flourish underneath his name, shaped like a hunting horn. It was so like him, to add that to a document he regarded as important. Then the thought flashed through her mind that it was as if he'd signed his own death warrant. She shuddered; she mustn't think that way. When he'd signed in the presence of Mr Liversedge he would have been brimming with excitement. Better to retain that image than a grotesque one.

On her return, she found herself at the back of the queue – a fact the boys lamented loudly. As a consequence, it was some time before they found themselves in front of Mr Hollett. The boys were restless and her mother tired.

Kate explained their situation.

'I'm grieved to hear of your bereavement, Mrs McAvoy.' Hollett put a cross next to their name. 'Please accept my sincere condolences.'

'We can still journey to Colville, can't we?' said Hannah. 'My daughter is the schoolteacher.'

'I see no reason why not.'

Kate thought she detected some uncertainty in Mr Hollett's response.

She butted in. 'It's our destination.'

'Of course.' Hollett turned to leave.

'Excuse me, I have a further question. I've been taking my father's place as schoolteacher on the ship since he passed away. Captain Fleming appointed me on behalf of the Company. I will be able to continue in the position in

Colville, won't I? Captain Fleming will speak for me, I'm sure. And Dr MacDonald.'

Mr Hollett hesitated a moment. 'Mr Wilson is in charge of community education. He will speak with you. That's the most I can tell you at this moment.' He smiled encouragingly and, seeing the two boys eyeing his buckskin jacket, knelt and whispered, 'When we get to Colville, I'll take you scouting with me.'

'What's that?' Seamus whispered back, eyeing up the tall gentleman in the jacket with the peculiar strings hanging from its sleeves.

'It means going out into the forest searching for bears and Indians.'

'Will you really?' Seamus's eyes grew round and large.

Mr Hollett's face grew stern. 'I'm a Hudson's Bay Company man. A man of my word. If I say I will, then I will.' He relaxed his fierce expression and the two boys laughed. Disembarking from the ship, Kate wondered if she'd misjudged him.

✵ ✵ ✵

Governor Douglas arrived with an escort and climbed onto the hastily erected dais. He was a big, dark-complexioned man, somewhat stern in appearance, with broad shoulders, thinning hair, and large bushy grey whiskers. He appeared to be a man very much at ease with his own importance. He was flanked by Captain Fleming, Dr MacDonald and Mr Ward. The dais being rather narrow, Mr Hollett was forced to remain standing to one side on the quay, and Stag thought he didn't look very happy about it.

Squatting close by was a native Indian. It was the first the emigrants had seen close to. A leathered face peered out from under a battered black hat. He was wearing fawn buckskin trousers and a loose linen shirt, and was holding a rifle. Had his manner not been so assured and dignified, the marriage of native Indian and Company attire could have made him appear incongruous but Stag thought him most dignified. His facial expression never changed, yet Stag was certain he missed nothing.

The governor spoke. 'It is indeed a proud moment for me, James Douglas, as Governor, to welcome you all from the *Princess Rose*. This is a day we have all looked forward to and one that will go down in the annals of British Columbia's history as a day to be remembered by our descendants with pride and honour. You see around you an as yet undeveloped Crown Colony, declared so in 1849 by the Colonial Office. It is with the courage and hard work of those of you assembled here today that we will build settlements that will stand for time immemorial on this island. Settlements that will do justice to our glorious Queen Victoria, on whose namesake soil you have today landed, and we are asking you to make your homes and raise your families in her name. I think it fitting we remember our Queen today, and I ask you all to join with me in the customary salute of three rousing cheers.'

The assembled passengers, crew and Fort Victoria inhabitants threw their hats in the air and joined in the cheering. So enthusiastic was the response to the governor's request, it took some time before order could be restored and horse and cart transportation organised for the three miles to Fort Victoria, for their overnight stay.

Before returning to the ship the crew shook hands all round and there was much slapping of backs amongst the men. Strong friendships had been forged and there was sadness on both sides. The captain accompanied the emigrants to the fort for dinner with the governor.

* * *

Outside the fort's wooden palisade, Indians were gathered in small groups around large fires. Mr Hollett explained to the boys that they were from different tribes on the island.

'They're called Nootkans, Songhees, Salish and Kwakiutl.'

'Are they here to fight?' asked Bartley.

'No, they come here to trade furs and buy tools. In Colville, when you see them going past in their canoes, they'll be on their way here to the fort.'

'What do they buy?'

'Kettles, soap, buckets, that kind of thing. In Colville they bring us salmon and venison, among other things.'

After they'd passed through the fort gates, Mr Hollett directed most of the new arrivals to a reception area, to be allocated a billet. Dr MacDonald and the McAvoys were taken to the fort's bachelors' quarters.

The McAvoys were shown into a dormitory.

'A bed,' said Hannah. 'We've all got beds. This is wonderful.'

'Do you think we'll be able to sleep in such luxury?' Kate pressed a hand on the mattress. 'In Liverpool I'd have thought this bed hard, but here it feels soft. It will seem strange not to be rocked to sleep.'

'I don't know about you, but I'm still rocking. I can feel the movement of the ship as if I'm still onboard,' replied her mother.

Despite having proper beds, their first night on dry land after over six months at sea was a strange and unsettling experience. Kate was right – without the perpetual motion they'd grown used to on board ship they all slept fitfully. In addition, the noises of the fort and the chanting of the Indians outside continued all through the night. Being unfamiliar to their ears, everything combined to upset the whole family's sleep far more than a strong swell at sea would have done. It was with relief that they embarked on the final leg of their journey to Colville.

CHAPTER TWENTY-TWO

The *Beaver's* tall chimney belched out a trail of black smoke as she steamed her way north, tracking the island's coastline. The fast-flowing waters between the island and Canada's mainland were clear and clean. All along the route the coastal woodland was dark, dense and strange. The ferns and shrubs covering the forest floor were protected by a thick umbrella of tall Douglas firs and cedars. Angular grey boulders, dropped by glaciers thousands of years ago, rested amongst fallen trees and washed-up driftwood lay on pebbles the size of cobbles on the beaches.

Mr Hollett, clutching a notebook to his chest, made his way through the passengers on deck, all of whom were absorbed by the unfamiliar scenery, and after exchanging a few words with Dr MacDonald, he approached Kate, who was standing with her mother and the boys.

'Mrs McAvoy, Miss McAvoy. How nice to make your acquaintance once more.' He lifted his hat and smiled at the boys. 'I am finalising the accommodation details. The schoolteacher's cabin is not yet finished, and alas, neither is the schoolhouse itself. We are placing you in temporary accommodation. It is a little smaller than you are entitled to, but we are doing all we can.'

'How long do you think it will be before the schoolhouse is finished?' asked Kate.

'I'm hoping no more than six weeks. Do not worry, there is a community building that will suffice for the immediate future. In the meantime, I must bid you farewell.'

After he'd moved on, Hannah said to Kate, 'He seems very efficient.'

'Yes, but a little stiff in manner, don't you think?'

'He smiled at the boys. I think he likes them.'

'Yes, he did. Maybe it's just that he's a Company man.'

'Well, he has a pleasant face. Perhaps he has a kind nature to go with it.'

Kate was delighted with her mother's comments. It wasn't what she'd said – it was that she had momentarily come out of her grief and noticed something in the world around her.

❖ ❖ ❖

It became apparent that Mr Hollett did like the boys. After they'd disembarked and were on the quay with their mother and Kate, he came over and stood with them and identified the welcome committee.

'That man with the big hat is Mr George Wilson. He's in charge of the mine and oversees the general running of the community. Next to him is his wife.'

'Look at all those children,' said Seamus, eyes bright and interested. 'They're standing up really straight like soldiers. Look, Kate, look, Mama.'

'Yes, you'll have lots of playmates. That's the Wilson children, all five of them. I can't remember their names, but you'll soon get to know them, I'm sure.'

'Who's that very tall man?' asked Bartley.

'That's Long Ben Sloane, the carpenter in charge of the mill.' Hollett turned to Kate. 'If you need any furniture making or mending, he'll see to it for you in his spare time.'

'He's huge,' said Seamus.

Hollett pointed to two men holding rifles. They were wearing beaver hats and jackets similar to his own, but not nearly as smart. 'You see those two, with the fur hats?'

The boys nodded.

'They're trappers. Woodsmen. They go into the interior of the woods and trap beaver, deer, land otters and other animals.'

'They look really old,' said Bartley.

'Hush, Bartley, don't be rude,' said Kate.

Hollett laughed. 'That's because they spend a lot of time outside in all weathers. It makes them wrinkly. They're very friendly – not as fierce as they look.'

'There's more Indians,' said Seamus.

'They're standing by to help us unload.'

'They look scarier than the ones we saw at the fort.'

'No need to worry. They're very friendly too. I must leave you now, but I'll be seeing you often, I'm sure.' He put his hand out and shook each of the boys' hands in turn. He bowed to Kate and her mother then began talking to one of the Indians.

After he had gone her mother said, 'Yes, he's a nice man. I think he likes you too.'

'Oh, Mother, don't be silly. He was just being polite, that's all.'

Kate turned her attention to Mr Wilson who, in his tall top hat and fitted coat, looked as if he was wearing his Sunday best. *That must be a good thing*, she thought. He obviously had a sense of occasion. That he was not smiling to greet them made him appear stern, but then he was the mine manager and probably thought he should command respect from the start. His general demeanour was as unpleasant as Mr Hollett's was pleasant. His nose was pointed like a chisel and his eyes were small, shaped like a fox's, and almost lost in the fullness of his cheeks, which he sucked in at regular intervals as if drawing on a pipe. Mrs Wilson matched her husband's unfortunate demeanour, although she was stouter. Where her husband had wet, fat lips, she, as if to counter him, sported thin ones that drew back to show her gums when she smiled. Kate thought Mrs Wilson looked the sort of woman who loved to give little boys a sound thrashing and claim it was for their own good. She hoped that after the formal greetings had been made the Wilsons would be more approachable. Certainly, their five children – two boys and three girls, who also seemed to be in their Sunday best – were eyeing the new settlers with interest. *My new pupils*, she thought. The oldest boy caught her eye, then, as if he had done something wrong, quickly looked away again. Kate looked more closely at the children. Each one had a sad look to them. Perhaps it was just the occasion. She was sure they'd all rather be running around than standing stock still like soldiers on parade.

Compared with Governor Douglas's speech, which had been relatively short and to the point, Mr Wilson took the opportunity to drone on and on. The new arrivals' interest soon drifted past him to take in the settlement creeping up the hill away from the water's edge, which was now to be their home. To Kate there seemed little rhyme or reason in the way the squat wooden cabins had been laid out. It was as if someone had taken a pile of stones, turned to face the water and thrown them backwards over their shoulder, with the cabins being built wherever the stones landed. Perhaps a drunken surveyor had wandered around placing markers where he felt a building could be slotted in between tree stump, track or creek. To be charitable, the settlement looked promising, if untidy, although she was astonished at how small it was. There were perhaps only twenty log cabins of varying sizes, and two much larger buildings, whose functions were not immediately apparent, but Kate thought might be community buildings. There was not even a church.

One building overlooking the harbour was very different from the others: Mr Wilson had referred to it in his speech as 'the bastion'. The three-tiered building was octagonal, with the top tier overhanging the bottom two so that it resembled a mushroom. There were square ports for cannon and narrow slits through which rifles could be pointed. It was possible to fire from each of the bastion's sides, on two levels. Mr Wilson said it was spacious enough to hold all Colville's inhabitants in the event of Indian attack. A use for which so far, he told them, it had never been tested.

Beside the bastion was a store, and in a separate cabin what looked like the Company offices, where the Company flag, a red ensign with the initials HBC in the lower right-hand field, was rippling in the late November wind. Behind the two largest buildings was the mine. She wasn't surprised when, one by one, the miners and their families turned to look at the wheel driving the lifting gear. It was probably the only construction that was familiar to them, reminding them of home.

The first few days were taken up with settling in and exploring. Luggage was lost and retrieved, working schedules set, rotas organised and a general dearth of stout footwear lamented. The McAvoys were allocated a cabin next to the Jeffersons and Lavinia. It was no time before Queenie rushed round.

'Isn't this jolly? Here we are as neighbours. This is such a blessing, isn't it?'

At first Kate's heart had sunk when she realised who their neighbours were to be. She guessed Stag would be beating a path next door, and right under her nose. Secondly, they would have the talkative Queenie on their doorstep, and her mother had always said she found her bothersome. Then it struck her that things had changed, and it was possibly good to have someone talkative next door who might engage with her mother.

At the end of the first week Kate, having heard nothing from Mr Wilson about the teaching position, went to the HBC Offices next to the Company store and made an appointment. She received a reply: Mr Wilson would see her at home.

What would have been a five-minute stroll to the Wilson cabin in spring or summer quickly turned into a trek in the persistent winter rain. Kate looked with envy at the clogged feet of the women overtaking her in the mud; they had a much firmer footing since their clogs had straps to keep them secure, and yet even they laboured up the slope dividing Main Street from Harbour Street. There was no question in Kate's mind – the miners, whether from Brierley Hill or Whitehaven, were better suited to the pioneer life than she was. Trying to ignore the squelching underfoot she fixed her efforts on her goal.

The cabin was befitting the mine manager's position. Set apart from the general miners' cabins, and next to the Community Hall, it was a most agreeable spot, with an unrivalled view over the harbour. Kate stopped to wipe the mud from her shoes on the hem of her skirt, but it was a futile gesture, and only made things worse. She knocked on the door with some force so the noise would carry over the wind, which blew with greater vigour away from the sheltered harbour area., Miss Betsy, their nanny and maid, opened the door, flat iron in hand, and ushered her into the cocoon-like warmth of the Wilson's kitchen.

'Close the door, quickly, child,' said Mrs Wilson, sitting at a table surrounded by account books. She shivered and adjusted the shawl around her shoulders.

Both Miss Betsy and Kate went to close the door, unsure which of them was the 'child'. Then for a short time, as Mrs Wilson scrutinised her visitor, there was only the sound of the flat iron being replaced on the stove and the curdling of Miss Betsy's spit when she licked two fingers, before tentatively using them to test the heat of the hotplate.

Kate looked at the children and smiled. Receiving no response, even though they were all looking at her intently, she returned her attention to their mother.

'Mrs Wilson,' she began, unsure of the welcome she was receiving. 'I have an appointment with your husband.'

'He will be here shortly. Normally by that I take it you mean *Mr Wilson*. Mr Wilson conducts interviews at the mine offices, but under the circumstances of this inclement weather he's attending to you here. Please sit.' She peered pointedly at Kate's unsuitable footwear then indicated a high-backed pine chair, before turning her attention to the thick marble-edged ledger open on the table in front of her, which she was completing in a spidery hand.

Unsure as to whether it was necessary to respond, Kate turned her attention to two of the children – a blonde-haired girl and her darker-haired brother. They were building a brick tower on the floor, while the younger ones watched. Despite their efforts, it kept toppling over.

'You're making it top heavy,' said Kate, 'May I help you?'

The girl looked to her brother for permission and, seeing he was in agreement, nodded.

'The base is too narrow for the height you want to build,' said Kate, going over to them. She knelt down and laid out four bricks, leaving a small space between each one, before inviting the children to add more, straightening them as they went along. When the tower was finished, she smiled at the two beaming faces. 'You see, you must have a strong foundation if you want to build tall and straight.'

'My own sentiments exactly,' said Mr Wilson as he entered the room holding some papers. The whole family rose as one. 'Sit down, children,' he said, before acknowledging his wife. Then he turned to Kate. He consulted the papers.

'Dr MacDonald has provided you with an excellent reference. He says you are "of strictly religious principles and unblemished character and that you keep an excellent head in a crisis".'

Kate imagined Mr Wilson struggling to match the reference with the drenched young woman in front of him with inappropriate footwear.

'I have no reason to believe I ever gave Dr MacDonald cause for complaint.'

'Tell me, Miss McAvoy, as a young woman – in fact, your appearance is somewhat that of a girl – how will you command respect and oversee our school in an efficient manner?'

'With respect, sir, I may appear young to you, but I think you will find that young children do not see me in the same light.'

'My own children require a firm hand,' he said as he glanced over at them, 'and I am sure there are unruly boys who would aim to try your patience.'

'When I was assisting my father in Liverpool, I was able to silence a whole classroom of unruly boys with a single look. I do not anticipate I will have any problem controlling my pupils here.'

'Your father, I understand, held the position of schoolmaster on the ship and you undertook to carry out your father's duties after his untimely death.' Mr Wilson fiddled with the high back of his starched collar. He was smartly attired again and it was obvious to Kate he enjoyed a certain vanity regarding his appearance, although he had long skinny fingers with nails shaped to a point like claws.

'Captain Fleming asked me to take up the position,' she said. 'He told me he was the Company representative on the ship and therefore able to make such an appointment. I did not volunteer my services, he invited me.' Kate was feeling at a distinct disadvantage under the scrutiny of wife, nanny and children, all hanging on her every word, ready to rake them over as soon as she took her leave, no doubt.

'I assume Mr Hollett has told you it is Company policy to employ a male in the capacity of schoolteacher. In fact, it is even more usual to engage a man of the cloth.'

'No, he did not. Captain Fleming told me I must make allowances for living in a new country and that many of the values I've been brought up to believe in will no longer apply here. I took him to refer to just this sort of situation.'

Mr Wilson pursed his lips. 'I'm sure the captain was well meaning in his intentions. However, you must remember the Company has spent a great deal of capital erecting a school and –'

'A school and schoolteacher's accommodation that's not yet finished. I think what you are implying is the Company does not want to allow a mere woman to have control of that investment.' She could have bitten off her tongue when she saw the expression on Mr Wilson's face. She had spoken far too candidly, but she knew she was right.

Mr Wilson smiled a slow smile that was almost triumphant. 'You must understand, Miss McAvoy, that life here is very…how shall I put it?' He paused as if to think, but Kate felt sure he already had the words formulated in his mind and was only savouring the moment. 'Life here is very difficult for the gentlewoman. Whilst it is true we must adapt, I am sure you realise that we gentlemen are doing our utmost to protect our dear ladies from the trials and tribulations of this young country.' He turned and smiled at Mrs Wilson, who dutifully, albeit automatically, matched his smile before returning her attention to the household accounts.

'Confirming my appointment as schoolmistress will help both myself and the Company.'

'And how will that be?'

She knew he was now mindful she was no fool. 'I am here, I am certificated, I would like to continue in the position. The Company need waste neither time nor money finding a replacement. My understanding is that the salary is £50 per annum, with the schoolteacher's cabin.'

'That is the remuneration for the schoolmaster, yes.'

Kate noticed he stressed the word 'master'.

'And you are correct that the position does include a larger cabin than the one you have been allocated.'

'Then surely all that remains is for us to draw up my contract on the same terms as my father's –'

'You'll be well able to support yourself and your family,' interrupted Mrs Wilson, in a tone that could only be described as sharp. 'There would be plenty to spare with frugality.'

Kate ignored her. 'There is also the question of my mother's pension. My father's contract allows for a widow's pension to be paid to my mother if she chooses to remain here.'

Mr. Wilson was staring at her, mouth open, seeming lost for words.

'Miss McAvoy, I think we need to clarify things before we discuss this further. The Company is prepared to honour Captain Fleming's offer for you to continue in the schoolteacher's position. However, it will be at a reduced salary of £30 per annum, with a one-year contract.'

'And my mother's pension? What will she receive?'

'The Company has decided to grant your mother a pension of £20 per annum. That will bring your household income to what your father would have brought in.'

'But my father had a five-year contract and I will have the same duties and responsibilities as my father. I do not see why I am not entitled to the same in contract length and salary.'

'My dear girl, your father was a headmaster, I understand, at a respected school in Liverpool, and the experience he was bringing to our community was far greater than any you are bringing. Beside him, you are a mere child. You cannot expect the Company to regard your work or presence as equal. Besides, your father was a man and you are a woman. Surely as a woman, some of your reward will be in the accomplishment of your duties.'

'That I am a woman is irrelevant. I may bring less experience than my father would have done, but I am not an inexperienced amateur.'

'You are certificated, I will admit.'

'To be clear, I attended the Miss Holland's Teacher Training College at Gateacre and boarded there for six months, where I sat quarterly examinations. I also received additional training at the Society of Friends' evening school, and attended public lectures in Liverpool to extend my professional knowledge. I then taught at the Lynton School for two years under the leadership of my father.'

'This is as may be, but I cannot offer you the same five-year contract. We must see how things progress. However, if it is your honour that is at stake here, were can offer you the full £50 per annum and revoke your mother's pension.'

'This is outrageous. My mother is entitled to her widow's pension. She has two young boys to raise. Boys who in time will be an asset to the community. It is in his contract that upon death and in the Company's employ she will receive a pension of £30.'

'There is another option open to you. You can always return to Liverpool. You are all entitled to a free passage.'

Mr Wilson stood up and pulled out his pocket watch. 'I have a meeting. I would like to get this settled by the week after Christmas, so we begin in a month's time in the

New Year on a solid footing. We'll discuss this again the week after Christmas. You are dismissed.'

He's treating me like a servant, thought Kate, *when I am nothing of the kind and certainly intellectually, I am an equal, if not better educated.* She smiled at the children and was pleasantly taken aback when the oldest boy, out of sight of his parents, gave her a wink before returning her smile.

On the trek back, the wind and rain were just as bad as they had been on the trek up, but Kate was too angry to notice. It was all just too much. Pa was dead; here she was trying to keep the family afloat. Her mother remained deep inside her private tunnel of grief, they were probably going to be short of money and everything was on her shoulders. Thank goodness her parents had seen the world was changing and that women needed to be trained for things other than marriage and domesticity. Her father was the only one she could turn to who would have known what to do, and he was with God. *If you're looking down on us, Father*, she prayed, *help me. Show me what to do. I need you.*

She stormed down the hill and along Harbour Street to the cabin they'd been allocated. She went to open the front door, then remembered the wood had swollen and it was stiff. She put her shoulder to it and pushed against it. The door gave way suddenly and she fell inside. It was the last straw. She burst into tears.

❊ ❊ ❊

An hour later there was a knock on the door and, after wrestling with it again, Kate found Miss Betsy standing there, holding a small tin.

'I'd have been here sooner, but I wanted to wait until the rain stopped.' She looked up at the sky. 'I think it'll hold off for a while longer.'

Kate invited her in, hoping she wouldn't notice she'd been crying.

'Mrs Wilson lets me bake sometimes for my own tin. After this morning, I thought I'd bring something down for you and the boys.' She opened the lid. The tin was full to the brim with delicious looking golden-brown biscuits.'

'That's so kind of you,' Kate said.

'That was an awful time you had this morning. He's so full of his own importance.'

'No, it wasn't easy, but the children seem friendly.'

'Oh, they're like real children when I've got them on their own, but when he's around, or Mrs Wilson, they're afraid to say or do anything.' Miss Betsy laughed. 'He thinks you've got a mind of your own and that you're too pretty for your own good. I know I shouldn't be repeating all this, but I hear everything. I'm just the nanny to them and they think I don't have ears. I was so pleased when you stuck up for yourself. He said all that new country, different ideas stuff was nonsense and that he's here to make sure traditions don't die. He's wrong of course. Everything's different here.'

'I can see that. Will you take refreshment?'

'Oh no, I must be getting back. Give my respects to Mrs McAvoy.'

'I will. She's not herself these days, but I'm sure she'll appreciate the biscuits, and that the boys will goes without saying. Thank you again.'

Kate put her shoulder to the door and closed it with mixed feelings. It seemed she had found a new friend in Miss Betsy, while at the same time made an enemy.

CHAPTER TWENTY-THREE

The next morning, Stag called on Lavinia and her parents. It was always at the back of his mind that he might catch a glimpse of Kate now she was living next door. It troubled him that she was still on his mind, so he tried not to think about it.

Lavinia was feeding Jonty. The little boy smiled when he saw Stag and waggled his fingers in greeting. Stag ruffled his hair.

'That's a good breakfast you've got there, young lad. Pieces of hot buttered toast and red jam. My favourite.' He went as if to help himself to a piece. Jonty immediately began to protest, until Stag withdrew his hand and began laughing.

'He's always pleased to see you,' said Queenie. 'I'm beginning to think his first word will be "Stag".'

'I'm glad you've come,' said Lavinia. 'Ma's upset.'

'What's the matter, Queenie?' She was looking cross rather than upset.

'It's just nothing like I expected, is it?' Queenie was standing by the kitchen range, arms akimbo, looking round, shaking her head. 'I've never had to deal with this sort of thing, have I? There's holes in the cabin walls. Look.' She took a large wooden spoon and thrust the handle between two logs. It disappeared right up to the spoon neck. 'There's only moss and mud 'tween these logs, isn't there? Folks'll be able to see my spoon handle waggling about outside and the wind'll howl through as it crumbles, won't it?'

'Don't fret, Queenie. I'll help you seal it when I get some time. Maybe tomorrow.'

'Bless you, Stag, my thanks to you. You know it's not just for our comfort, don't you? I'm thinking of the bairn over there.' She pointed her wooden spoon at Jonty, whose face was now smeared with the red jam.

'Ma, his name is Jonty,' said Lavinia, giving what Stag thought was a rather unkind look to her mother. 'He's not "the bairn" anymore.'

'What were you expecting?' said Owen, who had come in from the back room. 'It's exactly as they said it would be. A log cabin covered with shingles, a cooking range and a sink.'

'At least they've whitewashed the interior walls with clam shell,' said Stag. 'It makes it bright.'

'Well, whatever it is, the place is clean and the windows and doors are of good quality, even if the front door has swollen a bit with the rain.' Owen rapped his knuckles on the door frame. 'They've not skimped on these. We're the first. I'm sure we can make it homely given time.'

'And we're lucky, I suppose,' said Queenie. 'They've given us one of the bigger cabins, letting Lavinia and Jonty live with us.'

'Saves them a cabin, that's why they've done it,' said Owen. 'I doubt it's for our benefit. Gaffers always do what's reet for them first. What's it like in the men's hostel, Stag?'

'It's warm and dry. A lot better than being on the ship. The food's good and we can get an ale or two if we want. I can't complain.'

'I'm thinking you'll not be there o'er long, will you?' said Queenie, glancing at Lavinia.

Owen frowned at his wife. 'With ale on tap I doubt he's in any hurry to find anywhere else.'

Stag left after making arrangements to help Owen sort out the walls on his next free day. On an impulse that his head was telling him he should ignore, and his heart urging him to follow, he decided he would call on Kate. If the Jeffersons and Lavinia were having settling in problems, perhaps she and her mother were too.

❖ ❖ ❖

Kate struggled again to open the sticking door and was delighted to see Stag standing there in his working clothes.

'I'm just calling to see if you're settling in all right. I can see you need help rehanging the front door, for a start. Maybe just wants a bit planing off the edge. They've got the same problem next door.'

'Come in. My mother's resting, the boys are out with Evie.' Kate pulled two chairs out from under the kitchen table and they sat down.

They both began speaking at once, then laughed.

'I was going to ask if there's anything I can do to help you. I expect you'll be beginning your teaching soon. I saw you yesterday battling with the wind and rain. Even the weather seems against us.'

She frowned. 'I'd been to see Mr Wilson about my position.'

'Surely there isn't a problem?'

'It's about the pay and my mother's pension.' She related her discussion with Mr Wilson, and how he'd given her the ultimatum of accepting the terms offered or returning home.

When she'd finished, Stag thought for a while. 'Your mother is entitled to a widow's pension. That was in your father's contract. He passed away on Company business. They have to pay that.'

'That's what I thought.'

'You have to point out that if they were hiring someone different for the position, your mother's pension would have nothing to do with it. They would have to make the position attractive to applicants, which would mean the going rate. The £50 and the five-year contract.'

'So, what he's doing is trying to save money by not regarding me as he would a different applicant.'

'Exactly. He's trying to treat your mother and yourself as one unit, when you're not. On the ship you were a Company employee in your own right – in fact, you probably still are.'

'What am I going to do?' Kate felt she shouldn't be talking about her family's financial affairs, they were private, but she couldn't discuss the situation with her mother. Really there was only Stag and he was proving most helpful.

'I think you're overlooking something important. Without you he has no schoolteacher, so you're useful to him right now. He won't want to lose you – the returning to England is an idle threat. He's using you. That's obvious by the fact he won't give you a five-year contract. He's planning to keep you on for a year while he makes arrangements for someone new to come over from England. When your contract is up it won't be renewed, and you'll be without a job left living on your mother's reduced pension.'

'I hadn't thought of that,' said Kate. Thank goodness she'd mentioned it all to him.

'He'll probably be hoping you marry too.' He looked down at the floor. 'You should check to see if there's a clause that you have to resign if you marry.'

'I have no plans for anything like that.' She felt herself blush.

'Even so, it would be wise to cover this point. Five years is a long time. You can't see that far ahead. You must confront him. Let him know you understand exactly what he's doing and see what he says. Right now, all he can see is you and your mother sitting pretty on £50 a year.'

'You really have got a business brain, haven't you?' She was seeing him in a very different light.

'As for having a business brain. I think it's always been there, but it's only since I left Whitehaven that I've had to call upon it.'

'But what to do? He wants it all settled by the New Year. That's three weeks. I know he'll try and fob me off.'

'Well, what you do then is tell him you'll go over his head and appeal to the governor about your mother's pension, since it's her entitlement. He really won't want that – Governor Douglas thinking he can't handle a simple matter of engaging a schoolteacher.'

'Then what? What about Mr Hollett? Do you think he can step in?'

'I'd keep him in reserve. He's the link with Governor Douglas. I'm not sure what next, until things unfold. There is one thing, though – he may have a valid point over experience, which justifies a reduction on your father's salary, but not £20 less. The least you should be offered is £40, but if that's the case you must demand a clause that takes your increasing experience into account, so your income increases each year to cater for that.' He scratched his brow in thought then shook his head. 'An arrangement like that is not ideal, because he would be forever looking at ways to undermine it. No, you should aim for £45 per annum and your mother's pension.'

'Thank you, Stag, you're really helping me.'

'Owen Jefferson, who's used to dealing with gaffers, swears by negotiation. That's what you must do, you must negotiate, all the while remembering he needs you right now. It's in the miners' contracts that a schoolteacher and schoolhouse be provided. Already they've come down on that, with neither the schoolhouse nor the cabin being finished.'

'I hadn't thought of the children.' Kate was fascinated

by the new Stag. 'Maybe you should be a lawyer, not a shop keeper.'

'There's another thing you've overlooking, his children's education.' He seemed to be flying with ideas. 'He has five children who require educating. But never mind that, your main argument is, your salary's got nothing to do with your needs, it's about your entitlement.'

'Yes, I can see it all clearly now. I'm indebted to you. You've given me the ammunition I need.'

Stag stood up and made for the door. Kate wanted to ask him to stay a while, but she knew she couldn't. Tom's death seemed to have stepped in and dashed any hopes of a future with him. She wondered if he harboured similar regrets.

At the door, he hesitated. 'I miss the lessons we had on the ship. I've been busy settling in at the mine, helping out the Jeffersons, and…' His voice trailed off and he sighed.

'Yes, I know, we've all been busy.' *There are unsaid things between us*, thought Kate.

'Maybe I can start again when the days lengthen.'

Kate nodded. 'Yes, maybe.'

'I'll be in touch about your door.'

After he'd left, the room seemed empty. Kate sat pondering what might have been until the boys burst in with Evie, full of excitement over the three huge canoes they'd just seen go past, full of Indians.

'I suggested they wave at them,' said Evie.

'And did you?' Kate asked the boys.

'Yes,' said Seamus, 'They were all paddling so fast I thought they wouldn't wave back, but one at the back without a paddle did.'

CHAPTER TWENTY-FOUR

It was towards the end of the week when Evie called on Kate again. As soon as she opened the door, Kate could see she was in a state. Her eyes were sad and weepy. Kate sent the boys into the back room to keep their mother company.

'There was trouble yesterday,' said Evie.

'What kind of trouble? Where?'

'That storekeeper's been cheating us again. I was in there when he tried to charge a Brierley Hill woman twice as much as he should have done and diddle me at the same time.'

'Again?'

'Aye, it wasn't the first time. You're the only one he daren't cheat,' said Evie. 'He knows a teacher can add up quickly without writing it down. You can't imagine what it's like for us. He's cheated everyone ever since we've been here. What made me really angry today was the woman didn't even know she was being cheated until I told her. Same with the fiddler's wife the other day.'

Kate shook her head. It was true, she didn't know, but she could imagine – trying to remember the figures, then adding or multiplying, only to find the original figures had floated off somewhere out of reach. 'Perhaps he'll stop doing it now you've noticed.'

'For a few weeks, or even a month maybe, but he'll start again. I know that sort. Apart from anything he's got a shifty look and a tight mouth. Sign of a miser. I can tell he's as bent as a seven-penny piece.'

'We'll have to report him if he starts again.' Kate wondered whether it really was possible to interpret people's characters quite so clearly from their physical features.

'But who to? Mr Wilson or Mr Hollett?'

'Probably Mr Wilson to begin with. Mr Wilson is in charge of the mine and the community and he reports to Mr Hollett, who is in charge of the higher things, like Indian matters and general overseeing of administration. Mr Hollett reports to Governor Douglas. That's why he sometimes disappears to Fort Victoria. I think the governor plays them off against each other to keep them sharp and on their toes. It's quite complicated, but they all work for the Company in the end.'

Evie pulled a face. 'Aye, the high and mighty Hudson's Bay Company. As far as I can see there's no other company here, no competition.'

'You're right, the Company has a monopoly on all trading.'

'So no one can set up in competition?'

'That's right.'

'That doesn't mean they can cheat their own workers though, does it?'

'No. Certainly not. I'll see if I can catch him doing it. It won't be easy, with him only being open two days a week.'

'That'd be a great help. Anyways, I was thinking. If you'll help us and go over our numbers, then we'll be able to know exactly what's going on.'

'I don't know if the women have got time. Everyone's so busy now. They're still settling in and some have even begun clearing their land allocations. Even if you want me to help you, there's no saying the others will.'

'Then just teach me. We can do practice shopping. I'll be one less he can cheat and can keep a better eye on him for others. I'll wager the rest'll be lining up for lessons, seeing me save brass.'

'I will happily help anyone that wants it, you know that. Perhaps on a casual basis in someone's cabin for now.'

'It's not that we're stupid or anything like that. Back home we were all canny shoppers. Things are very different here. The amounts are strange. We never bought flour by the sack before, and it takes a quick mind to see how much everything costs and then work out if it's the right price for the weight you're buying. There's bags and sacks all of different sizes and weights. The storekeeper rambles on all the time about nothing. I'm sure it's to distract us from adding up straight.'

Kate sympathised; she'd also had to think differently when buying supplies. She'd missed an opportunity on the ship. She could have prepared the women for this, had she known.

'That storekeeper put his finger right on the problem. He said it's us that can't add up, and you know, he's right. Half of us can't tell when we're being cheated and when we're not.'

'Can you ask around and then come back to me? I'm sure we can organise something.'

'I'll do that.'

Evie stood up. She was looking a bit better, although her eyes were still sad and she had lost weight.

'Evie, are you all right? When you arrived, I saw you'd been crying, and I don't think a cheating storekeeper is worth sobbing over.'

'Sam and I have had another disappointment. After we lost our baby, we called him Stephen, by the way, I lost another just before we arrived in Honolulu.'

Kate put a hand on Evie's arm. 'I'm sorry to hear that.'

'I've just lost another one here.'

'Oh, I'm so sorry. Is it worth speaking to Dr MacDonald?'

'That's what Sam says. I said I'd go and call on him, because it's not just the loss of the baby, it's the disappointment for Sam too. I owe it to him to do everything I can and going to see Dr Macdonald is something I can do.'

'That's absolutely the right thing. I'm sure of it. You'll make a wonderful mother – our boys love you.'

'Yes, I suppose I'm using them for practice.' She laughed.

'That's better. You're smiling now.'

Kate was beginning to think of the boys' tea and what she must do in preparation when, just as she was leaving, Evie said, 'What do you think about Stag and Lavinia? Do you think he'll ask for her hand?'

Kate was unable to prevent a look of dismay passing over her brow. 'Her hand? You mean get engaged?'

'I think Stag needs to be locked up, if only for his own good, if he's thinking of it. You can tell he doesn't love her.' Evie's face creased into a mischievous grin. 'You know, at one time we all thought he had his buttons turned to you. I saw your face and often enough it was rosy-cheeked, and you'd eyes that were dancing when he was talking to you.'

Kate shook her head, then realised she'd done it far too vigorously to be convincing. *Not only were my eyes dancing*, she thought, *my heart was too.*

'I only gave him lessons for a short time,' she said.

'No, afore that – even from the first dance on the ship. Before Tom died. It's funny how life turns out. Stag must feel he has some sort of obligation to Lavinia and the boy. He spends a lot of time with them. You could have done worse. Stag's no bad lad and he's grown up a lot recently.'

Kate couldn't hold back. 'Do you really think they'll get married?'

'We're all sort of expecting it. She won't stay in mourning for ever and soon a decent period will have passed. Then there's the worry she may have to go back home when the next ship comes in.'

'They won't send her back with her mother and father here and her having a tiny baby, will they?'

'Well, it's not for me to say, but if she marries Stag then they won't be able to, will they?'

'No, I suppose they won't.'

✻ ✻ ✻

Kate and the boys went up to the schoolhouse to see how things were progressing. Although it was not yet habitable, the roof was finished, and when they peeped through the open gaps left for the windows, they saw doors and window-frames stacked against the walls, ready for insertion. The schoolteacher's cabin was further along and had not only a weatherproof roof, but also a front door.

'Are we really going to live in this bigger cabin?' asked Seamus, standing on tiptoe so he could see inside.

'I hope so,' said Bartley. 'It looks like we can have our own bedroom.'

'I hope so too,' said Kate.

On the way back Mr Hollett saw them at the junction of Front and Harbour Streets. He called out and ran to catch up with them.

'This is a stroke of luck,' he said. 'I was just going to call on you. I brought you this. Here.' He handed Kate a small earthenware pot.

'What is it?' asked Bartley.

'It's honey. They have it in the store at the fort. It comes in from Fort Langley. I'm thinking of getting our storekeeper to stock some. Let me know what you think of it.'

Kate took the proffered jar and thanked him.

'Think of it as an early Christmas gift. Are you walking home?'

'Yes, we've been to look at the schoolhouse and the cabin.'

'We're working on it as fast as we can. There was a delay with some of the windows. They're made at the fort. Mr Wilson tells me he is in negotiation with your contract.'

Kate wondered whether to tell him she now thought Mr Wilson wasn't being fair to her, then remembered Stag's advice to keep him in reserve.

'As you're going home, may I escort you to your door?'

'Yes, thank you.'

They walked in silence for a short while as the boys ran around them in circles, using up their spare energy.

When they reached the cabin, Mr Hollett said, 'My early Christmas gift is not the only reason I'm calling.'

'No?'

'I'm sure you've heard that the Company are putting on a Christmas Eve dance. I wonder if you would do me the honour of accompanying me? It's to be held in the Community Hall and my understanding is there are some amongst you who are accomplished musicians. It will be quite an event for Colville.'

Kate was both flattered and amused by the formality of his invitation. To turn him down after such a request would be rude, she told herself. He looked almost boyish, standing in front of her in his buckskin jacket. She wondered if he was cold. He didn't seem to be. She guessed he was in his mid- or late-twenties. She was about to make an excuse when out of the corner of her eye she saw Lavinia looking out of the window. *Why not?* she asked herself.

'Yes, I would be delighted to accompany you, Mr Hollett. Thank you.'

❄ ❄ ❄

It was a few days before Christmas before Stag was able to find the time to mend the sticking doors. He rehung the Jeffersons', accepted some dinner, played with Jonty before his afternoon nap, then went next door to see to Kate's. Lavinia had looked at him with her irritated face when he'd told her what he planned to do.

'Mind you don't trip over that Mr Hollett when you're there,' she said. 'I've seen him hanging around. I think he's got his eye on the schoolteacher.'

The news came as a shock, yet when Stag thought about it, he wasn't surprised. She was a lovely looking girl and Hollett was a single man. It made sense that Hollett had an eye out for Kate, but this thought did not ease his discomfiture at the news.

As it was, Mr Hollett was nowhere to be seen. Kate and her mother were clearing away their dinner dishes and the boys were at Evie and Sam's.

Stag had nearly finished and was testing the door when Kate asked if she could have a word before he left. He assumed it was more news on her contract, so he was surprised when she said, 'Have you heard anything about the storekeeper?'

'What about him?'

'The women say he's cheating them.'

'I didn't know that. I hardly every go there. Most of my meals are at the men's hostel and I've had no need for anything else yet.'

'Has Lavinia or Queenie said anything to you?'

He shook his head. 'I'll check with them. Who was it who told you?'

'Evie. She told me he tries to confuse them by talking and taking advantage of those whose arithmetic is shaky. I've been in but he doesn't do it to me – he knows I can add up quickly.'

'Can you go when he's busy, so he doesn't notice you're there?'

'I'm going to try that. I can't do anything until I see him do it, and he's not open every day, so chances are few. I've begun helping some of the women. We do practice shopping.'

She's so competent and willing to help others, Stag thought. He began to make a comparison with Lavinia, then stopped himself. 'Your contract? Has there been any movement there?'

'No. Mr Wilson said we'd discuss it in the week after Christmas.'

'He's trying every trick under the sun. Making you worry about it.'

She turned round to check her mother wasn't listening, saw she was dozing, and leaning forward, said in a whisper, 'I haven't said anything to Mother. I don't want to worry her.'

There was a loud knock on the door. Hannah's eyes opened and Kate went to open it.

Stag's face fell as Mr Hollett walked into the room holding a miniature fort. It was complete with a wooden barricade and a bastion. He saw Stag sitting at the kitchen table and, looking at the hammer and some nails lying there, said, 'I see you've got a workman in. Don't bother with him next time. If there's a fault with the cabin's structure I can get one of the mine's carpenters to come in.' He made to put the fort down on the table, so Stag had to move his tools.

Stag clenched his jaw and narrowed his eyes. The man was an idiot. Kate looked embarrassed, but Mrs McAvoy was beaming from ear to ear at the interloper. Well, he couldn't blame her. A Company man was probably a better wager as a son-in-law than a Whitehaven collier.

'No need to escort me to the door,' he said.

'Thank you very much,' said Kate. 'We really appreciate it.'

Before he could escape through the newly fixed front door, Stag heard Hollett say, 'I thought the boys might like this for Christmas.'

'Oh, it's wonderful,' said Hannah. 'And look. There's a little red flag on the flagpole, just like in real life. They'll love it.'

A new kind of sadness rolled over Stag as he trudged back to the men's hostel. He'd thought he was doing the right thing helping Lavinia, but now he wasn't so sure he could sublimate his feelings for Kate. In fact his feelings for her were, if anything, becoming more intense. It was now apparent that Mr Hollett also found her attractive.

What are you going to do? he asked himself. *Just what are you going to do?*

CHAPTER TWENTY-FIVE

'Are you sure you won't come to the dance, Mother? It's a big occasion.'

'I can't. It will bring back all the memories of my last dance with your father. Anyway, I'm in mourning. It wouldn't be seemly. Evie and Sam are collecting the boys and it will be good that I'll be here when they return them. I can put the boys to bed and Sam and Evie can go back to the dance.'

'I could see to the boys.'

'Oh no, this evening you are Mr Hollett's guest. Sam and Evie offered to take them along – I think they'd be disappointed if we changed our minds at this late stage. We don't want to upset them, especially as Evie's just lost another baby.'

Kate had to agree. Although her mother needed to start living again, even if only by taking tiny steps, a Christmas Eve dance was probably not the right kind of social occasion for her to consider attending.

She wondered what people were going to think when she arrived at the Community Hall on the arm of Mr Hollett. She couldn't stop thinking how she would much rather be on Stag's arm. What was it Evie had said? 'We thought he had his buttons turned towards you.' She smiled; it was an expression she'd never heard before, but she knew what it meant. After this evening they'd probably think she was turning her buttons towards Mr Hollett. *How wrong they will be*, she thought.

※ ※ ※

With a red-and-white neck cloth tied loosely around his neck, and wearing a clean white shirt and his best grey breeches, Stag's spirits lifted as soon as he entered the Community Hall. He'd been looking forward to the dance ever since he'd heard about it – a chance to play his mouth organ again in company and the hope of some dancing with Kate. Looking after Lavinia didn't mean he couldn't ask others to dance, he'd told himself.

Hanging from two of the ceiling cross-beams was a makeshift banner with 'MERRY CHRISTMAS' stitched on it in a contrasting fabric. The letters were a bit lopsided. He'd seen Queenie fashioning it in haste the previous day.

Quite a number were already gathered and there was an air of expectancy and excitement. Stag nodded to one of the trappers, who'd recently returned from up island and had been boasting in the men's hostel bar about the stack of furs he'd brought in. Dr MacDonald was in deep conversation with Owen. As he approached, Owen broke off to tell Stag that Lavinia was settling Jonty and would be there soon. As far as he could see, everyone was in grand cheer and Stag felt the evening could only get better. He made his way to the drink table and helped himself to an ale.

The door opened and Stag was horrified to see Mr Hollett come in with Kate on his arm. It was a terrible shock that coursed through his body. He'd not expected Kate to be on the arm of anyone, and least of all Mr Hollett. His mood changed from one of expectation to one of intense disappointment. Although she was wearing a dress he had seen many times before, she had added an ivory-coloured lace fichu that framed her shoulders. He had never seen her looking so pretty. Mr Hollett had forsaken his Company attire and was wearing a yellow-and-grey striped waistcoat with blue trousers that Stag thought made him look foppish and a bit of a rake. His shirt sleeves had been carefully folded back to just below the elbow.

'You,' said Mr Hollett, waving Stag over. 'These benches need placing around the room.'

Stag began moving the benches as Mr Hollett stood and watched.

'You're one of the musicians, are you not?'

'Aye, I play the mouth organ.'

'Well, make sure you play your best this evening.'

Stag wasn't going to be told how to hold a Christmas dance. 'We miners know how to put on a *Merry Neet*.'

'What's that?'

'It's the Cumbrian name for a Christmas dance.'

'A merry night,' said Kate. 'He's very good. He played a great deal for us on the ship.'

'Well, thank goodness those days are over for you,' said Mr Hollett, scanning the room over her shoulder as if looking for someone more interesting than Stag to talk to. 'It must have been very difficult as a gentlewoman.'

'It was difficult for everyone,' said Kate.

'Aye, we all had bad times,' said Stag.

'Yes, I'm sure, but some of you must have been used to living in difficult conditions all your lives.' He addressed his remarks to Stag. 'Although I suppose working in mines you're used to the dark and the odious smells.'

Stag put the bench down in the middle of the floor and walked away, leaving Mr Hollett looking after him open-mouthed.

Mr Hollett spent the first hour close by Kate's side, drinking freely, becoming quite red in the face. At one point he put his hand on hers. When Lavinia arrived, Stag asked her to dance. Whether it was his mood or something else, Stag wasn't sure, but she seemed heavy of step. Over her shoulder he could see Mr Hollett smiling and fawning over Kate, and he wondered how she could stand it. Perhaps she was flattered. He remembered the dance on the ship, when they'd spoken properly for the first time. He'd felt a spark straight away, despite their different backgrounds, and she appeared to accept him for who and what he was.

Mr and Mrs Wilson, who, with their older children, were sitting slightly apart from everyone else, seemed to share Stag's discomfiture over Kate's partner, judging by the expression on their faces. This impression was compounded when they summoned Mr Hollett to their table and offered him a seat, leaving Kate stranded on her own on the other side of the room. Stag couldn't rescue her without leaving Lavinia.

Kate waited for Mr Hollett to return then, seeing him settled at the Wilsons' table, went to see the boys, who were taking turns dancing with Evie. Mr Hollett didn't seem to notice Kate had been snubbed when he sought her out fifteen minutes later, even redder in the face. Stag watched him sway as he held the front door open for Mrs Wilson, ushering her and her children out the door, while she informed everyone it was too late for them and for her. Mr Wilson waved his family off, with what Stag interpreted as an undisguised expression of relief.

❊ ❊ ❊

Kate had not been amused when Mr Hollett left her standing on her own. When he found her talking to the boys, she noticed his eyes were glassy.

'Mr Hollett, I think we'd better dance some of the beer from you,' she said. She'd seen Stag dancing with Lavinia and felt twinges of jealousy.

To her surprise, Mr Hollett turned her down.

'I don't care to dance in this fashion. It's workers' dancing. I used to see it at the harvest supper on our farm in Yorkshire. Clod-hopping, we used to call it.'

He had snubbed her again. Kate was surprised at his response. It seemed there were two Mr Holletts: the pleasant sober one and the contrary inebriated one.

It seemed he had read her thoughts. He stood up, swaying slightly. 'But of course, if you'd like to.'

Kate took his arm to steady him. 'You'd better sit down.'

'No, no. If you desire to dance, then we will.' He led her into the throng of dancers and, for someone who said he didn't dance, was soon spinning her around the floor. Stag was leading the music and Lavinia was standing next to her mother, watching him. Kate saw Stag look across at her with Mr Hollett and frown, and Lavinia follow his gaze with narrowed eyes. The bench episode had been embarrassing and she guessed Stag had taken a dislike to her partner.

Stag kept a fast pace going for fifteen minutes until she and Mr Hollett were forced to sit down. She saw him smile when they left the dance floor.

'I think you and I should consider an arrangement, Miss McAvoy,' said Mr Hollett.

Kate turned to look at him to see if she'd heard correctly.

'I think it will be most acceptable if we begin walking out together.'

Kate laughed. 'It's drink talking, Mr Hollett. I have no plans to commence an acquaintance with anyone more than friendship at this time. There has been a grave misunderstanding if you think I've encouraged you in any way. I agreed to come to the dance out of civility, nothing more, and you've forgotten about my application to teach. I expect to be very busy.'

'Oh,' he said, looking piqued. She saw he was going to say more, but their conversation was halted by Dr MacDonald.

'Miss McAvoy, Mr Hollett, kindly excuse me for interrupting. I am wondering how your mother is?'

'She's taken father's passing very badly, as you would expect.'

'Yes, that's why I'm enquiring. I had thought she might be here this evening.'

'She's not ready for a social occasion yet.'

'I wonder, would it be permissible for me to call? Purely on medical terms of course.'

'I would appreciate that, Dr MacDonald. Whilst it is fitting that we should all mourn, I fear she has no interest in life at the moment, and some conversation with you would be most agreeable to her, I'm sure.'

'I could bring her some books. She reads, does she not?'

'She used to. Perhaps some new material will spur her on to read again.'

After Dr MacDonald left, Kate saw Mr Hollett had wandered off to the bar and, with a full glass in his hand, was talking to the fur trapper. Evie and Sam were putting coats on the boys. She found her shawl and made her way over.

'I'll take the boys home. You two stay and enjoy the dance.'

'We're happy to take them home and we said we would.'

'I know, but I'm ready for home myself and I suspect Mother may already be asleep. If I go, I can put the boys to bed without waking her.'

Stag had his back to her, and Mr Hollett was still talking to the trapper. No one would see her leave.

'If I could just ask you to pass on my apologies to Mr Hollett. He may be seeking me out later.'

CHAPTER TWENTY-SIX

Kate and Hannah spent Christmas Day watching the boys play with the fort. Evie had made some peg men with painted faces to go with it. The boys set them up and threw marbles at them, pretending they were cannon balls. Kate could not deny that the fort was a great success and, in the cold light of day, felt some regret that she had slipped away without thanking Mr Hollett for the evening.

The start to Christmas Day had been very different from previous years. Mr Wilson had led a short service in the Community Hall and, although it drew everyone together, Kate had remarked to her mother that without a proper minister, or being in a church, it had not seemed like Christmas. On the other hand, because it was so different they had been saved from rituals that would have reminded them of happier Christmases spent in Liverpool as a complete family.

It was a relief when the holiday period was over, although Kate knew she had to do something about the storekeeper and his cheating.

She'd worked out he was always busiest on a Friday, around dinner-time. When Friday came, she waited outside until she could see the store was busy and the storekeeper's back was turned. It was a large room and the lighting was not bright. She slipped in and remained in the shadows by the door.

The storekeeper was a balding, middle-aged man sporting a wobbly double chin. A half-apron was tied round his waist at the front.

A young Brierley Hill woman asked to see the ticking cotton.

'How much is it?' she said, feeling the quality between her fingers.

'Eight pence a yard.'

She drew in a breath. 'That's expensive,' she said.

'It's the best quality and remember, it has to come from San Francisco. How much would you like?' He began measuring out the cloth, even though she hadn't yet said she wanted it.

She consulted a piece of paper. 'I'm not used to buying so much ticking. I've always cut my worn sheets and put the ends to the middle. This time I thought I'd make some new ones.' She was starting to look uncomfortable.

'How much?' he asked again. There was just a hint of impatience in his voice.

'Two and a quarter yards then.'

'That's one shilling and eight pence.'

No it's not, thought Kate, *it's one shilling and six pence. Two times eight pence plus tuppence for the quarter yard.*

'Anything else?'

'I'll take half a plug of twist baccy. Not the most expensive, the middle one.'

Kate watched as the storekeeper put the tobacco in a bag. It was four pence a plug. She could see the price on the box.

'Anything else?'

'No, not today. How much is all that?'

'Three pence for the baccy. One shilling and eleven pence thank you.' He put out his hand.

'Can I put it on our account?'

'You can put the baccy on,' said the storekeeper. 'But the cotton is a luxury good. It has to be paid for in cash.'

'A luxury? Cotton ticking?'

'Oh yes, definitely.'

The young woman opened her purse and handed over the money, and the storekeeper opened a small book with marbled covers that Kate took to be a sales ledger.

The young woman was oblivious to the fact that he had overcharged her by tuppence for the baize and another penny for the tobacco. That was three pence in total. Kate also doubted very much whether cotton sheeting was a luxury item. If he was doing this to everybody, he was making a great deal of money on the side. She said nothing and watched as he turned to the next customer, the fiddler's wife, with her clog-dancing daughter.

'What can I do for you?'

The woman began reading from a list. 'A pound of rice, a bag of coffee, a pint of vinegar and a bag of currants.'

The storekeeper leant over his counter, 'Now then, young lady,' he said to the little girl. 'I bet you'd like a sugar sweet?'

She smiled and nodded while he took an orange barley sugar from a glass jar and handed it to her. The mother was forced to turn her attention to unwrapping the waxy paper covering the sticky sweet and, while she was doing this, the storekeeper began putting the order together and weighing the ingredients. Kate watched him under-weigh. When he'd finished, she calculated the cost to be two shillings and two pence. He asked for two shillings and four pence.

She decided not to confront him immediately and left. She would make sure he refunded the money he had stolen, but she'd wait until later, when the store was less crowded. Lest she forget, she wrote down the sales and noted the discrepancies. She had no doubts he'd been carrying out this form of pilfering since they'd arrived, and there would be plenty of women who could back her accusation.

It was mid-afternoon and the storekeeper was cashing up when she returned. He looked up.

'I'm closing the store. What was it you wanted?'

'I would like a word with you,' she said.

He looked surprised.

'How long have you been cheating the women?'

His jaw dropped. 'I don't know what you mean.'

'Yes, you do. Some of the women may be slow with their arithmetic, but others are quicker than you think and have noticed short change and overcharging.'

'That's all lies. It's them that can't add up.'

'I might put some trust in that statement if I hadn't seen it with my own eyes.' She related how she'd watched him that afternoon. A bead of sweat appeared on his brow.

'Look, it was busy this afternoon – so busy I didn't even notice you in here. I get rushed off my feet. I can make mistakes too, you know.'

Kate had a sudden hunch. 'You make entries in a cash book, don't you? For all purchases?'

'Yes, it's Company policy.'

'Well then, we can check the price you charged for the cotton ticking.'

'That ledger's private Company information. I can't show you that. Company accounts is private.'

'Then I'm right. There's no entry for the cotton ticking, is there? You've not only overcharged the customer, you've pocketed her money as well. Mr Wilson is going to be very interested in this, I am sure of that.'

She leaned forward and snatched the ledger. 'I'm going to put a stop to this,' she said, and before the storekeeper could get himself out from behind his counter, she had run out of the store, clutching the accounts.

She arrived out of breath at the Company offices and asked to speak to Mr Wilson. He had his coat on and looked as if he was just about to leave.

'Miss McAvoy. This is unexpected.'

'I need to speak with you urgently. It's about the storekeeper.'

Mr Wilson raised his chin and looked down his nose at her. 'Come into my office.'

Inside the office, Mr Wilson seated himself behind his desk and invited Kate to sit opposite.

'I would rather stand,' she said, knowing if she sat, he would be able to look down on her. She gave a full account of what she'd seen and how she knew it had been going on for some time.

Mr Wilson glanced over at a pile of papers on his desk and only looked back when she produced the sales ledger. She placed it on his desk and turned it round so he could read the entries. She pointed with her finger. 'There, today, no entry for the ticking cotton.'

He turned back a page, as if to check the entry hadn't been made on an earlier date, then looked up at Kate. 'You are correct. It would seem there has been no entry. However, I'm sure it's just an oversight on our storekeeper's part and, if you will forgive me, I'm sure some of the women are not as adept at arithmetic as you are, Miss McAvoy. It could indeed be that they feel they have been overcharged when in fact they have miscalculated costs themselves.'

'You're not going to do anything, are you?'

'It's not a question of not doing anything; it's that I have no proof.'

'No proof? You have my testimony and I have no doubt I can gather together many other testimonies from the women and probably the men too.'

'I know it seems cut and dried to you, but to imply that a trusted employee of the Company has wilfully set out to steal from settlers is a strong accusation and one, as I have already mentioned, I do not think will stand up to close scrutiny. It's possible he didn't have time to make the missing entry and intended to do so later.'

'What you say is true. It most certainly is a strong accusation and settlers are the last people who should be cheated. You leave me little option but to take my accusations to Mr Hollett, as the Island Liaison Officer. I will ask him to present my findings to the governor.'

Mr Wilson sat up in his chair, and as he often did when he was thinking, he put his fingers together and looked over them. 'There's no need to act hastily. I can see you are angry. Involving the governor is not a wise move. He is a very busy man.'

'I can see why you may not want the governor to be involved. In his welcome speech he spoke of the new arrivals as being the founders of settlements that will grow into the towns and cities of the future. He will be appalled to think that some of those very first settlers have been treated in such a paltry way. The reality is, Mr Wilson, it is your settlement, your community and you are the one in charge. It is to you that the governor has entrusted his dream. He will not be happy to learn that his trust has been squandered. He will expect you to act immediately upon learning of this matter for the good of the Company and Colville's future.'

From his furrowed brow Kate imagined Mr Wilson was mulling over the information, working through any consequences he thought might affect him directly. It was all true. The settlers had been treated appallingly by the very Company that was supposed to be nurturing them, and it was on his watch.

'All right, Miss McAvoy, I understand what you are saying. Let us speak no more of Mr Hollett.'

'No, indeed. Let us instead speak of my contract.'

Mr Wilson's head shot up. 'Your contract? What about it?'

'We need to settle it. Here are my terms. My mother is to receive the £30 pension. She is entitled to it, whether or not I take up the school-teaching position.'

Mr Wilson opened his mouth, but Kate kept her eye upon him, and her gaze was so firm he closed his mouth and met her eyes. She raised her chin, as he had done, and squared her shoulders. He could not know that beneath her dress her legs were shaking and her stomach was turning over.

'I accept that my father had much more experience to bring to the position, so I am prepared to accept an income of £45 per annum.'

Mr Wilson's eyebrows shot up and he spluttered.

'My contract will be for five years and there will be a clause that enables me to decide for myself, should I marry, whether I continue in my position.'

'This is outrageous. You and your mother would have an income of £75 a year. That is almost the same as a working miner.'

'And you think we are not worth that? You know I am a fully certificated teacher. What price do you put on education, Mr Wilson? It is surely as beneficial as the work of a miner? We bring two healthy young boys who will grow up as valuable members of the community. They are possibly the schoolteachers of the future. And you know my mother is entitled to her pension in her own right. It has nothing to do with my obtaining a position.'

'It is usual for a woman to cease work when she marries. Do you have plans?'

'I do not, but I feel strongly that a woman can continue

as a useful member of a community if she marries. Especially a schoolteacher.'

There was a long pause before Mr Wilson said, 'Allow me a moment to consider the Company's position.'

He picked up a pencil and rolled it between his fingers. Then he placed it on the desk top and rolled it back and forth with his left hand.

'Can we agree on your mother's pension of £30 as stated in your father's contract, the remuneration for your position at £40, a contract of three years and the marriage clause?'

Whilst his offer was most acceptable to her, Kate could hear Stag's voice saying 'negotiate, negotiate'.

'My mother's pension at £30, my salary at £43, a four-year contract and the marriage clause. And there's the matter of the storekeeper.'

'I will transfer the storekeeper to the fort and bring in a replacement from Fort Langley and we will agree there is no need to trouble Mr Hollett with the arrangements. I will consider some way of making retribution to everyone. It may not be financial, since that will be difficult to dispense, but I will think of something and it will be fair.'

Kate remembered Mr Hollett had described Mr Wilson as 'fair' that first day on the Beaver. She didn't think he'd been very fair so far with her.

'We are agreed.' She smiled at him. 'Everything is settled then for the New Year, as you hoped.' She extended her hand. 'Shall we shake hands on it like two gentlemen?'

Mr Wilson accepted her hand, albeit with a rather sour expression. She wasn't surprised to discover he had a limp handshake.

When Kate got home with the good news about her contract, she saw a pile of books on the table.

'Has someone called?'

'Yes, Dr MacDonald. He's left me some books to read.'

'Was it a pleasant visit?'

'Yes, it was. Very nice.'

'Will he come again?'

'He said he would.'

'Then everything is good, Mother. Everything is good.'

CHAPTER TWENTY-SEVEN

Miss Betsy was at the door. 'I've an invitation for you,' she said, holding out an envelope. 'I'm to wait for your answer.'

Kate invited her in.

'What is it?' asked her mother.

'It's an invitation to an afternoon tea on New Year's Day. It's from the Wilsons.'

'The Wilsons?'

'Yes, in their cabin.'

'It's just for you two, not the boys,' said Betsy.

'And you need an answer right away?'

'Mrs Wilson said, "Wait for the answer." So I'm here waiting.'

'Indeed, you are,' said Kate. She looked at her mother.

'I'm still in mourning, I can't go.'

'Didn't you tell me that Dr MacDonald said it was acceptable for you to begin with small social visits?' She turned to Betsy. 'Please tell Mrs Wilson we are delighted to accept.'

'I will.'

Hannah picked up a hairbrush from the table and, pleading the onset of a sudden headache, retired, leaving Kate and Betsy alone.

Kate sensed Betsy was in no hurry to leave. 'Is there more?' she asked.

'Well, I shouldn't be telling you, but Mr Hollett will be there.'

'Really, well that will be jolly,' said Kate, pulling a face and laughing.

Betsy joined in the laughter. 'And Dr MacDonald too.'

'Is it a special occasion other than New Year's Day?'

'Not exactly. More a bit of matchmaking.'

'Oh goodness me. Surely not. My mother and Dr MacDonald?'

'Well, I don't know about that, no. You and Mr Hollett. I reckon it's only right you should know in advance, but look surprised when you see him or I'll be in deep trouble. We unattached women must stick together. I heard Mr Wilson say to his wife he thought it would be good to get you married off and that a couple of babies would soon put you in your place.'

Kate raised her eyes to the ceiling. 'Am I looking surprised now?'

'Yes. Make sure you look as surprised when you see Mr Hollett. And Mrs Wilson said Mr Hollett needs a wife for advancement within the Company.'

After Betsy had left, Kate smiled to herself. Of course, they'd seen her on Mr Hollett's arm at the dance and had no reason to think the evening had ended badly. So, this was Mr Wilson's new tactic. He would get her married off, then there would be hints she was overtaxing herself or not supporting her husband enough. If she had a baby, that would definitely end her school-teaching days. But even if she did marry, it certainly would not be to a Company man; it would be to someone who was going to be there for her, someone who loved her for who she was, not for any advancement in rank. It would be someone like Stag. A hard-working man with sound principles. She was sure Stag was someone who could be trusted.

Poor Betsy, she felt sorry for her. Although she was proving to be a mine of information, it must be awful for her stuck in that house under what appeared to be a very strict regime. For such a friendly, lively girl it must be a great trial. It was small wonder she found satisfaction in passing on gossip snippets.

Kate saw Stag pass by. She opened the door and called to him. He stopped, seemed delighted to see her and retraced his steps.

'Good morning, Miss McAvoy.'

'I was able to negotiate.'

For a moment he looked puzzled, then he remembered. 'Your contract? Has it ended well for you?'

'Indeed, it has.' She told him about the storekeeper and how his cheating had given her the opportunity to raise the subject of her contract.

'I'm very happy for you.'

There was only one question she wanted to ask Stag and that was if he was going to marry Lavinia, but she couldn't possibly. She settled for a vaguer way to make an enquiry.

'How is everyone next door?'

'They're all well.'

Was that all he was going to say? 'Jonty's first Christmas?' She'd meant to make a statement, but it came out as a question. Of course it was Jonty's first Christmas.

Stag nodded. 'Did the boys enjoy playing with the fort?' he asked.

'Yes, very much.' She couldn't lie. *Oh, this is all so awkward*, she thought.

'Well, if there's nothing more I'll bid you farewell. Lavinia is expecting me.'

Kate watched him walk away. She didn't care that all the while they'd been talking, Lavinia had been standing at her cabin door watching them. What she was thinking, Kate had no idea, but she didn't look pleased.

❖ ❖ ❖

New Year's Day was upon them and Hannah had still not decided what she should wear. She was shaking her best blue-and-grey striped dress with the lace collar in a vain attempt to straighten the creases. 'Should I still be in mourning dress for this social visit to the Wilsons? Maybe I shouldn't even be going. It's probably breaking all the rules.'

'We've already discussed this. It doesn't matter about rules anymore, we're not in England now. That's a pretty dress, but perhaps not suitable. But you can't go in your day mourning dress; that will indicate you have no sense of occasion.'

'It should be a full year of full mourning dress, then two years of half-mourning. I feel disrespectful.'

'Why don't you wear your Sunday mourning dress? Take that white double-flower spray from your best hat and attach it to the collar at the front. People then won't feel as uncomfortable as if you were all in black.'

Hannah put her best dress away and brought out her Sunday mourning dress. She held it up against herself. 'When I packed this, I never thought I'd need it for your father's death. I only put it in our trunk at the last moment. How does it look? Is it too bad?'

'Nothing that a good steam from the kettle won't sort out, along with a strong brush down. It's the Wilsons, Mother, not the governor. What a "to-do" this is turning out to be.'

'I know, I know. I just want it to be right and I'm still not sure I should even be going. I'll be glad when it's all over. I can't imagine why they've invited us.'

'It will be genial, I am sure. Some tea, some cake, some pleasantries and that will be it.' Kate also wished the whole thing was over and done with. It was going to be tedious.

Evie arrived full of smiles to look after the boys, holding a box containing a fresh batch of biscuits. 'Oh, you do look handsome, Mrs McAvoy. Take your time, no need to hurry back.'

❊ ❊ ❊

Miss Betsy ushered Kate and her mother into the Wilsons' parlour. The fire must have been lit some hours earlier as the room was warm and welcoming. Mr Wilson was sitting in a large armchair and Mr Hollett was standing slightly to the right of the fireplace, close enough to warm himself while not blocking the heat. Dr MacDonald arrived shortly after Kate and Hannah. Greetings were exchanged and Mrs Wilson began fussing over the seating arrangements. When everyone was settled to her satisfaction, she rang a small brass bell and Miss Betsy entered with a large tray, placing it on a table to the side of her mistress.

Mrs Wilson, who seemed even fuller of figure than Kate remembered her, was wearing a voluminous green tartan dress that spilled out over the side of her chair. She poured a cup of weak tea and passed it over to Hannah, saying, 'Our tea service is bone china. We had it shipped out on the last boat.' Without giving Hannah time to comment, she turned to Mr Hollett. 'I expect your family has a number of china tea services in Yorkshire?'

'I expect so.' Mr Hollett was eyeing up the fancy cakes on the table. 'I've never given it much thought.'

Kate suspected that had Mr Hollett known the other guests would be herself and her mother, he would have made an excuse. He had greeted her politely enough, but when their eyes met he'd looked away. She wondered if the others sensed the awkwardness in the room. Dr Macdonald had greeted Hannah with a wide smile. It was early days, but she sensed a strong friendship was going to develop between the good doctor and her mother. There was nothing wrong with that – her mother needed all the support she could get.

Happily, Mrs Wilson was well able to oversee the conversational duties required of her as hostess, although she couldn't stop herself from turning to Hannah and stating the obvious.

'Your family are from Ireland, are they not, Mrs McAvoy?'

'Indeed they are. My late husband and I left Dublin and moved to Liverpool some years ago. He obtained a good position as headmaster in a school there.'

'Such a bad business with all that famine,' said Mrs Wilson. 'All those farmers leaving and flooding the boats to North America.'

'Only the ones with funds to purchase passages,' said Mr Hollett, sounding relieved there was now something he could comment upon intelligently. 'Many Irish came across to England. In fact, my family engaged quite a few to pull potatoes on our estate. They were good workers and we placed them in one of our old barns, and named it "The Paddy House". They lived there on potatoes and bread and drinking beer in the evenings. When the season was over, we had to let them go, and I think most of them repaired to the cities. I understand Liverpool has quite a large Irish community, does it not?'

They all turned to Hannah. 'It does,' she said.

Kate felt herself bristle. 'I can assure you our family are not from the Irish bogs, Mr Hollett. Neither have any of us ever pulled potatoes for a living or lived on bread and potatoes.'

'I am sure, Miss McAvoy, Mr Hollett is not implying that.' Mr Wilson turned to his wife. 'Why, I'm certain some of our Scottish relatives worked the land going back. I cannot think of any right now, but there will be some.'

'I can proudly say the same. My relatives in Scotland still reside in the Lowlands,' said Dr McDonald.

'How are we getting on with the schoolhouse?' asked Kate.

Mr Wilson added two more logs to the fire before speaking. 'I will admit that things have not progressed as rapidly as I would have liked. There was a problem with the ditches at the mine and we had to set some of the carpenters on to help the miners.'

'I passed by yesterday and the men were there,' said Mr Hollett. 'I stopped and had a word. They're making the schoolhouse and the cabin their top priority now.'

'Then I suggest you and Miss McAvoy walk up to Millstone Creek together to the sawmill tomorrow. There will be interior items to plan. Benches, desks, a blackboard. It's important that you two liaise over the school furniture.'

Mr Hollett look startled. 'Colville's educational requirements are surely your responsibility?'

'Strictly speaking yes, however, as Island Liaison Officer I've been thinking you may be involved in overseeing schools in other parts of the island, and this could be good experience for you.'

Mr Hollett turned his attention to his fingernails and made no comment.

'Yes, of course. I will be happy to escort Miss McAvoy to the sawmill tomorrow.'

Satisfied smiles crept across both the Wilsons' faces. Looking at Mr Hollett's expression, Kate could see he wasn't foolish – he knew exactly what was going on.

Dr MacDonald accepted more tea from Mrs Wilson and said, 'Are you going to have an official opening for the school?'

Everyone looked to Mr Wilson. 'What a splendid idea. When is the next festive day?'

'Easter?' suggested Mrs Wilson.

'Oh, that's too far away,' said Kate. 'Although I suppose by then we can be absolutely certain the schoolhouse will be finished.'

'St Patrick's Day?' said Hannah.

Kate frowned. 'That's the middle of March.'

'May I suggest St Valentine's Day?' said Mrs Wilson, looking first at Kate and then at Mr Hollett.

'Excellent idea,' said Mr Wilson, pointedly not bothering to consult anyone else. 'I'm glad that's settled.' He was obviously used to making unilateral decisions.

'May I suggest a concert?' said Kate. 'The children can perform, and perhaps some of the parents will agree to participate.'

'Oh yes, our children will simply adore that,' said Mrs Wilson. Kate could imagine her in that moment, wondering what they would wear, and how she was going to make them the stars of the show.

'February the 14th.' Mr Wilson straightened his cuffs and brushed some crumbs from his trousers. 'May I ask you to place a notice on the Community Hall board, Miss McAvoy?'

'I will be most happy to do so and I would like to express thanks to Dr MacDonald for suggesting we have an official opening.'

CHAPTER TWENTY-EIGHT

The following morning, the sawmill manager broke off from directing operations to attend to Stag. There was a harried expression on his face.

'I've a ship in the harbour hungry for timber spars for San Francisco. That city swallows them down and spews up saloons and whorehouses by the dozen. They can't get enough of either. What can I do for you today?'

'I'm here to collect some shingles for the Jeffersons' place.'

He pointed to a small shed. 'They're in there,' he said. 'Make a pile of what you want and I'll get one of the men to deliver them. Thursday evening? We're doing the rounds. They're not the only ones needing some.'

'Any time. There's always someone there.'

The sawmill manager's attention passed from Stag's face to over his shoulder. 'I've got more visitors. Just when I'm up to my ears.'

Stag turned to see Mr Hollett and Kate. It was painful for him to see them together again. Mr Hollett nodded in passing and, to Stag's surprise and delight, carried on, while Kate turned back to speak with him.

'The schoolhouse is to be finished. Mr Hollett and I are here to organise the desks and chairs and a blackboard. We'll know in a day or two for sure. If all goes well, we'll have an official opening on February 14th.'

'Valentine's Day. That's grand news for you and for us all. Congratulations.' Stag was genuinely happy things were going so well for her. 'I don't see you as often as I used to.

'No, that's true. You've been good to Lavinia and Jonty.' She couldn't stop herself, she had to ask. 'Do you still call there?'

Although her mouth smiled, it seemed to Stag her eyes were sad. He felt the need to explain. 'Yes, Tom asked me to see to them.'

'I know. It's common knowledge.'

'I have a debt to repay.' When the time was right, he would tell her. She had a right to know, because he felt sure she cared for him; he could see it in her eyes. He suspected his affection for her shone no less brightly.

✻ ✻ ✻

'Good afternoon, stranger,' said Owen. 'It's well over a week since we saw you. The shingles've been delivered. Thank you.'

'I've been working extra stints, then straight to the hostel,' said Stag.

Jonty, giggling, put his arms up, and Stag bent down and picked him up.

'Where's Lavinia?'

'She and her mother have gone off to a prayer meeting with Mr Wilson. I think they only go for the biscuits.'

'That's a nice idea.'

'Anyways, that's why I'm left with the bairn. Although it gives me a chance to speak with you.'

Stag had a feeling he knew what was coming.

'You've been spending a lot of time with us helping us out, and we do appreciate it. The bairn's comfortable with you and I dare say our Lavinia is comfortable with you too.' Owen straightened up and Stag braced himself. He put Jonty back down on the floor and set some toy bricks beside him.

'Just what are your intentions towards our daughter?'

Stag cleared his throat. 'You're asking me if I'm going to propose marriage to her?'

'Yes, I am. I'll not beat around the bush over it. I'm a man that speaks his mind, you know that.'

Stag nodded. 'Tom asked me to "see to her and the bairn" and that is what I have been trying to do.'

'Aye, well no one can fault you on that, lad. What about the future?'

'It may seem to you that I'm holding back. However, my thoughts are that it's appropriate Lavinia has time to think, and I've regarded the time since Tom's death as a period for her to mourn. Because Tom was my marrer, for me to take his wife as my own is a big step, and people like to talk. The last thing I want is to tarnish her reputation or Tom's memory. Don't you think it's best we don't give them anything to gossip about?'

'You're saying it's respect for Tom and Lavinia's reputation that's held you back?'

'Yes, I am.'

'I understand, lad, but it's been six months and Lavinia and the boy need stability in their lives. Who's to say that when the next boat comes in, the Company won't say she has to return? That would tear our family apart.'

'I doubt they'll do that.'

'That's as may be, but you can't deny it could happen, can you? They could say they needed this bigger cabin and that Queenie and I are to move into one of the smaller ones. Something like that.'

Stag nodded. 'I suppose they could.'

'Listen, lad, it's not for me to push you, but what say you to Eastertide? Come to me and ask for her hand then. I'm sure she'll accept you. It'll be spring, a time of new beginnings. No one will think anything unseemly about it by then.' He stepped forward and put out his hand. Stag reciprocated and they shook hands.

'It's a man-to-man talk we've had, lad. No need to say owt to the womenfolk. Let's surprise them.'

Stag had known this moment was going to come and that a voice inside his head was going to tell him he was making a mistake. What he hadn't bargained for was that the voice would scream and shout at him for all it was worth. So loudly, in fact, he thought Owen must surely be hearing it.

✽ ✽ ✽

The notice announcing the schoolhouse concert was greeted with much excitement. Kate was holding classes for the children and a few of the women in the Community Hall.

'It's open to all,' said Kate. 'Adults and children alike.'

As the children were leaving and Kate was preparing for the women's class, the fiddler's wife came up and offered her husband's services. Seamus was at Kate's elbow. Suddenly his voice rang out, 'We can get Stag to play. He can play and you can sing.'

'That's a nice idea, but you can't just volunteer someone like that. You have to ask them.' Kate turned to her left to speak to another mother.

Seamus persisted. 'Really, it won't be a concert if Stag doesn't play.'

'He's right,' said Evie. 'You and Stag should sing a duet.' She grinned. Kate knew she was being mischievous.

'Really...'

'Can you sing?' asked the fiddler's wife. 'We've never heard you.'

'Of course she can sing,' said Seamus, as if he thought it was something that was obvious to all, just by looking at her. He clapped his hands. 'Hush, everyone. Who thinks my sister should sing a duet with Stag for the concert?'

Evie corrected him. 'You mean the schoolteacher.'

'Yes, all right, my sister, Miss McAvoy, the schoolteacher.'

The fiddler's wife knitted her brows at him. 'Steady, young man, let's not have any cheek from you.'

'If I ask him, will you do it?' asked Evie. 'You really

ought to do something, and it would be fun for everyone to see. Make a change.'

Against her better judgement, Kate agreed. The thought both frightened and excited her. They would have to practise. She knew he would agree to play, but maybe asking him to accompany her could be going too far. He might say no.

CHAPTER TWENTY-NINE

Hannah greeted Stag at the door. 'We're in such disarray. We're making ready to move to the schoolteacher's cabin in a few days and, while we don't have much, it's proving more than we thought.'

'Don't fret yourself, Mrs McAvoy. I'm here about the concert, not to judge the tidiness of your cabin.'

'On top of everything, Mr Hollett is taking the boys out tomorrow afternoon on a bear hunt. He promised to do that some time ago. They're excited already, just when I need them to help me.'

Stag wasn't surprised to hear about the bear hunt. Mr Hollett was a puzzle to him. Most of the time he was the Company official, high-handed and somewhat pompous, yet Stag had to admit he seemed genuinely fond of children. He'd had the fort made for Seamus and Bartley, and now he was entertaining them in his off-duty time. Was it all a ploy to be close to Kate? Or maybe he just liked children. He always stopped to ruffle Jonty's hair and Stag had seen him talking to other children in the street.

'It seems I've come at the wrong time.'

'Oh, no,' said Kate, putting a pile of clothes down on the table. 'We're both pleased to see you.'

'Indeed we are,' said Hannah. 'I often see you going next door to visit Lavinia.'

'I visit the whole family, not just Lavinia,' he said. He wasn't exactly sure why he felt he had to explain himself, he just knew it was important he did so. 'Evie has said we should sing a duet together at the schoolhouse opening.'

'You don't have to,' said Kate. 'Seamus just came out with it, and some of the women heard and well, you know...'

'We need to practise, then.'

'When would be a good time, Mother?'

'I'm going to Dr MacDonald's for afternoon tea and the boys will be out with Mr Hollett. So, tomorrow afternoon would be an agreeable time. And you'll be here when the boys get back, so I needn't worry about what time I return home.'

Stag spent the next twenty-four hours looking forward to his visit. To be able to spend time with Kate, with no competition for her attention from family or Mr Hollett, was time to be savoured.

When he arrived, she greeted him with a laughing face. 'I'm prepared.' She pointed to a small pile of sheet music. 'My favourites – all I could bring with me.'

Stag examined the music. The third sheet was *Scarborough Fair*. He picked it up and began humming. 'One of my favourites, too.'

'I know,' she said. 'I saw how your eyes lit up when you saw it.'

'You're a soprano?'

'No, an alto.'

Stag took his mouth organ from his pocket, played a short introduction and nodded to bring her in. At first she was self-conscious, and some of the notes wavered. She stopped, cleared her throat, and began again. Stag stopped playing to listen to her. She had a rich voice, clear and steady, with no hint of unintentional vibrato. He imagined her seated at a piano, small children around her singing in harmony, himself singing with them. *Stop it*, the voice in his head said in a whisper. *Why are you torturing yourself thinking such things? Because I can't help it*, he shouted back.

It was soon apparent they didn't really need to practise, but only twenty minutes had passed.

'I'm afraid we have no ale to offer you, but we have some ginger beer. We get it for the boys.'

'That will be grand,' said Stag. 'I'm still a boy at heart.' He watched her as she collected a brown earthenware jar from a shelf and two glasses. She was graceful in movement, without appearing fragile.

'How are things at the mine? I heard there was some disagreement.'

'Aye, there was, but it's sorted now. The bosses put us on digging ditches, and that meant we didn't qualify for bonus payments. We get those for bringing coal to the surface, and if we're not hewing, then no coal's being brought up.'

'It's written in your contracts, isn't it?'

'Aye. Owen negotiated on our behalf.' Stag was talking

about the mine, but he wasn't thinking about it. All he wanted to do was take Kate in his arms and kiss her. Not in an overpowering way, rather in a gentle, supportive way. It was her he wanted to be looking after, not Lavinia. He'd given support where he could, advising on her contract and the storekeeper, now he wanted to touch her, to provide support other than in words.

'Are you all right, Stag?'

She was looking at him with concern and he realised she'd been talking while he was mulling over his thoughts.

'I was just asking if you still wanted to open a store?'

'I do. I think about it when I'm working. I tell you, I could transform that Company store. Everything about it is all wrong. For a start, it's so dark people can't see the goods properly. Although the displays are so poor, I don't suppose it matters.'

They laughed.

The cabin door opened and the boys burst into the room, tired, hungry and full of their adventure. Mr Hollett followed.

'Look, Kate, we didn't see any bears, but we got something else.' Seamus opened a canvas bag and pulled out a dead chicken. 'We ran into one of the woodsmen and he said we could have it.'

'And we can keep the feathers,' said Bartley.

'Chicken pie for supper then,' said Kate, laughing at their exuberance.

'Will you pluck it for us, Mr Hollett?' said Bartley.

'I think we should ask Mr Liddell,' said Mr Hollett. 'I'm sure he'd like to do it for you, unless it's not something he's acquainted with.'

Stag allowed himself a moment of smugness.

'I've dressed chickens since I was a boy on my grandfather's farm.' He'd registered the flash of disappointment on Mr Hollett's face on seeing him. It was momentary, but he'd caught it. Was it just that Mr Hollett simply didn't like him as a person or was it that he was irritated to find him there with Kate?

CHAPTER THIRTY

Mrs Wilson and the five little Wilsons, all dressed up again as if for a Sunday school outing, arrived for the Valentine's Day School Opening Ceremony and took up all the best seats on the front row. The McAvoys sat behind, with Kate on the end. Mr Wilson welcomed everyone, then subjected them to a long and boring speech about 'the unending perseverance of teachers and the importance of book learning.'

Bartley and Seamus, sitting in between Kate and their mother, began swinging their legs back and forth – at first randomly, then in unison, with increasing speed. Kate put a hand on Seamus's knee and whispered, 'If you don't stop doing that, I'm going to go and fetch a box for you to put your feet in.' She knew, if left to their own devices it was only a matter of time when, through boredom, they would start kicking each other.

Stag had entered earlier with Lavinia and the Jeffersons. He'd smiled and nodded and patted his pocket, to indicate he'd not forgotten his mouth organ. Looking at Kate, Lavinia had put her gloved hand on Stag's arm. Around her shoulders was the same shawl she'd been wearing on the quayside when they'd all first encountered each other. Kate took it as a public sign she was now in half-mourning for Tom.

When Mr Wilson had finished and was handing over to Dr McDonald, Hannah leaned across the boys.

'Are you nervous?' she said to Kate.

'Yes, I am a little.' It was unexpected. Whether it was that she was going to sing in front of everyone and wanted it to go well, or whether it was because she was singing with Stag, she wasn't sure. Possibly a combination of both, but she knew she would feel easier when it was over.

While Mr Wilson had extolled the virtues of education, Dr MacDonald concentrated on the human aspect: how a schoolhouse was solid bricks and mortar, whereas the teacher was the life blood. He invited Kate to the front.

'Think of this building as the body of Colville's teaching, and here,' he paused and with an open hand indicated Kate, 'here is the beating heart of Colville's teaching. Not only its heart, but its lungs as well. We are fortunate to have Miss McAvoy with us. I know many of you, young, and old, have already received instruction from her, and that you will support me in saying that she is competent, capable, and cheerful.' He began clapping and everyone joined in.

Kate was embarrassed. She hadn't expected such a public appreciation of her efforts. She glanced at her mother, who was smiling through tears. She just knew she was thinking of her father and how proud he would have been to have heard Dr MacDonald's praise.

After the applause had died down, a voice from the back shouted, 'Speech, speech.'

Dr Macdonald inclined his head towards Kate and she stepped forward.

'Our doctor's kind words are much appreciated and I will do my utmost to live up to his expectations. I may be the heart and lungs but where would I be without my hard-working pupils? Those of all ages who have put so much effort into studying in what have, on occasion, been very trying circumstances. What I want to say is that each one of us has a part to play in doing our best for the next generation of Colville citizens. Let us confirm our commitment to education in Colville with another round of applause.'

Then Dr MacDonald invited Mr Hollett, as the governor's representative, to declare the schoolhouse open. Everyone sang the National Anthem and cheered the Queen, then the doctor began looking around for a seat, since it appeared no one had thought to save him one. He made his way towards Hannah and the boys.

'Mrs McAvoy, a wonderful day for you and your daughter. A splendid new schoolhouse. How proud you must be.'

'Indeed, I am. I see you're looking for a seat. Will you sit with us?'

Kate was standing by, having returned for the concert programme she'd left on her seat. 'I will not be returning, Dr MacDonald, please take my seat. Move along, boys. Mother, move up so you're next to Dr MacDonald.'

He accepted the invitation, the boys moved along and settled down, and they all waited for the concert to begin. Kate made her way back to the front.

Each performer was introduced by name. She and Stag were last on the programme. A Wilson girls' trio preceded them. Kate thought, once again, how they all had a sad look in their eyes when on parade, and how different they were in class. When they'd finished, Mrs Wilson rose to her feet and began clapping her girls with great gusto. She then turned and bowed to the audience as if she herself had performed. Several people laughed, including Seamus and Bartley, and although Kate too thought it most amusing, she gave them one of her looks.

While Mrs Wilson was accepting her applause, Stag made his way to the front. As he was walking up, he smiled at Kate then, knowing his back was to the audience and no one could see, he winked at her. She found it hard to keep a straight face. She moved a music stand into the centre and settled her music on it. It was just a safety net – she knew the words, but she didn't want anything to go wrong. She checked the height of the stand and, finding it a little low after the Wilson girls, raised it. As she looked up, she saw her mother smiling and she smiled back.

'Are you ready?' she said in a low voice to Stag. He nodded.

Kate stepped forward. 'Stag Liddell and I would like to entertain you with *Scarborough Fair.*'

Stag played a short introduction, Kate found her note and they began. She sang the first two verses, with Stag providing a gentle accompaniment on his mouth organ. Then Stag sang the third verse as a solo, and it was then that Kate noticed Lavinia, sitting with Jonty on her lap. Everyone else was smiling and looking at them with encouraging, interested faces, which made Lavinia's expression all the more noticeable. It was furious. She had clenched her jaw and her eyes were narrow, but what was most noticeable was that all colour had drained from her face. Kate had heard the expression 'white with anger' – now she knew what it looked like. *She's jealous*, thought Kate. *Lavinia's jealous of me.* She was so immersed in her countenance, she almost missed her fourth verse entry, the vocal duet. Stag was looking at her with affection in his eyes as he sang. In fact, it was more than that: he was looking at her with love in his eyes, and it was in front of everybody. They entered the fifth and final verse, with Stag returning to accompany her. There was so much approving applause, Stag invited everyone to join them with a *Greensleeves* encore. When they'd finished, Kate stole another glance at Lavinia. Even before the applause had died away, she was up on her feet. Kate watched as she made her way to Dr MacDonald. The doctor placed a hand on the boy's forehead then spoke to Lavinia. Before Kate reached her mother, Lavinia had left.

'Where did Lavinia go?' Kate asked.

'She was worried Jonty had a fever,' said the doctor.

'Is he ill?'

'Just a slight rise in temperature. Nothing that some cool air won't take care of.'

'It's very stuffy in here,' said Hannah. 'She has him so well wrapped up, I'm surprised he can breathe at all.'

'I suggested she leave the menfolk to put the room back in order and take the boy home with her mother.'

* * *

One minute the room was busy and then suddenly it was empty. After the benches and stools had been put away, Kate and Stag found themselves alone in the schoolroom.

'That went well,' he said.

'They really liked it.'

'I think some of it was the schoolmistress singing with the collier lad. I'll wager that was something they never thought they'd see.' Stag's deep-throated laugh filled the room.

'We'll have to be careful or we'll be singing at everyone's birthday party.'

He put a hand out and touched her arm. 'Would that be so bad?' he asked.

She was about to make a light-hearted response when she saw he was serious. She felt herself blush. Then she remembered how he had looked at her and she blushed even more deeply.

'I've always thought you're lovely to look at,' he said, 'You're even lovelier when you blush.'

She turned away. 'Stag, you mustn't speak to me like this. What about Lavinia?'

He turned her round to face him. 'On that I need to explain. Do you remember at the sawmill we talked about my looking after Lavinia?'

'Yes.' Kate wondered if he too had noticed Lavinia's angry face during the concert.

'Sit with me now, lass, and I'll tell you why I've an obligation.' He pulled two benches out and placed them so they were able to sit opposite each other while he talked.

'Do you remember when Tom was dying, he spoke of a pact?'

'Yes, I heard about it,' she said, nodding.

'When we were young – that is to say, I was ten, Tom was nine and his brother, Ruari, was eight – Tom got a pig's bladder from the butcher for running some errands. We stuffed it with newspaper and tied it up with string to make a football. It was quite a blowy day and we took it up to the cliff and walked along the top for a while, kicking it about. Anyway, the wind got up and the football was picked up and carried to the far side of the marked path by the cliff edge.' He hesitated and Kate wondered if the memory was so far in the past, he was having trouble recalling the events, or whether it was too painful to relate.

Stag coughed and continued. 'Ruari and I raced to retrieve the football. As we crossed the footpath, the grassy edge on the far side crumbled away. We both went over and landed on a ledge, not too far below. Tom reached down. We put our hands up and he chose mine first. Tom and I locked wrists and he began to pull me up. Then, just as my feet left the ledge and I was scrambling up, the whole thing gave way and Ruari fell. It was where the rock comes out in horizontal layers like steps. He hit his head on the way down and it killed him. I've often wondered if it was my feet pushing down on the ledge that caused it to give way – but how can I know when I didn't feel anything?'

Kate reached out and put a hand on Stag's shoulder.

'Because I was facing the cliff, I didn't see him fall, but I heard his scream. The thing is we both had our hands up and Tom chose mine, which meant his brother died and I lived. I don't know why he took my hand first. He never said, I never asked, and he never blamed me. On that day we made a pact there and then never to say what really happened to protect his mother, who would never have forgiven him for not taking his brother's hand first. We lied and said Ruari fell over and bounced off the ledge. I can still hear that scream as he went down, even the pitch of it. You see now why I make sure Lavinia and the boy are looked after.'

'Tom saved your life.'

'Aye, at the cost of his brother's. I've always felt I had a debt to repay and now my chance has come for…what's the word?'

'Redemption? A way of paying off the debt?'

'Aye. I was going to say deliverance. I've carried the guilt with me ever since. Tom never asked me to bear any responsibility, and he never laid any blame on me, so I suppose I shouldn't feel this way. I can't help it.'

'If you find deliverance, do you think it will help? Is that something you're looking for?'

'I think I'll know I've found it when I stop having the nightmares.'

'Nightmares?'

'I dream I'm falling off a cliff and I hear Ruari's scream. Although I always wake up, I never hit the ground as he did. I think if I can repay this pact, maybe I'll be released from the dream. It doesn't help that Jonty looks a lot like Ruari.'

'You're an honourable man, Stag. I understand what you're doing and it's worthy of you.'

'I've told you because I want you to know the whole story. I've wrestled with how I should look after Lavinia. Tom's words to me were to "see to Lavinia and the boy".'

'He didn't ask you to marry her?'

'No, there's no actual obligation, but everyone expects it. Owen has had words with me and more or less instructed me to ask for her hand at Eastertide. I've never spoken to her of marriage, although I suspect, as time has passed, she has reason to have expectations.'

'Does she care for you?'

'She cares more for the boy than for anyone else. I've struggled with what my commitment should be and recently I've become more confused. When you and I were singing just now, that which I've suspected – that I care more for you than for Lavinia – was made clear to me. Now I'm torn between doing the right thing and following my heart.'

'Do you think Tom would want you to be unhappy?'

Stag considered her words. 'No. I don't think so, but he would put the happiness of his wife and child before my happiness. As he rightly should.'

'I should tell you I could not think of a future for myself based on someone else's unhappiness.'

'You mean Lavinia's?'

'Yes. She has had pain enough this last six months or more. I will confess we'll never be friends, but I wish her no ill.'

'You're saying I should do the right thing and marry her?'

'Not necessarily. Is it possible to be there for her should she need you, without committing to marriage?'

'At first I thought I had to marry her and I reasoned that love would grow with familiarity. Fate has played a cruel trick on me. I've experienced the growth of love through familiarity, but not for her.'

'If there is no obligation to marry her, can you not step back, be like a brother to her and a godfather to Jonty? Much as you are now?'

'I'd been thinking that way more and more. But then Owen told me there's a risk she may be asked to return to England with the next boat on a free passage if she doesn't have a husband.'

Kate wondered if this was just a trumped-up idea to put pressure on him by Lavinia's family. 'That would be dreadful for them all. Surely the Company will not insist on her returning? Are you sure?'

'It's possible they could send her back.'

'You could ask Mr Hollett.'

'That may run the risk of planting the idea in his head.'

'I hadn't thought of that. But to return to your own predicament, you said Tom wouldn't want you to be unhappy.'

'But neither would he want Lavinia separated from her parents and Jonty from his grandparents. I have to ask, could you see a future for us if it didn't cause unhappiness to Lavinia? I'm assuming you've feelings for me, as I do for you.'

'Yes, I have feelings for you. If I allow them to grow with the risk they cannot be reciprocated then I'm setting myself up for a road to misery along which there will be much pain. Please don't ask me for a commitment on those terms. I couldn't stand it. Let us see what the future brings. I have Mother to think of and the boys. There is much in our way.'

'Have I overstepped?'

'No, no, not at all, we've much in common despite our different backgrounds. Not least a shared interest in helping Colville grow and develop – you with the opening of the mines and your plans for a store, myself educating the next generation. You've opened your heart to me, explaining the pact, and I have much admiration for you. You know, sometimes things have a way of working out, and in the way we least expect.'

Stag touched her cheek, all the while staring deep into her eyes. Kate had to look away, the emotion emanating from him was so intense. Her senses were sharpened by his touch. He made her feel more alive. She wanted to run out into the street to shout out that she loved him so everyone would know.

Later, reliving the moment, she remembered how much she'd wanted him to touch her. She was ready to be loved. How different it could all have been if Tom had not died.

CHAPTER THIRTY-ONE

Inside the schoolhouse Kate was tidying up, straightening benches, and gathering up dip pens and ink pots to put on a tray. A stack of slates was balanced precariously on the edge of her table. Mothers were arriving outside to collect their children, standing around in small groups, gossiping. There had been a slight hold-up when the youngest Wilson daughter couldn't remember where she'd left her bonnet, but Kate had soon found it, and Miss Betsy, after grumbling to her charges about the windy weather, set off, leaving Kate alone.

With everyone gone, a welcome peace descended on the classroom. When the door opened, she expected it to be a child who had forgotten something. She looked up and was startled to see Lavinia – the last person she expected to see.

'What brings you up here on such a blustery day?' she asked.

'I've need to talk with you.'

Kate walked forward to meet her, feeling uneasy. 'What about?'

'About you and Stag.' Lavinia's face was giving nothing away.

Kate put the ink pot tray to one side. 'What can you have to say about Stag and me?' Her unease was growing.

'You probably noticed at the opening I wasn't very happy seeing you and Stag singing together.'

Kate said nothing. However she answered, it was going to trap her into something, although quite what she wasn't yet sure.

'You two clearly have a special connection – perhaps even an understanding, and this troubles me. For you and for Colville.'

'Why?'

'Because there's something about Stag you don't know.'

'What's that?'

'He's a thief.'

Kate drew in a quick breath. Surely that couldn't be? All she could say was, 'Stag?'

'Aye. He was involved in a robbery just before we left.'

'There must be a mistake.'

'The manager of the offices was badly beaten with a shillelagh – beaten so badly the police called it attempted murder.'

'Are you sure Stag was involved?'

'Well, his bait tin was left there, by the safe. It's got his grandfather's initials on it and the name of his farm.'

Kate's fingers were curled so tightly her nails were digging into her palms. 'What does Stag say?'

'He told Tom he'd lost it, but it does look peculiar that he left Whitehaven in a hurry the week of the robbery. He said he went to Liverpool, but what's to say he didn't lay low somewhere, carry out the robbery, then head off to Liverpool so he could get on the ship and make off with the money? They could have worked it all out.'

'They? What they?'

'I don't know who the others are, but there were three of them.'

'Stag doesn't look as if he has any money.'

'He won't, they didn't get any. The safe was empty.'

A thousand questions were flooding into Kate's head. She reeled with what the repercussions might be. 'Why hasn't anyone else mentioned this?'

'The robbery was the talk of steerage for the first couple of days, and you weren't down there, were you? Only Tom knew the bait tin was Stag's and he wasn't going to shop him. No one other than me – and now you – know he was involved.'

'How do you know all this?'

'Tom told me and swore me to secrecy. My advice to you is to ask Stag 'bout it. See what he's to say.'

'Why have you told me?'

'Wouldn't look good for a schoolteacher to be married to a common thief, would it? I'm just trying to help you before things go too far.'

And if you hadn't told me no one apart from you would know, thought Kate. 'I want you to leave.'

Lavinia pursed her lips. Kate got the impression she was trying to suppress a laugh.

'I'm going. Jonty'll be wondering where I've gone. Like I say, see if Stag's got owt to say on this.'

After she'd gone, Kate sat completely still. Too much was going on inside her head for her to be capable of moving. If it was true, the news was going to affect everything she'd striven for. Lavinia was right – as a schoolteacher she couldn't associate with a man who was a thief, never mind have an understanding with him. However, it wasn't just that he'd committed a crime. If he was dishonest, how could she personally ever trust him over anything he said or did?

Her eyes fell on an ink stain on the side of one of the desks. It was a fresh one, for had she noticed it before, she would have dealt with it immediately. It was in the shape of an upturned triangle, wide at the top, culminating in a sharp point at the bottom where the ink had run out of momentum. Was her association with Stag going to be like that? A promising beginning ending in a single speck, followed by nothing? Her eyes remained fixed on it as her brain struggled to make sense of the shattering news.

She had to speak with him; she knew that. She also knew doing so was probably going to change everything. There had to be some truth in it, Lavinia couldn't have made it up, she'd know Kate would ask Stag. The things that made her happy – being with Stag, discussing things with him, perhaps having a future with him – were all going to slip out of her grasp. She put her head in her hands and wept.

✶ ✶ ✶

Stag was on his way home from his stint at the mine when he saw Kate waiting for him at the junction of Main and Harbour Streets. He noticed immediately that she seemed tense, and there was no welcoming smile.

'Is something wrong?'

'Lavinia came to see me.'

'What did she have to say?' Stag trawled through his recent associations with Lavinia. Nothing obvious came to mind.

'She says you were involved in a robbery.'

Stag gasped; he hadn't anticipated anything as vicious as this. 'No, that's not right. It's all flim-flam. It's true there was a robbery, but I was in Liverpool.'

'She said you could have been laying low, been part of the robbery and then gone to Liverpool. That you were planning to emigrate with the proceeds.'

'That's make-believe. I did go to Liverpool on the Monday, and I stayed in a guest house until Saturday. People saw me there. The robbery was on the Wednesday.'

'Then why was your bait tin left by the safe?'

'She told you that, did she? I lost it a few weeks before I left. It must've been found – or more likely stolen – and left there to make it look as if I was part of the robbery.' Even as the words came out of his mouth, Stag knew they sounded weak. How could he prove he'd been in Liverpool? No one on the ship saw him there during the week. It was, in fact, quite possible for him to have been in Whitehaven, or Cockermu'th even, return for the robbery and then leave for Liverpool with no one seeing him. There was no doubt it looked odd that he'd left earlier than the others. He could've been planning on emigrating to get away with stolen money.

'Who would want to incriminate you?'

If he told her about Stevens and the other two, it'd prove he knew about the robbery in advance. Then she'd think he should've done something to stop it, especially since Dolan was so badly injured. There was nowhere for him to turn.

He lied. 'I don't know. Don't you believe me?' He didn't need to hear her answer – he could see the doubt in her eyes.

'I don't know what to believe.'

'You're worried about being seen with a thief? Your reputation as the schoolteacher? You needn't be. I'm not a thief, I just can't prove it right now. Maybe when the next boat comes there'll be news that'll clear me.' Stag could see he was fighting a battle he couldn't win; the warmth he was used to seeing springing from her face and body was no longer there. In its place was confusion and doubt. She'd put up a barrier and he didn't have the ammunition to break it down.

'I want to believe you, but...'

'But you can't take the chance.' Why would Lavinia do this? he asked himself. Surely she must realise this alienated him from her.

'You're right,' he said, 'about what you said yesterday. Things do have a way of sorting themselves out and most definitely not in the way we expect.'

She looked puzzled.

'Ask yourself why Lavinia would do this.'

'She said it was to stop me making a mistake. That I needed to know.'

'For your standing in the community and the good of Colville?'

'Well, not exactly, but my standing in the community is something this would affect.'

'Only if I'm guilty, which I'm not.' He had raised his voice when he hadn't meant to. 'She told you to put a barrier between us.'

'I know it was our duet at the school opening that caused her to say something. She said she thought we looked as if we had an understanding and that I needed to know before things went too far.'

'As I thought. She was jealous, don't you see?'

'Yes, I think you're right, but knowing that doesn't mend anything between us, does it? It *is* something I should be aware of.'

'If it were true, then aye, she'd be right to tell you.'

'She must think it true.'

'Perhaps, but she's never said anything to me, or asked me about it. I didn't know Tom had told her about my grandfather's bait tin. If I could only prove I was in Liverpool.'

'Yes, if only, but you can't.' Kate turned to walk away. Her message was clear. 'I'm sorry, Stag,' she said. 'I really am. It's best we have some time apart.'

'Please keep this to yourself. I don't know how I'm going to do it, but somehow I'll prove I was in Liverpool.'

'Don't fret. This is hardly something I want to talk to anyone about.'

When her mother came home from walking the boys, Kate pleaded a headache and said she wanted to rest in her room. At supper she could hardly eat a thing and with Hannah remarking how pale she looked, she took refuge in her headache and retired to bed early.

* * *

Stag trudged back towards the men's hostel, head down, shoulders hunched. Why would Lavinia do such a thing, when he was watching over her and her child? Did she really believe he was a thief? She must surely realise that bringing up the robbery, without ever having talked to him about it or given him a chance to clear his name with her, made no sense. It was a terrible breach of trust that gave him a valid excuse not to marry her – but at what cost? She'd certainly put a stop to any future for him with Kate. Was she really so jealous that she would forfeit a possible marriage with him just to obtain some sort of revenge? He would ask her; he would confront her. He changed direction.

Lavinia was sewing when Stag arrived. An untidy pile of linen lay on the floor beside her open workbox. Jonty was sitting at her feet, playing with some laundry pegs.

'I've been expecting you,' she said.

'Did Tom think I was a thief?' He had already decided he would get straight to the point. His voice had a sharp edge to it. He was trying to appear calm whilst raging inside.

'No. I don't think he could allow himself to think that. He was very loyal to you.'

'That's no answer. Do you think I'm a thief?' His voice had grown louder.

'I'd like to think not, but facts is facts.'

'Have you told anyone else about the bait tin?'

'No. I told Kate to stop her making a mistake.'

'That's not true.' He was almost shouting. Jonty looked up at him, his face crumpled, and he held his arms out to his mother to be picked up. 'You told her because you didn't want us to be happy. You just wanted to put a sneck in our wheel. You've never liked her since the moment you set eyes on her on the quay in Liverpool.' He paused for Lavinia to settle Jonty on her knee and waited for her to deny it. He hadn't meant to upset the boy. He continued in a softer voice, although he was no less agitated. 'Do you know what happened when Tom and I made the pact?'

'No, he never said owt about it. First I heard was when he was dying.'

'The details are of no matter to you. He saved my life. I owe him. Let me tell you, if you so much as spill one word about the bait tin to anyone else, or imply I'd anything to do with the robbery, I'll consider breaking my pact with Tom. I'll not look out for you and Jonty. You'll be on your own. Not because I want to hide my guilt. Oh, no. It's because I'm innocent.'

'Please don't talk this way, Stag.'

'You didn't think it through, did you? You just wanted to see the look on her face and tip up the apple cart. Well, I hope it was worth it, Lavinia, I really do, for we all have a high price to pay.'

He bent down to make sure Jonty had recovered from his distress then turned and walked out. He met Owen outside. He nodded and carried on.

Back at the hostel, Stag wondered if Tom had told her he'd left Whitehaven early specifically to be in Liverpool when, or if, the robbery took place, and to get away from Stevens' threats. If so, it proved he knew about the robbery – although knowing and taking part were very different. He thought Tom must have kept that information to himself or she would have said something. Perhaps he'd thought it too incriminating, and information that could so easily be misinterpreted.

CHAPTER THIRTY-TWO

Queenie called a meeting in the Community Hall for all the women. When Kate arrived, ten minutes late, Queenie was in full flow.

'Look at this.' She put her hand into a large box and brought out various pieces of fabric. 'The new storekeeper has donated this to us, and he says there's another box if we want it. We want it, don't we?'

'Why is he giving it to us?' asked the fiddler's wife. 'The old one would never have done anything like this. He'd have sold it all on the side.'

'Mr Wilson told him to. He found some boxes full of offcuts in the store room.'

Ah, thought Kate, *this is Mr Wilson's way of making amends for the cheating. It's a clever idea.*

'What do they want us to do with it?'

Queenie stood up and pointed to the wall behind her. 'Don't you think that wall is crying out for decoration?'

There was some murmuring. Then Lavinia spoke up. 'Come on, Ma, tell them.'

'The truth is, Mr Wilson thought we might like to make a quilt. A memorial quilt.'

'In memory of who?' asked Kate.

'Oh no, that's not right. I meant a commemoration quilt, to hang up.'

'Commemorating our arrival,' said Lavinia. 'A settlers' quilt.'

'You mean we each do a bit, then stick it all together and hang it up?' said the fiddler's wife.

'Aye,' said Queenie.

'We could put our names on and the date we arrived,' said Hannah. 'I think it's a wonderful idea.'

Kate was delighted to see her mother express enthusiasm. She hadn't seen her so animated since before her father's death.

'Some of us don't have the time for anything like that,' said one of the Brierley Hill women.

'We could make a special time. For instance, on a Sunday afternoon for an hour, or maybe a bit longer. We can bring the bairns and they can play, and we can sew and chat. Will they let us store the fabric here do you think, Kate?'

'We can ask,' said Hannah. 'That's a good idea.'

'It'll take a while to make,' said Evie.

Queenie began pulling more fabric from the box. 'It'll take as long as it takes. Let's take a vote. All those in favour of the idea of a quilt. You're not voting to take part, just whether it's a good idea or not.'

Everyone except two of the Brierley Hill women put their hands up.

'Right, the idea is passed.'

'If we don't want to do the community quilt, can we still have some of the bits? After all, it's for all of us, isn't it?' It was the fiddler's wife.

Displeasure showed on Queenie's face. *There's always someone who has to be different and make things difficult*, thought Kate.

'I'm just asking. There's more isn't there?'

'I'm sure we can sort something out. Let's move on for now,' said Queenie.

Evie put her hand up. 'I'd like to help with the memorial quilt and with –'

'Commemoration quilt,' corrected Queenie.

'Yes, I mean commemoration, but what I really want is to make a cot quilt.'

There was an awkward silence. Kate looked around and suddenly everyone was either looking at the floor, or at the walls or inspecting their nails. They all knew that Evie had lost two more bairns after the still birth and that all she wanted was a bairn of her own.

'I'm sure there'll be enough for that,' said Queenie. 'Now, let's agree on a time for our commemoration quilt.'

Kate wanted to tell her it was a commemorative quilt, not a commemoration one, but didn't want to correct her in public.

✳ ✳ ✳

The following week, Dr MacDonald invited the McAvoys for afternoon tea in his rooms at the men's hostel. Kate had visited his surgery with the boys when Seamus had earache soon after they'd arrived, but this was the first time any of them had visited his private quarters.

They were shown into a warm, spacious and comfortably furnished room. It seemed he'd brought several items with him. In pride of place was an old walnut desk over which were strewn piles of books. A small area had been cleared for a silver tray holding several short-stemmed glasses, and a decanter that looked as if it was filled with whisky.

After greeting them Dr MacDonald made tea, which he served in bone china cups, after giving the boys a glass of lemonade each.

'Such delicate cups, Dr MacDonald,' said Hannah.

'I brought them with me. They were my mother's.'

Kate wasn't surprised; she'd always thought him a man interested in history and tradition.

'Did you bring the desk with you?' asked Hannah.

'Yes, indeed I did. That desk was my father's. He was also a doctor and saw many patients while sitting at it. I've chosen to keep it as my reading desk.'

'Is your father still alive?' Hannah asked.

'Oh no, he is long gone, and my mother a few years after him.'

Kate wondered if the doctor was lonely. He didn't seem to have any male friends. He wasn't like the other Company men, and the miners and carpenters regarded him with awe. It was early days, and although Dr MacDonald was probably fifteen years or so older than her mother, Kate again hoped they would continue to have a strong friendship. It need not be more, although perhaps in time it would lead to something stronger, and

– with no disrespect to her father's memory – that would be a good thing. She was sure of that. He was kind, and that was what her mother needed: kindness.

Dr MacDonald removed two books from a bookcase.

'Here you are, Seamus, an illustrated book of European birds, and for you, Bartley, an illustrated book of Scottish wildlife.'

The boys' eyes lit up.

'If you're quiet and behave well I'll let you take the books home with you. You can think of me as your library. I'm sure your mama and sister have taught you how to look after books.'

'Oh, yes,' said Seamus. 'Always take them from the bookcase by the spine; never put your finger on the top and pull them out that way.'

Kate looked at Bartley. 'And what else?'

'Never, ever turn the pages over at the top.'

'I see you have them well trained,' said the doctor. He turned to face her. 'Stag called to see me the other day.'

'Is he ill?' asked Kate. She hadn't seen him for two weeks since their confrontation. Just the mention of his name gave her a jolt.

'No, it was a social call. If it had been a medical visit, I wouldn't have mentioned it. I put a notice up that I was hoping to begin a lending library with some of my books. He was the first to come along. Well, actually he was the only one to come along. I have a feeling he's going to make a great go of it here. He has such bright, alert eyes. I'm sure he will go far.'

'We used to see him a lot,' said Hannah. 'But since we

moved into the schoolteacher's cabin, we don't see him so much.'

'I miss him,' said Bartley.

'Me too,' said Seamus.

Kate felt her mother was expecting her to say she missed him too, but she wasn't going to. Moving to the schoolteacher's cabin had not only given them more space, it meant she no longer had to see him visiting Lavinia and the Jeffersons all hours of the day. However, just because she no longer saw him didn't mean she didn't want to see him. She didn't even know if he was still visiting their house. He had seemed so cross with Lavinia, maybe he had had an argument with her.

'Kate.'

Her mother's voice brought her out of her reverie.

'I'm telling Dr MacDonald about the quilt.'

'It sounds just what your mother needs. Apart from that, I've always found Sunday afternoons rather tedious. When is your first meeting?'

'This coming Sunday. As it's our first, we're having a tea party with buns and cakes to celebrate.'

'I have to say, colliers' wives are great cooks and bakers, and the colliers themselves will take any excuse for a celebration.' Hannah laughed and Dr MacDonald grinned and raised an eyebrow at Kate, as if to say 'Don't worry about your mama. She'll recover, given time.'

'Well, it all sounds most worthwhile. A community quilt. Such a good idea of Mr Wilson's.'

Yes, thought Kate, *an excellent idea in many ways. Well done, Mr Wilson, you have surpassed yourself and come up in my estimation.*

CHAPTER THIRTY-THREE

From early morning it was apparent it was going to be a bleak Sunday. The air smelled of rain, and the clouds coming in from the west were heavy and dark. The Community Hall was abuzz with activity.

Kate and her mother had been there for a few minutes when Queenie bustled in. 'We should've asked for the schoolhouse. It's not good for the children being in here with the smell of ale from the men's Saturday night grog. I'm right, aren't I? I wasn't sure how many we'd be. Turns out we're eighteen, so we could've fitted in there with room to spare.' She opened a tablecloth and walked towards an empty table.

'Wait a minute.' The fiddler's wife, damp cloth in hand, cut across her path. 'I've to wipe that table down.'

Mumbling something under her breath, Queenie stepped back and began tapping her foot. She shouted across the room. 'Miss McAvoy, there's a box of Evie's oatmeal cakes and some jam by the door. Can you bring it in for me, please? Evie's not coming. She's not feeling very well.'

'Cramps?' asked the fiddler's wife.

Queenie nodded and pulled a face.

Oh no, thought Kate. *Surely not again, so soon? Poor Evie.* At the door she met Lavinia, with Jonty on her hip. He was clutching a small, bright red wooden canoe that Stag had bought him, one of the toys Billy Botcher had made on the ship. Lavinia looked as if she was about to say something, but Kate picked up the box of biscuits and the jam and turned away.

Queenie arranged the tablecloth and opened her arms to signal she would take the boy, who was sucking two fingers. Lavinia passed him over to her mother.

'He wouldn't go down for his nap, so I thought I'd come early and bring him.'

'You'll want a sleep now, won't you, my bonny lad?' Queenie beamed at Jonty with grandmotherly pride. Right on cue, the boy produced a huge yawn.

Dr MacDonald had arrived and was pinning another sign about his library to the noticeboard. 'You can make a little bed for him in the storeroom,' he said. 'It's the door on the left as you come in. It will be peaceful for him there. It's warm, and you can keep looking in to check on him. There are some Company trading blankets in the cupboard in case the boiler breaks. You can make a bed with those.' The doctor gathered up his papers. 'I hope you enjoy your afternoon, ladies.'

'Thank you,' said Lavinia, as he made for the door. 'Stag's coming by later to collect him. He'll entertain him.' She began filling plates with Evie's oatmeal cakes.

Despite the distractions, Jonty's head was beginning to flop and his eyelids to droop. The warmth of the room was increasing his drowsiness.

'He'll have to go down. I'll take him,' said Queenie. 'Then I'm needed, aren't I? I can't stand here all afternoon and cuddle when there's work to be done.'

With Queenie pronouncing Jonty comfortable, and the other children settled in a corner with some crayons and paper, the women put their chairs in a circle.

'It's my view we should have someone in charge,' said Queenie. 'And I put myself forward.'

'What about Mrs McAvoy?' said the fiddler's wife. Queenie wrinkled her nose.

Kate waited for her mother to decline the proposal and was pleasantly surprised when she didn't.

'Anyone else want to be in charge?' asked Queenie. When no one came forward, she asked, 'Shall we have a secret ballot?'

That's Owen's mine-manager's voice talking, thought Kate.

There was a general consensus that there was no need for secrecy and that a show of hands would suffice. Queenie counted the votes. Then her shoulders sagged and she looked at the floor.

'That's ten for Mrs McAvoy and eight for me. Mrs McAvoy it is, then. Isn't it?'

Kate wondered if her mother had really thought through the amount of work the project would involve. It would be good to have her occupied with something to think about, but the last thing she needed was for it all to go wrong and to get caught up in it.

Hannah put her hand up. 'Ladies, I have an idea. My skills lie with organisation. May I suggest that Queenie sorts out the actual making of the quilt, the design, sorts the material, and that kind of thing, and I organise the meetings, keep track of where the materials are stored and, if necessary, be the spokesman should we require more fabric or need support from the Company in any way.'

Queenie beamed. Looking around, Kate saw the other women were nodding in agreement. It was the perfect solution. Certainly, her mother was a good organiser and much more likely to obtain results from any Company interaction than Queenie. Queenie knew the women better than her mother, so she could marshal them more easily if enthusiasm waned.

Everything settled, Queenie emptied one of the fabric boxes in the centre of the circle so they could see the colours and types of material. There were now two additional boxes. Kate guessed Mr Wilson had either added more pieces to the Colville offcut box or had asked the new storekeeper to bring pieces from his last position, which had been Fort Langley.

'Let's spend ten minutes or so sorting the materials,' suggested Queenie. 'I think by colour rather than texture first. We can sort things further when we have a design.'

'Who's going to do the design?' asked Kate.

'I'd like to suggest something,' said Hannah. 'Let's have a competition. We'll ask Dr MacDonald, Mr Wilson and Mr Hollett to choose a winner. How about that?'

'Can anyone enter?' asked one of the Brierley Hill women.

'I would suggest anyone. Even children, if they want to.'

They were just putting the piles of material to one side when Stag arrived. Kate felt her heart sink to her boots. Lavinia rushed forward to greet him.

'Jonty's in the little store room. By the main door.'

A few moments later, Stag returned and began looking around the room at the women setting out the tea things and the children running about.

Lavinia looked at him as if she thought he was stupid. 'He's not in here. I told you, he's in the store room.'

'No, he's not,' said Stag. 'I've just been in and he's not there.'

Lavinia frowned. 'He must be; he'll be under the blankets.' She pushed her way through several groups of people and left the room. She returned almost immediately, her face bright red. 'He's not here. He's gone.'

Despite still being angry with her and barely on speaking terms, Kate immediately caught Lavinia's anxiety. She watched her looking around the room, putting her hand to her throat, eyes wide, and felt suddenly cold, despite the warmth of the room.

Lavinia began calling, 'Jonty, Jonty, where are you?'

Apart from her voice, the room fell silent as everyone stopped what they were doing and began looking under tables and in foolish places where a child could not possibly be. Kate assumed they did this because it gave them something to do. Queenie was white-faced. Unable to do anything, she was propelled to a chair.

Kate crouched beside her, holding her hand.

'It'll be all right, Queenie,' she said. 'Just you see.'

Queenie, always ready to chat and ask her questions, was for once lost for words.

Stag voiced what everyone else in the room was thinking. 'Someone must've taken him. Someone fetch Dr MacDonald and anyone else in the men's hostel.'

'Maybe he's wandered off,' said Kate, trying to be positive, although she knew an unsupervised child could quickly fall foul of danger.

'Don't be stupid,' said Lavinia. 'He's still only crawling. Someone's taken him.'

As if hearing the words aloud made the situation real, some of the women began sobbing.

Men began arriving. No one had seen him on the way to the hall. Mr Wilson, looking pale, was briefed on the disappearance.

'Are you sure he's not here?' he asked.

Mr Hollett said, 'Quite sure. He's gone. I've checked the surrounding area. I'll organise search parties.' He picked up his knife and used the handle as a gavel to bring the room to silence. 'You, you and you.' He pointed to three of the Brierley Hill miners. 'Up to Millstream Creek to the sawmill. Search it thoroughly.' To another three he said, 'You, you and you, to the mine. Listen as well as look. You may hear him crying. Everyone meets back here to report to Mr Wilson.'

At this, Lavinia burst into agonised sobs.

'Stag, Sam and I will search the route down to the harbour and the lumber dock. Everyone else fan out and keep looking. Women and children, return to your homes until we know there's no immediate danger.'

As he was leaving, Mr Hollett called to Kate. In shock, he'd forgotten the first thing he should have ordered. 'Run down to the store and get the storekeeper to ring the bastion bell.'

CHAPTER THIRTY-FOUR

The new storekeeper was undoing his apron and about to close the store when Kate arrived. He rang the bastion bell straightaway then checked the immediate store area and the Company offices. There was no sign of the boy. Despite the rain easing off, it was still wet and soggy underfoot.

Her message successfully delivered and the area around the bastion clear, Kate wasn't sure what to do. She walked down to the harbour, thinking she would meet up with Mr Hollett, Stag and Sam and see if she could aid them in any way. She could see no point in going home to sit it out with her mother and the boys. When she was within sight of the harbour, she saw Stag and Sam at the coal wharf checking the quay. Mr Hollett was talking to the crew of a San Francisco barque engaged in loading coal. She looked to her left to the lumber dock where there was a small shed with an overhanging roof. Perfect for shelter from the drizzle. She began walking towards it.

She heard her before she saw her. Evie had Jonty on her knee and she was singing. Kate advanced cautiously and began speaking in what she hoped was a calm unthreatening voice.

'Hello, Evie,' she said. 'What are you doing here in this drizzle? You'll get wet.'

Evie smiled and gave Jonty a piece of gingerbread. He appeared to be unperturbed and was dry. 'My lad likes to see the boats. Look, he's got one of his own.' She pointed to the red canoe Jonty was clutching in his fist.

'Evie, you're making a mistake. He's not your lad, he's Lavinia and Tom's. You remember, don't you?' Kate ruffled Jonty's hair. The boy giggled.

'I love him more than she does. When I arrived at the hall, he was sobbing his little heart out and no one was with him. His father's dead, you know. Sam'll make a good father.'

'And you'll make a good mother when you've a baby of your own.'

Evie was in her own world. She was alarmingly serene. 'God won't let me be a mother, you know. I'm a geld wife.'

'A geld wife?'

'That's what women like me are called in Cumberland. I'm a wife that can't have children. I must be a bad person.' Evie started humming.

'No, Evie, that's not true. You're not a bad person, you're just not well now. You'll get better, I'm sure of that, and when you're well again, you'll have lots of children.'

'You don't know about losing bairns.'

'Not myself, but have you wondered why there are so many years between myself and my brothers?'

'No.' Evie looked at Kate with sudden interest.

I must keep her engaged, thought Kate. *Keep her talking.* 'My mother, Mrs McAvoy. Hannah. You know her? You know her very well, don't you?'

Evie nodded.

'She lost several babies between me and Seamus.'

'That's not the same. That was her, not you.'

'No, but I saw her pain and shared it with her, each time. I'm thinking you've pain like she had inside you now.'

'Aye, I've a lot of pain right now. Every time I get a lot of pain, but I never get a bairn for it.'

'Have you thought that Lavinia's feeling pain now, when she doesn't know where Jonty is? She's worried about him, and soon Jonty will be wanting his mother.'

'I don't want to think about her. She left him in that store room to cry.'

Kate looked up at the sky. 'It's clearing up. Let's show Jonty the canoes in the harbour.' She put out a hand.

Evie's face brightened. 'Do you think he'll like that?' She took a comb from her pocket and combed Jonty's hair.

'I'm sure he will. Shall we go and see the boats, Jonty?' The boy looked at Kate, then back at Evie, before stretching his hand out for more gingerbread.

'Aye, I think he'll like that.' Evie stood up, settling Jonty on her hip.

As they began walking alongside the dock, Kate could see Stag, Sam and Mr Hollett in the distance. She wanted to signal, but thought it might distress Evie and make her fearful.

Mr Hollett was the first to see them. He set off running, with Stag and Sam calling to the crew of the barque to follow.

Evie stopped and began looking from side to side. 'They're coming for him. Where can I go?'

'They're going to take Jonty home. They're not going to hurt you or him. It's time for his milk and his nap.'

'No!' Evie transferred Jonty to her other hip and, before Kate could stop her, she stepped off the side of the dock onto a log boom. The logs responded to their weight and realigned themselves in the water. Evie shifted to fall in with the motion. When the men drew close, she called out, 'Play me a tune, Stag, we want to dance.' She used the tip of each clog to pull off the other and, standing barefoot for a better grip, began moving from side to side as if swaying to music. The logs responded in the water, matching her rhythm, and the clogs bobbed up and down with the logs.

Stag took out his mouth organ. 'I'll play you a tune, Evie, but I need to come a little closer, or the wind'll carry it away.'

Jonty began fighting against Evie's tight hold, moving his legs up and down. He knew Stag very well, but Mr Hollett and Sam were almost strangers. With the men's faces all showing alarm, it was no wonder he was becoming restless.

Stag began to play *Greensleeves*. Evie smiled and began moving in time to the music. To her horror, Kate saw the logs begin to separate.

Jonty wriggled and fought for release from Evie's arms. His face was puce with rage and his chubby legs beat against her body. Stag stepped onto the boom, easing his right foot forward, aiming to keep the logs steady. Evie scrutinised him as he inched forward, all the while playing his mouth organ. As Mr Hollett made to follow him, Evie, without looking directly at him, screeched, 'No, not you.'

He took a step backwards.

Stag stopped playing and put out a hand. 'Evie, Jonty will fall in the water. It's too cold for him.'

'He won't. I'm holding him tightly.'

'He's upset. He's crying,' said Kate, wondering how close Evie was going to let Stag get to her. If they fell in the water, they would freeze in a minute.

Evie began singing again, seemingly oblivious to Jonty's distress. Stag moved closer, but she took a step back. He shouted to Mr Hollett and Sam, standing by. 'Get the doctor! We're going to need him!'

'She's not going to come off,' said Sam to Mr Hollett, after a man had been sent running. He looked up at the sky. Then in a louder voice, so Evie could hear, he said, 'The rain's coming in again too.'

'Did you hear that, Evie?' asked Stag. 'It's going to rain again and Jonty's frightened already. You don't want him to get cold and wet, do you? Look at those clouds.' He looked purposefully over her shoulder.

Evie turned her head to follow his gaze, and he seized the moment. Taking two steps forward, he reached out and took hold of the boy. Evie screamed in frustration as Jonty was wrenched from her grasp and the logs began dancing to their own discordant tune. With his upper body projected forward, and the boy's additional weight unsettling him, Stag fell, crashing down onto the logs, his knees taking the full force of the impact. His mouth organ bounced off into the water. He grimaced with the pain but managed to keep hold of the struggling boy, whose whole body was juddering as he screamed. The effort was not without a price; Stag could feel the rough irregularities of the bark against his knees and the pointed splinters burrowing in. The thick breeches that might have afforded him some protection split on impact, thus his flesh was rubbing directly on wood.

The only thing Stag could do was throw the boy the few feet to Mr Hollett. He couldn't risk slipping and pitching him into the water. But would Mr Hollett catch him? And would the boy's wriggling swerve him off to one side? He decided the risk of injury was worth it and by adjusting his hold on the child he managed to get a firm grasp of his hips. Although he knew it was going to cause him pain, he twisted his body round, so he had a better angle and, all the while looking straight into Mr Hollett's eyes, he pitched the boy towards his open arms. He held his breath. It was as if time stood still. It was an awkward catch, but Mr Hollett managed it and passed Jonty to Kate. Despite his terror and screaming, the lad's fingers were still clasped around the little red canoe, as if it was a talisman. Stag turned back to retrieve Evie. It was even harder on his knees than standing had been. His blood mingled with the saps and fluids of the slippery surface, but he knew if he tried to stand, his footing would be even less secure than before.

He began to ease forward and, just as he put his hand out to grasp Evie's skirt, her foot slid out from under her, and she went down. Stag stretched out and managed to grab her wrist as she fell through the gap where the logs had separated.

'The weight of her clothes is pulling her down,' he shouted.

'His arm's gone into the water with her,' gasped Kate, her eyes fixed on the horrific scene unfolding in front of her.

'Can you keep hold of her?' cried Mr Hollett.

'I won't let go,' Stag shouted. 'Tom didn't and I won't.'

'What's he talking about?' asked Sam.

'It's all right,' said Kate. 'It's something important from his past. He's all right.'

'Look,' came a voice in the crowd, which was growing bigger as each second passed. 'The logs have closed. Stag's arm's trapped!'

'And she's right under!' added another voice.

The nerves and muscles in Stag's arm were screaming. Tears of pain rolled down his face. He gritted his teeth, telling himself he must not let go, he could not let go, he would not allow himself to let go. He could feel Evie thrashing about in the water under the surface.

On the dock people were rocking from side to side, calling out offering help, while others were standing silently in shock, clasping their neighbours' hands. Several women were twisting their skirt sides. All sported anxious faces. Sam shouted for Evie, and rushed to grab a log hook from a nearby pile, but they were tied together with thick rope. Mr Hollett leapt forward, cutting the tie with his hunting knife, and the hooks tumbled onto the gravel in an untidy sprawl. Sam seized one and, stepping onto the logs, began trying to separate them.

'The angle's wrong. I can't do it!' The logs dipped below the surface and freezing cold water washed over his feet. Dropping to his knees, he shouted, 'If Evie's in this water much longer she'll die, even if we get her out.'

He pushed again with the hook. This time the angle was better, and a small gap appeared between the logs, but it wasn't enough. It did, however, show them that with the right angle and strength, the logs could be separated. Catching a hook expertly thrown to him by one of the crewmen, Mr Hollett began stabbing an opposing log. Unifying their strength and working in tandem, Mr Hollett and Sam were able to open the logs wide enough for them to reach Evie. Stag could feel nothing in his arm, although whether it was from nerve damage or the anaesthetising effect of the cold water, he wasn't sure. He held on through sheer willpower, despite Evie becoming heavier every second. He was now aware she'd stopped thrashing about.

'Here, catch this.' Frank Richardson threw a small spar to Sam. 'Lodge it between the two logs, then you can wedge the gap open.'

'Can you get her?' Stag's voice quavered.

'I've got her,' said Mr Hollett.

Sam put his hand down into the water. 'And I've got her.'

They pulled, and Evie came up ramrod straight. For someone so slight of build, she seemed a dead weight of unbelievable mass.

'Is she breathing?' asked Sam.

No one answered. The crowd, growing with every second, was now silent apart from a few women's sobs.

As the water gave Evie up, her bare feet caught the spar wedge and, in turn, it knocked her clogs off the boom. The water swallowed them up as if exacting payment for her release. Stag, pale-faced with blood dripping from his arm, watched as Sam and Mr Hollett struggled to manoeuvre Evie off the boom. As they neared the edge of the dock, several onlookers came forward to help lift her. They laid her on the ground. People began taking off their coats for blankets. Her face bore the mask of death and the sodden strands of hair plastered to her cheeks created a macabre frame.

Mr Hollett put his ear to Evie's mouth, then a hand on her chest, but there was nothing. He felt for a pulse in her neck then shouted, 'Where's the doc?'

'I can see him running. He'll be here soon,' said Kate.

'Turn her on her side,' someone shouted. 'Turn her on her side to get the water out.'

When she was returned to her back, Mr Hollett began pressing on her chest and lifting her arms. 'I saw them do this at school a long time ago,' he said, uncertainty in his voice.

'I'll rub her feet,' said one of the Brierley Hill wives. Stag remembered stories about women putting hot bricks on the feet of miners with choke damp, in fruitless efforts to revive them. Other women laid their coats over Evie's legs.

'It seems forever since she went under,' said Sam.

'It's not that long,' said Kate. 'There's hope. We must pray.'

'Aye, everyone, pray, pray!' shouted Sam.

Some of the onlookers began praying silently, others mumbled and put their hands together, all fearing the worst.

Lavinia came running, followed by Queenie, eyes red from crying, her hands clutched to her chest. Lavinia scooped Jonty up from Kate's arms and Queenie, now laughing uncontrollably, put her arms around them both.

'Thank you, thank you,' Lavinia said.

'He's upset, but he's all right. Stag saved him,' said Kate, adding pointedly, 'Remember that.'

'That looks like Evie,' said Lavinia.

'It is,' said Kate.

'Hush, Lavinia,' Queenie said. 'You've got Jonty back and that's what matters right now.'

Lavinia opened her mouth to protest, but the look her mother gave her caused her to close it again.

The spectators parted as Dr MacDonald ran in to kneel beside the woman on the ground. He leant forward and, putting his fingers inside her mouth, pulled out a thin strand of green weed. He tilted her head back so her chin pointed upwards, held her nose and began breathing into her mouth. With his free hand, he motioned to Mr Hollett to keep pressing her chest.

Sam rushed forward. 'Evie! Evie!'

Stag held him back. 'Let them do their work, Sam, they know what they're doing.' They stood side by side, Stag praying to God and willing Evie to start spluttering and coughing, but she did not.

After ten minutes, Dr MacDonald motioned to Mr Hollett to stop. 'Thank you,' he said. He got up and made his way towards Sam, who was standing by, tears rolling down his face. Sam bypassed the doctor and went straight to Evie, touching her cheek, before pushing her hair back from her forehead and kissing it. His tears fell onto her motionless face. He put his arms around her, as if to warm her, and partially lifted her up. As she rose in Sam's arms, Stag had to turn away. He couldn't bear to look. He wanted to remember her as she had been, little Evie, always wanting to help others, not as she now was. He heard Sam say, 'My poor Evie. All you ever wanted was a little family of your own to care for.'

'She's got one now,' said Dr MacDonald. 'They've been waiting for her.'

'Yes,' said Sam, his voice heavy with immeasurable grief. 'Yes, she's a mother now.'

Dr MacDonald turned to Stag, whose lower arm was beginning to throb.

'You've at least one broken bone and I see exposed sinews, Stag. Let's get you up to the sick room. You're still numb from the cold water. You'll be needing something for when the pain starts up, which is probably any minute now.' He opened his bag, took out a bottle of laudanum and handed it to him. 'Take a fulsome swig.'

Stag, using his good arm, felt in his pocket for his mouth organ, then remembered he'd lost it.

CHAPTER THIRTY-FIVE

The following day, Kate called in at the hostel's sick room. Stag, looking drawn and exhausted, was propped up, his right arm bandaged from wrist to shoulder.

'Dr MacDonald said I could call.' Seeing Stag's face light up, she wished she could turn the clock back to when they were happy. She handed him a jar of honey. 'This is for you.'

He thanked her and she thought how colourless he looked against the white of the pillows.

'Are you in a lot of pain?' she asked, sitting down on a stool by the bed.

'I'm better than I was last night. When Dr MacDonald was cleaning the wound out and seeing to my knees it was bad, but better than losing the use of my arm or ending up like Hooker. It reminded me of helping the doctor when we went round the Horn, only this time I was the patient. He says it'll heal, but I'll only be fit for light duties. No hewing or loading.'

'Ever?'

'He says it's always going to be weak and it may not set straight, so no heavy lifting, which is a blow. Still, better to have a lame dog than a dead one, I suppose.' He gave a weak smile. 'Mr Hollett called earlier and confirmed they're going to try me in the office on a reduced temporary wage, and if I'm acceptable then I'll be re-contracted. They can manage because they've got new colliers coming in next month.'

'Does that mean no access to bonuses?'

Stag shook his head. 'I've been awake half the night worrying. Everything has changed so quickly.'

There was a light rap on the door and Owen came in. He appeared startled when he saw Kate. He doffed his cap and stood holding it.

'I won't stay. I just wanted to thank you for all you did yesterday. We owe you a thousand thanks. And you, Miss McAvoy, you were the one who found Jonty.'

'No thanks are needed. Jonty is safe and well and that's all that matters.' Kate wondered, briefly, if Owen would think Stag such a good prospect as a son-in-law with no access to bonuses. She could see he was uneasy. He was fiddling with his cap, running his hands over its peak.

'Well, I'll not stay. Lavinia's still in a bad way, you know. I don't like to leave her. It's the shock.'

Stag extended his good hand. 'Before you go, I've a favour to ask you.'

'For sure, whatever it is,' said Owen.

'I lost my mouth organ when I fell on the boom, but I bought a spare when I was in Liverpool, for just such a mishap. Can you bring it? It's in my room.'

'For you, sir, anything.'

After Owen had left, Stag said, 'Well, that was an in-and-out visit.'

They laughed and then an awkwardness descended. Despite his reaction when he first saw her, Kate sensed Stag was uncomfortable with her being there. He'd smiled at her, but not in the open way he used to.

'You're a good man, Stag,' she said. 'What you did yesterday was more than Tom could ever have asked of you from your pact. You saved his son's life. You've delivered yourself from any guilt over his brother's death.'

'Any one of us could have saved the lad. I went forward because Evie asked me to play.'

'No, he'd have been frightened of anyone else. He knows you, he sees you all the time. You were able to get much closer to him than anyone else would have been able to do.'

'We lost Evie. Evie who had her whole life in front of her.'

'I know, but you didn't let her go. It was the water and the cold that killed her. You held on to her, Stag, at great cost to yourself.'

'How's Sam?'

'He's terrible. I think he blames himself. None of us foresaw how upset she was or what she might do. I keep thinking about what we should have done. She wasn't one to talk about her troubles. We all thought she was stronger than she was.'

'You weren't to know. She was such a slip of a lass.' He looked down at his bandages. 'I've paid a heavy price. A gammy arm.'

'I know things seem bleak now,' Kate said. 'But perhaps there's some future there if you step back and think about it. In the office you'll learn how to do accounts, write letters, make connections with people. All the things you need to know to start a business when the time comes. Dr MacDonald says you can lead a normal life and you'll get a lot of the use of your arm back. Think of your future as being above ground now. You can't look back – you'll be taking important steps towards opening your store.'

'It may be above ground, and I'm less likely to be injured now, but I'll not make enough money to start a shop.'

'The way things were going you had to finish your five years with no experience. Most likely you'd have found it hard going. Now, like I say, you've just over four years and then you're going to be released, with all the business and administrative expertise you're ever going to want. If you show yourself capable, which you most definitely are, you'll soon be reading Company letters, making decisions, learning everything. It's likely you'll be promoted within the Company and end up with a better wage and no going underground. Think about it. In the long run this could be the making of you.'

'I can't see Hollett promoting me.'

'I think you'll find he sees you in a different light now. As does everyone. You're the miner who saved Jonty. Hollett will give credit and promotion to a man who deserves it, I'm sure of that. Trust me, you can turn this crisis into an opportunity.'

'I hear what you say.' He held her eyes with his. 'But it's a future without you. I'm not going to marry Lavinia.

I know that now. If it wasn't for the robbery, would we have an understanding?'

Kate looked away. The possibility he was involved in the robbery was just too damning, yet she knew he was right: they were made for each other. If it hadn't been for the cloud hanging over them, she would be telling him how they could save enough money together to open a business, how she would support him in any way she could. How maybe Seamus and Bartley could help him in the store. The Company wasn't always going to have a monopoly, she was sure of that, and she just knew he could succeed.

'I've one regret about being in Liverpool,' he said, when she turned back to look at him.

'What's that?'

'Instead of standing outside the Adelphi Theatre I should have gone inside. I'd have bought a ticket and most likely I'd have kept it as a souvenir. I'd be able to take it out of my pocket and show you I was in Liverpool that Wednesday, the day of the robbery.'

'You were outside the Adelphi? What were you doing?'

'Playing my mouth organ. The maid from the lodging-house came with me to collect the money. She suggested it when she heard me play.'

'Can you remember what you saw there?'

'Aye.'

'Describe it to me.'

'Why?'

'Please, just do it.'

He looked into the distance. 'It's very busy, there's lots

of people. A man in the market where I bought my clothes tells me to watch out for pickpockets.'

'Ah, dippers,' Kate said, laughing. She could see and hear the city's crowds in her own mind. 'What else can you see?'

'Aye, "dippers", that's what he called them. There's a juggler with a big crowd watching him, a tin-whistler and a fiddler. Is this what you want to know?'

'Yes, go on. Tell me more. Where are you playing?'

'We're by the noticeboards. The ones outside that tell you what's on.'

'Who's playing?'

He thought for a moment. 'Er, someone and their wonderful dogs, and some singers. I think they're American singers.' He was still looking into the distance, as if he could actually see it all happening.

'Anything else?'

'There's lots more. The dancing monkey is there with a grubby little ruff around its neck. Is this some kind of test?'

She ignored his question. 'Did you go more than once?'

'Aye. We went together on Wednesday because it was the maid's – Our Mary she was called – it was her afternoon off, and she said it was the best day to go, because it was matinee day. She called it "double day". You can play for the people going in and the people coming out. I went on Thursday and Friday by myself. I needed the brass, I'd had mine stolen.'

'And did you get two crowds?'

'Aye, we did.'

'You really were there, weren't you, that Wednesday?'

'Aye, I told you I was. You sound as if you finally believe me.'

Kate detected a tone of annoyance in his comment and she could understand why. 'I believe you because I know now you're a good man, loyal, brave and true to your word. I should never have doubted you. You proved all those things yesterday. I also believe you because the Adelphi has two matinee days: Saturday and Wednesday. It can't be Saturday – you were on the ship – so, it has to be Wednesday when you were playing your mouth organ in the city. I also believe you because I think I saw you.'

'What?' Stag's face lit up brighter than she had ever seen it.

'Well, not you, but I remember Our Mary. She was holding out her hat saying, "Put your pennies in here. This Cumberland lad's had his purse pinched. Let's show him Liverpool people care." Something like that. I remember because I thought it was a good line, appealing to people's hearts like that.'

'Did you think it was true?'

'Not for one minute, but there was something about her I liked, so I gave her a penny.'

'Do you remember me?'

'No, I didn't pay much attention to the man playing, and his hands were in front of his face holding the mouth organ. I was just passing through. What you're describing is what I saw too. The way you're describing it, I can see it. I can tell by your expression you're reliving it. Your face is alive, your voice is alive; you're recalling it, not making

341

it up. You were there, Stag Liddell, you were there, and I owe you an apology. I'm sorry, truly sorry.' She was smiling and laughing.

'There's no need for that. I understand your doubts. You're my alibi – I never expected that.' His cheeks were flushed, his pupils large and round. He was smiling and laughing back at her. The barrier was breached. Kate put out her hand and he took it, stroking it gently with a light touch while he talked.

He told her about Stevens, Hibbs and Devlin, about losing his bait tin, and how he hadn't shopped them for fear of repercussions for his father. He told her how much he'd regretted that decision since he'd learned of Donal's injury. She listened carefully, without interruption, focusing on his face the whole time with such intensity it was as if she thought if she looked away, he would disappear.

'I'm an honest man. You need never worry I'll let you down. If we're ever in Liverpool I can take you to Mrs Hudley's.'

'I know that,' she said, still smiling.

There was a sharp knock and Dr MacDonald walked in with a book in one hand and a bottle of laudanum in the other.

'Stag's been telling me all about what he was doing in Liverpool,' said Kate.

'An exciting time, I've no doubt,' said Dr MacDonald, looking at their joined hands. 'Would I be hasty in assuming there may be good news for sharing at some date in the future?'

Kate felt herself start to blush and went to withdraw her hand, but Stag kept a tight hold on it.

'If I can give you one piece of advice for the future, it's this: keep no secrets from each other. The truth will always out.'

'Yes, indeed,' said Kate. 'We certainly know that.'

✷ ✷ ✷

Later that afternoon Lavinia visited. 'I still don't know how I can ever thank you, Stag,' she began. 'I know I've already said it, but it's true, and you've been badly hurt in the process.'

'I did what anyone would do.'

'That's not true, but I know my Tom up in heaven will be giving thanks you were on the dock when Jonty needed you. It's as if God made sure you were on hand.'

'I don't know about that. I couldn't save Evie.'

Lavinia's face darkened. 'She kidnapped my son.'

'She wasn't well, Lavinia. It was an accident. She didn't mean to put him in danger; she was desperate and frightened.'

'It was a kidnap, everyone knows that.' She set her lips into a tight line.

'You love Jonty more than anything in the world, I would say.'

'Aye, of course I do. I'm his ma.'

'In that case, you can understand how Evie felt when her stillborn bairn was thrown overboard. Not only did she have a dead baby, but also there was no committal, no chance to say a formal goodbye, no placing him in God's care. It was as if her son never existed. Since then, she's lost another three bairns before they were old enough to take breath. It's no surprise when we think about it that she lost her way, is it?'

'It happens. It happens to lots of lasses and they don't steal other folk's bairns. I tell you she kidnapped him.' Lavinia sucked in her cheeks and let out a sigh.

'But tell me this – you told me when you looked at Jonty after he was born you thought he was perfect.'

'He still is,' she said, smiling.

'Don't you think Evie looked at her bairn and thought he was perfect too?'

'He might have looked it, but he was dead.'

'Think for a moment. For Evie it must have been a bittersweet moment. A perfect child, but he'd never put his arms out to her like Jonty does to you. He'd never call out to her, or smile at her like Jonty smiles at you. I ask you to show some understanding that Evie was sick with grief from her losses.'

'Aye, it must have been hard, and I know she was desperate, but I can't forgive her. She took my Jonty and he could have drowned.'

'For Sam's sake, I'm asking you to have some understanding. He has to live as the husband of the woman who took the baby. Sam has grief enough to bear. They were his bairns too, and it won't help if you keep referring to her as the kidnapper. If you can't do this for yourself, then can you please do it for me?'

Lavinia bit her bottom lip. 'I know it's not his fault, but every time I see him, I'm going to think of her.'

'That will pass, Lavinia, I'm sure of it. Referring to Evie as the kidnapper will only drag things out.'

'I do owe you, I can set store on that, so I'll try. Which reminds me, there is something else I can do for you.'

'What's that?'

'I've thought about it and I can release you from your debt to Tom.'

'Release me?'

'When Tom was dying, he asked you to see to Jonty and me, but there was something more, wasn't there?' He said something about a plan, or a promise, or –'

'A pact. It was a pact.'

'Then I think what I'm doing is releasing you from your pact, whatever that was. By saving Jonty's life, you've paid whatever debt it was you owed Tom.'

'We had the pact and I suppose, aye, you could say I've repaid my debt to Tom, but –'

'I want you to be our friend because you want to be, not because you have to be.'

'We can be friends, Lavinia, and I'll watch Jonty grow with great interest. He's my marrer's boy and always will be. We can be better friends if you do the right thing. You need to be able to stand in front of your looking-glass and know that you see a compassionate woman looking back at you. Show compassion for Evie's memory and in later years, when Jonty learns of all this – which he will – he'll know you showed kindness to someone in distress.'

The door opened and Mr Hollett entered. Lavinia leapt to her feet, all smiles. 'Mr Hollett, how can I thank you? You and Stag are both heroes.'

Mr Hollett gave a short bow and extended his hand to her. 'No, no, we only did what anyone would do. We just happened to be there. However, I have recommended Stag for a Company bravery citation. The papers are on their way to Fort Victoria as we speak, by way of the express canoe.'

Stag drew in breath to express genuine modesty regarding the previous day's events, but Lavinia was in full flow.

'Oh, Mr Hollett, you should have one too. You're a hero to me.'

He straightened his back, lifted his chin and put his hand on his chest. 'I cannot recommend myself. That would never do.'

'I'll do it then – I'll write to the governor saying how you saved my boy.' The intensity of Lavinia's appreciation was causing her to bob up and down. Stag had never seen her so animated.

'Stag was the one who actually saved him.' Mr Hollett turned his attention to Stag, but words of praise were still gushing from Lavinia's lips.

'Mr Hollett, you're *my* hero.'

Suddenly Mr Hollett looked different, standing there lapping up the praise. It seemed to Stag there was no doubt in Charles Hollett Esquire's mind that Mr Charles Hollett, Island Liaison Officer, was indeed a hero. He wanted to laugh out loud. The answer to all their problems was right in front of him: Mr Hollett needed a wife, Lavinia needed a husband.

Stag knew he was on the right track when Mr Hollett gave a quiet cough and said, 'Lavinia – if you will allow me to call you that – it will please me greatly if you will refer to me as Charles in private.'

Lavinia blushed and toyed with a rogue curl that had freed itself from the constraints of her bonnet.

'Yes, of course, Mr Hollett, how gentlemanly of you.'

Mr Hollett laughed and raised an eyebrow, leaving Lavinia momentarily confused until she realised the jest.

'Oh, I mean, Charles, not Mr Hollett.'

They held each other's gaze – Lavinia's eyes bright and shining, Charles looking like the cat that got the cream.

Stag smiled. Lavinia was going to make a perfect Company wife. He wondered briefly if she would become too grand to buy from his store when he achieved his dream. His smile widened. New and promising beginnings for them all, it would seem.

THE END

SELECTED BIBLIOGRAPHY

Primary sources:

Provincial Archives of British Columbia, Victoria, B.C. Canada.

HBC Fort Nanaimo fonds, 1854-1861. Waste Book. (Daily accounts) PR-686

HBC Indenture made with John Thompson, miner, 1854. MS-1138

Leynard, Paul, Pamphlet, *The Coal Mines of Nanaimo*, MS-1983

Nanaimo Community Archives:

The Devlin, Beck family fonds. Maria Devlin. CA NCA1 – 212 Accessed online 2021.

HBC Letter book: correspondence between Joseph McKay (Nanaimo) and James Douglas (Victoria) August 1852 - September 1853, transcribed by Carol Hill 2014. PR-1683. Accessed online 2021.

HBC fonds: Transcription of Joseph McKay's Journal August 24th 1852 - September 27th 1854, transcribed by Carol Hill 2014. PR-1683. Accessed online 2021.

The Devlin Family Archive:

Personal papers, interviews, photographs, and newspaper cuttings.

Secondary sources:

Ackworth, John, *The Clog shop Chronicles,* London: Charles H. Kelly, 1896.

Adams, John, *Old Square Toes and His Lady,* Canada: Touchwood Editions, 2011.

Akrigg, G.P.V. and Akrigg, Helen, B, *British Columbia 1847-1971: Gold and Colonists,* Vancouver: Discovery Press, 1977.

Bell, R. C., ed., *Diaries from the Days of Sail,* London: Carter, Nash, Cameron, 1974.

Bowen, Lynne, *Boss Whistle: The Coal Miners of Vancouver Island Remember,* Lantzville: Oolichan Books, 1982

Bown, Stephen R., *The Company: The Rise and Fall of The Hudson's Bay Empire*, Canada: Doubleday, 2020.

Collier, Sylvia, *Whitehaven, 1660-1800,* London: HMSO, 1991.

De Bellaigue, Christina, *Educating Women: Schooling and Identity in England and France 1800-1867,* Oxford: Oxford University Press, 2007.

Dickinson, W., et al, *A Glossary of The Words and Phrases pertaining to the Dialect of   Cumberland*, London: Bemrose and Sons, 1899

Fisher, Robin, *Contact & Conflict: Indian-European Relations in British Columbia, 1774-1890*. Vancouver: University of British Columbia, 1986.

Hay, Daniel, *Whitehaven, A Short History*, Whitehaven: Whitehaven Borough Council, 1966.

Hocking, Silas K., *Her Benny: A Tale of Victorian Liverpool*. Original date of publication 1879, this edition Liverpool: The Gallery Press reprint, 1985.

Jollie, F., *Jollie's Sketch of Cumberland Manners and Customs: A Glossary*, Original date of publication 1811, this edition Cumberland: Michael Moon, 1974.

Lillard, Charles, *Seven Shillings a Year: The History of Vancouver Island*, Ganges: Horsdal & Schubart, 1986.

Lower, J. Arthur, *Western Canada: An Outline History*, Vancouver: Douglas & McIntyre, 1983.

Mannix & Whellan, *History, Gazetteer and Directory of Cumberland, 1847*, Cumberland: Michael Moon, 1974.

McCourt, Colin, *New Houses Revisited: The Story of a Whitehaven Mining Community*, McCourt, 2008,

Moon, Michael and Moon, Sylvia, *Bygone Whitehaven*, Cumberland: Michael Moon, Vol., 1, 1980, Vols 2 and 3, 1982.

Norcross, E. Blanche, (ed.,) *Nanaimo Retrospective: The First Century,* Nanaimo: Nanaimo Historical Society, 1979.

Norcross, E. Blanche, (ed.,) *The Company on the Coast,* Nanaimo: Nanaimo Historical Society, 1983.

Peterson, Jan, *Black Diamond City Nanaimo: The Victorian Era,* Surrey: Heritage House Publishing Company, 2002.

Pethick, Derek, *Victoria, The Fort,* Vancouver: Mitchell Press, 1968.

Reader, W. J., *Life in Victorian England,* London: Batsford, 1985.

ACKNOWLEDGEMENTS

This novel has been a long time coming to fruition. The seeds were laid in my childhood by my mother Eleanor Hunting, my grandmother Mary Devlin, and my great grandmother Eleanor Bell. Each one of them fired my imagination with their tales of our intrepid ancestors who arrived on Vancouver Island in 1854. Also, I must mention my two great aunts Rhoda Beck and Dorothy Martin (both nee Devlin), who were well respected grande dames within 20th century Nanaimo society and staunch members of the I.O.D.E. (Imperial Order Daughters of the Empire). To all these women I owe thanks. Of course, their stories were fact, mine is faction – fiction based on fact.

I have received a great deal of support in writing this novel and I thank these people now: My beta readers Dr Christopher Roberts and Carol Meads who had the unenviable task of commenting on my early drafts. Jeremy Gibbs, always helpful and encouraging, whose patience I must have severely tested. My editor Helena Fairfax who took these drafts and showed me how to turn them into a readable novel whilst encouraging me when the going got rough. My proofreader Julia Gibbs who did a wonderful job and corrected my erratic punctuation and dangling modifiers. My publisher Sarah Houldcroft of Goldcrest Books who has brought this novel to print saving me from the technical mysteries. Mr Matthew Bultitude, FRCS, who patiently answered my medical queries. Adrienne Vaughan for sharing her expertise and encouraging me, and I thank James Milton for introducing me to her. Emma Chatterton's thesis brought Katherine Mansfield's inspiring novels to my attention for which I am grateful. My second cousin Rhoda Preston Flint generously shared her portfolio of Devlin and Beck family photographs and history when I visited her in Bellingham.

My children, Kathryn, Thomas, and Hannah have always been there for me and I hope they see me as the keeper of the Canadian flame. I thank them along with my husband Jim whose encouragement has been boundless and who has supported me unstintingly through all the angst and rewrites.

ABOUT THE AUTHOR

Lorna was born and brought up in Lincolnshire. Her Canadian mother would often talk about growing up on Vancouver Island in the 1930s, and the family's early history there. This sparked an interest for Lorna that continues to this day. After raising a family Lorna studied and taught history at the School of Oriental and African Studies in London. She now lives in Stamford in a very old house with stone walls and lots of beams.

Contact Lorna:

www.lornahunting.com
Twitter: @lornahunting
Facebook: @huntinglorna
Instagram: lornahunting

If you've read and enjoyed this book, please leave a review on Amazon or Goodreads.

Made in the USA
Las Vegas, NV
28 December 2021

39723413R00208